Laurie Gilmore writes small-town romance. Her Dream Harbor series is filled with quirky townsfolk, cozy settings, and swoon-worthy romance. She loves finding books with the perfect balance of sweetness and spice and strives for that in her own writing. If you ever wished you lived in Stars Hollow (or that Luke and Lorelai would just get together already!) then her books are definitely for you.

Also by Laurie Gilmore

The Cinnamon Bun Book Store

The Christmas Tree Farm

The Pumpkin Spice Café

LAURIE GILMORE

Winner
TikTok
Book Awards

ONE MORE CHAPTER

One More Chapter
a division of HarperCollins*Publishers* Ltd
1 London Bridge Street
London SE1 9GF
www.harpercollins.co.uk
HarperCollins*Publishers*
Macken House, 39/40 Mayor Street Upper,
Dublin 1, D01 C9W8, Ireland
First published by HarperCollinsPublishers Ltd 2023
This hardback edition published in 2024
1

A catalogue record for this book is available from the British Library
ISBN: 978-0-00-872098-8

Printed and bound in the UK using 100% Renewable Electricity by CPI Group (UK) Ltd

This book is produced from independently certified FSC paper to ensure responsible forest management.
For more information visit: www.harpercollins.co.uk/green

To the beardiest, most-flannel-wearing guy I know. Thanks for always providing so much inspiration.

Playlist

We fell in love in october - girl in red
Dancing With Your Ghost - Sasha Sloan
invisible string - Taylor Swift
Autumn Leaves - Ed Sheeran
Amoeba - Clairo
Falling - Harry Styles
Remember That Night? - Sara Kays
Hands To Myself - Selena Gomez
Another Love - Tom Odell
ceilings - Lizzy McAlpine
Wildest Dreams - Taylor Swift
Before You Go - Lewis Capaldi
Haunted House - Holly Humberstone
cardigan - Taylor Swift
Video Games - Lana Del Rey
Flicker - Niall Horan
34+35 - Ariana Grande
The Night We Met - Lord Huron
Dandelions - Ruth B.
Kiss Me - Sixpence None The Richer
Everything Has Changed - Taylor Swift
Dreams - The Cranberries
Maroon - Taylor Swift

Chapter One

Jeanie Ellis had never killed a man before, but tonight might be the night. Desperate times and all. She clutched the baseball bat tighter in her fist and crept down the rickety, back staircase.

She hadn't slept in three nights. Not since moving into the apartment above her aunt's café. Well, *her* café, technically. Jeanie was officially the new owner of The Pumpkin Spice Café, her Aunt Dot's pride and joy until exactly two weeks ago, when the older woman announced she was retiring – and taking off for the Caribbean for a few weeks to work on her tan. Apparently, Dot could think of no one better to take over her beloved café than her favorite – and *only,* as Jeanie pointed out – niece. An idea that now seemed completely absurd as Jeanie tiptoed off the last step prepared for battle.

Every night, she'd heard strange noises. Scritchy-scratchy type noises with the occasional clangy-bangy type noise. At first, she'd tried to chalk it up to the wind, or maybe an animal scurrying through the back alley. She absolutely refused to let her mind take off down a path to the worst-case scenario, like she usually did. She would *not* allow herself to imagine an escaped serial killer creeping up her back steps. That banging was definitely *not* an armed robber, here to take the meager change her aunt kept in the cash register.

Jeanie was starting fresh.

Jeanie was a new woman.

The quaint seaside town of Dream Harbor and its inhabitants knew nothing about her, and she planned to take full advantage of that.

A shuffling noise at the back door caught her attention. She would take full advantage of her 'New Life, New Jeanie' plan as soon as she figured out what was keeping her up at night. No one could live a laid-back, quaint, small-town life with a murderer outside their back door. That was just logical.

She choked up on the bat and crossed the small hallway between the stairs and the door that led to the alley behind the café. Although 'alley' wasn't quite the right word for it. Alley conjured images of overflowing trash cans and scurrying rats. But Jeanie wasn't in Boston anymore. She was in Dream Harbor, which she was convinced someone must have actually dreamed up. It was far too idyllic to have sprung up naturally. No, the space behind the café and the other businesses on Main Street was more like its own little side street, with room for delivery trucks and tidy trash bins. She'd even seen some of the other shop owners taking breaks and chit-chatting back there during the day. Not that she'd talked to anyone yet. She wasn't quite ready for that, for being the new kid.

Jeanie shook her head. Her thoughts were way off track, and she was about to be potentially murdered. Alley or not, whatever was out there was keeping her awake, and after three nights without sleep, she was barely holding it together. She rested the bat on her shoulder and reached for the doorknob. It was nearly dawn and a weak gray light seeped through the window over the door.

Oh, good, Jeanie thought vaguely. At least I'll be able to see my attacker before I die. With that less-than-pleasant thought in her head – not at all the positive new persona she was shooting for – she yanked open the door—

And came face to face with a crate of small pumpkins.

Gourds? It didn't matter, because before Jeanie could get her produce names sorted, the giant man holding the crate of small pumpkins spoke.

Or at least he made a gruff startled noise that reminded Jeanie that she was currently holding a baseball bat in a very aggressive manner. She nearly dropped it to her side, but then she remembered; this was still a large, strange man. Gourds or no gourds, she probably shouldn't let her guard down just yet.

'Who are you?' she asked, keeping one hand on the door in case she had to slam it in this mysterious pumpkin-man's face.

His dark eyebrows rose a fraction of an inch as though he was surprised by her question. 'Logan Anders,' he said as though that would clear things up for her. It didn't.

'And what are you doing in my back alley, Logan Anders?' she asked.

He blew out a frustrated-sounding breath and shifted the crate in his arms. It was probably heavy, but Jeanie would not compromise her safety just because this man was the picture of autumnal bounty with his crate of vegetables and his worn, flannel shirt and thick beard. Her gaze lingered on his face for a beat longer. So she could pick him out of a line-up, she reasoned. She might need to know that above his beard was a long, straight nose and ruddy cheeks. The police officer might ask her if he had lashes for days, and the answer would be yes. It might be of the utmost importance to the investigation to know that even in the dim light of the morning she could see that his eyes were a devastating blue.

'It's Thursday.'

Jeanie blinked. Did the day of the week have something to do with why this man was here keeping her awake?

'And you've been keeping me up since Monday,' she said.

Now it was Logan's turn to look confused. 'I just got here.' He shifted the crate again, his forearms flexing under the strain. It really must be heavy, but he hadn't made any move to come in or set it down.

'Well, I've been hearing strange noises all week and I tried to pretend it was just the wind or a raccoon or something. But then I started thinking that's probably what people tell themselves right before the killer bursts through the door.'

Logan choked a little, his eyes going wide. 'Killer?'

Jeanie felt her cheeks heat up. Maybe she'd let her imagination get the best of her. 'Or something...' Her voice trailed off. She wasn't really sure what to say to this strange man and he seemed to be equally at a loss. 'So, what are you doing here?' she prompted.

'Right, uh, I deliver produce every Thursday.' He nodded toward the box of said produce.

Jeanie winced. The produce delivery. Of course. Aunt Dot had told her so many things in the day before she left and Jeanie had written none of it down. The café had been closed since she'd got here and she still hadn't wrapped her head around everything that needed to be done. Thankfully, Norman, the café's long-time manager, was here to help. He assured her they'd have the café up and running by the weekend.

Logan shifted the box again. The heavy box he was still holding.

'So sorry!' Jeanie stepped back and swept her arm toward the café. 'Come in. We'll find a place to put those ... uh ... pumpkins?'

Logan hesitated in the doorway, his gaze shifting between Jeanie and the bat still poised over her shoulder.

'Gah! Sorry. I won't hit you on the head. I promise.' She tried to give him a reassuring smile but it didn't seem to help. He still hovered in the doorway.

'I'm really sorry, I assumed you were a murderer. It's nothing personal. I just haven't slept in three nights, and something's been making noise down here, I swear. And

I'm still trying to wrap my head around this whole café-inheritance thing.'

Logan stared at her, a hesitance still in his eyes. Crap. She'd probably already scared him. Jeanie had been called 'intense' on more than one occasion throughout her life. She was pretty sure it was even on a report card or two. It was something she was trying to work on, part of her new, Jeanie persona. Less talking. Less overthinking. Less intensity.

She took a deep breath and blew it out slowly. Café Jeanie was calm, chill. Just your friendly neighborhood coffee-shop owner, ready with a smile and your favorite drink. Not her theories on who or what was trying to kill her on any given day, or the latest in ice-cap-melting news, or the eighteen things she had to get done later today.

She tried to channel Aunt Dot's free-spirit vibes even as she wished the woman had been slightly less laid-back and had actually left her more explicit directions. She attempted a gentler, sweeter smile. It felt strange on her face. 'Please, come in. That must be so heavy.'

Logan gave a slight nod in acknowledgment. 'I usually leave it out here.'

'Oh.' So it wasn't her monologue scaring him away, she'd just interrupted his usual operating procedure. She understood very well how that could throw a person off.

When her favorite coffee place on the corner was closed for a week, she could barely function. And it wasn't for lack of caffeine. There was no shortage of coffee shops in the city, but none of them were hers. She'd been in a bad mood all week.

Her smile this time was genuine. 'Well, you're here now and I'm awake. How about a cup of coffee?'

Chapter Two

Logan liked the new owner of the PS Café more when she wasn't about to knock his head off with a baseball bat. But that wasn't saying a whole lot. He had work to do, deliveries to make, and well-meaning townsfolk to avoid. He really didn't have time to be sitting here having a predawn drink with her, but he didn't seem to be able to escape. Or get a word in. Dot's niece hadn't stopped talking since she insisted he come in.

Every Thursday for the past five years, ever since he started managing the farm, he'd left Dot's four crates of produce next to the back door. He liked being in town before the sun came up and the people came out. He liked getting his business done before any other businesses were open.

Logan wasn't one for small talk. He hated speculating about the weather. He did not need to know about the latest town scandal. He liked being a part of the latest town scandal even less. So the quicker he was done with his deliveries, the sooner he could get back to the quiet of the farm. Or as quiet as a farm can be with half a dozen chickens, two senior goats, one rescue alpaca, and a grandmother who loved chatter. Thankfully, his grandfather was just as quiet as he was. His grandmother talked enough for the both of them. Almost as much as this Jeanie did.

'So, what do you think my aunt intended to do with those ... uh, little pumpkins?' she asked, glancing down at the crate he'd left by his feet. She stood behind the counter, a hand on her hip, the other swiping at the little wisps of hair that had fallen out of her messy bun.

'Gourds,' Logan corrected her from his spot on the other side of the counter.

'Right. Gourds. I thought so.' Jeanie still looked confused. 'But ... you don't eat them, right?'

He nearly laughed. Nearly. He was still too annoyed to laugh. 'No, you don't eat gourds.'

Jeanie's gaze roamed over the other three crates that he'd carried in instead of leaving them in their rightful place near the door. The place he always left them. The place he wished he'd left them this morning. 'I'm guessing the rest of it is for the smoothies she added to the menu.'

Logan nodded. This town loved their smoothies. Not that he was going to complain. Smoothies meant the café needed a lot of fresh fruit and veggies from his farm. Smoothies were good for business.

'The gourds are just decorative,' he said, saving both of them from more guesses.

Jeanie's eyes lit up like he'd solved the world's problems. He ignored how pride flared in his chest at the sight of her pleased face. It had been a while since he'd been able to solve anyone's problems.

'Of course! I really should have thought of that. It's the lack of sleep!'

She rested her elbows on the counter and her chin in her hands. She was wearing an old, oversized cardigan, the sleeves so long they covered her hands, over a threadbare T-shirt and pajama pants. He was pretty sure the pants had little hedgehogs all over them, but he'd tried very hard not to notice.

He was trying very hard not to notice a lot of things about Jeanie. Like how expressive her dark eyebrows were, and how she hadn't stopped moving – making his coffee with quick efficient movements. She was a study in contradiction. Competent, but lost at the same time. Quick to smile, but also quick to frown, every emotion clear in her eyes. Dark brown eyes, nearly black, the same as his coffee order.

Jeanie rubbed a hand down her face, breaking the spell. How long had he been staring at her? She yawned and stretched her hands above her head. Her T-shirt lifted with her arms and Logan averted his gaze from the exposed slice of skin above her waistband. He was definitely not going to notice that.

When he dared to look at her again, she was back to leaning on her elbows on the counter. Dark circles hung beneath her eyes, her black hair a messy nest on the top of her head. Her slumped, defeated posture tugged at something inside him. Something inconvenient. Something he did not have time for right now.

He opened his mouth to tell her he had to get going on his deliveries, but she was already talking again.

'It's just so weird. I keep hearing these sounds. Every night. Do you think maybe this place is haunted?'

Logan nearly choked on his coffee. 'Haunted?'

'Yeah.' She straightened, her eyes brightening with her new theory. 'Haunted. Like maybe the spirits who live here aren't happy with the new owner.'

'The spirits?' It was too early in the morning for this level of insanity.

'Ghost, spirits, whatever.' Jeanie waved her hand like

the semantics of the haunting didn't matter. 'Something is upset that I'm here.'

'I really don't think—'

'There's no other logical explanation.' She crossed her arms over her chest. Case closed. 'This place is definitely haunted.'

'No other explanation?' Logan thunked his mug on the counter. This was too much. 'Raccoons, old pipes, drafty windows, your own imagination.' He counted the other explanations off on his fingers. Jeanie narrowed her eyes at him on that last one, but he went on. 'Could be the kids in town messing around. There are an infinite number of explanations that make more sense than ghosts. Now I really need to go—'

'What do you mean kids messing around?'

Logan sighed and resisted tearing the hair from his head. 'I don't know. Maybe some kids were messing around in the back alley.'

Jeanie nodded slowly, taking in this new theory.

Logan slid his mug across the counter, a thank you and goodbye on the tip of his tongue.

But Jeanie was faster. 'So what are we going to do about it? I really need sleep.'

'We?' He backed away from the counter. Maybe he could just turn and run. The last thing he needed was to get further entangled with the new café owner. He could practically hear the book club ladies cackling about it. They ate gossip for breakfast.

Jeanie nodded. 'You're my only friend in town. I can't confront a gang of teenagers by myself.'

'*Gang* is being a bit generous,' he mumbled, still backing toward the door, but now Jeanie was following him. Definitely hedgehogs on the jammies. He refused to find that endearing.

'Please? I'm new here and I feel like I have no idea what I'm doing...' She shook her head, her words trailing off. 'Sorry. This isn't your problem.' She smiled. 'I'll figure it out.'

The smile she forced onto her face tugged at something inside him again. She looked so ... so lost. Even as she smiled and pushed the hair from her face, attempting to assure him she was fine. She clearly wasn't. And that scrambled him up even more than her constant talking.

Damn it. 'Come to the town meeting tonight,' he said.

'Town meeting?'

'Yeah.' He ran a hand down his beard already regretting his next words. 'They're every other Thursday. You can bring up your ... uh ... problem. Get some help.'

Her smile grew into something bright and real. *Oh, no.* Jeanie's real smile was even more endearing than the damn hedgehogs. How had his usual morning deliveries taken such a drastic turn?

'Thank you! That's a great idea.' Jeanie clasped her hands in front of her, like she was stopping herself from reaching out for a hug. Logan didn't know if he was relieved or disappointed by that.

He needed to go. He had one hand on the doorknob, nearly there. Nearly back to his normal morning, his blessed quiet.

'Will you be there?' Jeanie's question stopped him before he could escape. Logan usually only went to town meetings if forced to by some farm issue and only then if his grandmother was too busy with her knitting circle to come into town. His grandfather would rather have teeth pulled, without anesthesia, than attend a town meeting (his words).

Logan had no need to show up this week and yet for some reason found himself saying, 'Yeah, I'll be there.'

Jeanie's delighted squeak followed him out into the predawn light.

The book club was going to have a field day.

Chapter Three

Hello, I'm Jeanie Ellis, Dorothy's niece, and the new owner of The Pumpkin Spice Café. I've been having a little issue with a nocturnal disturbance...

Nocturnal disturbance? That made her sound even crazier than she had this morning. Jeanie's knee bounced up and down despite her attempts to stop. She was nervous. She wanted to make a good first impression at this meeting, and she'd gone over her little speech in her head at least a dozen times since she got here. Twenty minutes early, apparently.

She sat at the back of the room; the old floors and possibly even older chair creaking beneath her. There were only a handful of other people milling around the room, greeting each other with the easy familiarity she hadn't found since she was a kid. She'd missed it. The sense of belonging, of home. She hadn't realized she'd missed it. In fact, she'd run from the little town where she'd grown up as soon as she graduated high school, so ready to be free of its constraining borders. But somewhere along the way, the thrill of the city, the crowds, and the concrete had lost its allure.

She shifted in her seat and the chair groaned ominously. An older gentleman offered her a friendly smile and a salute as he walked by to join a group gathered near the podium. Jeanie raised a hand to return it, but he was already gone. Tucking her hands between her thighs in an effort to warm them and to keep from fidgeting, she watched the group greet the man with good-natured teasing about his bright-green tie. Jeanie couldn't remember the last time she'd joked around like that. The last time she had people like that to joke with. At least not in person. Somehow in the last several years, her closest friend had become her brother. And their relationship consisted of random texts, memes, and the occasional FaceTime chat.

Jeanie pulled her coat around her shoulders. It was freezing in here despite the rattling efforts of the radiators lining the walls.

The town meetings were held in the original town hall building, which according to the engraved brick out front was built in 1870. Jeanie couldn't really imagine what it looked like in 1870, but tonight it looked like a small auditorium with several rows of metal folding chairs and a podium up front. The stage behind the podium was decorated for what Jeanie imagined would be an upcoming fall performance. Hand-painted scenery with pumpkins and apple trees lined the back of the stage with hay bales scattered in front. Jeanie pictured kids in costumes dancing around up there, waving to their parents in the audience. It would be adorable, she was sure. Although she did question the safety of putting children on a stage that old. Would those old wooden planks support them?

She shook the thought from her head and glanced back toward the double doors that led to the meeting space. Still no Logan. Maybe he'd just agreed to come to get her to stop talking. It wouldn't be the first time someone had agreed with her just to get her to shut up. She'd come on too strong, as per usual. Laying out all her problems and sleep-deprived theories right at the quiet farmer's feet. The very handsome, very quiet farmer.

Jeanie smoothed her hands down her thighs, trying to wrestle her bouncing knee into submission. It didn't matter that Logan was handsome. Like, very, very handsome. Like, if there was a *Sexy Farmer Weekly*, he would be on the cover.

It didn't matter because getting involved with

handsome farmers was not a part of her New Jeanie plan. She had agreed to her aunt's crazy idea to take over the café so she could have a fresh start.

Jeanie had spent the last seven years as the executive assistant to the CEO of Franklin, Mercer & Young Financial. Until he had a heart attack and died at his desk one night. Jeanie had been the one to find him the next morning, his vacant eyes staring at her as she entered his office, coffee in hand. The coffee stain on the carpet from where she'd dropped the mug in shock was still there when she quit.

The doctor said the heart attack was stress-induced. That and Marvin's atrocious diet of mostly bacon and late-night takeout. But it was the stress-induced part that stuck with Jeanie. Was that her future? To work and work until her heart just gave out? Gave up?

Jeanie had a tendency to overthink. To over-talk. To overwork. She didn't do rest and relaxation very well. She didn't do calm or cool. But she was determined to try. For her health, she was determined to try. Suddenly, the fact that her life consisted only of work, a few office acquaintances she got drinks with on Fridays – when she wasn't too exhausted to join them – and her pitiful and sporadic attempts at dating, seemed like a very big problem. A deadly problem.

When, only a few weeks after Marvin's death, her

Aunt Dot had devised this plan for Jeanie to move to Dream Harbor and take over the café, it had seemed like the perfect escape. Except now Jeanie was certain she was failing already. Especially after her little performance with the handsome farmer this morning. She'd nearly taken his head off, and then she'd talked his ear off at a thousand miles per hour. She'd seen the horrified look on his face. He'd wanted nothing more than to escape.

She glanced at the door again. Nothing but a small gaggle of older women bustling in. They smiled at her as they took their seats.

It was for the best, really. Jeanie also wasn't good at relationships that lasted longer than a few weeks, and a fling in a town as small as this one seemed like a terrible idea. Not that Logan wanted to have a fling with her. Not that he'd even wanted to have a cup of coffee with her this morning, before she forced him into it . . .

'Hey.' His gruff greeting startled her out of her thoughts as he slid into the seat next to her. He smelled like the outdoors, like fall leaves and woodsmoke. Jeanie resisted the urge to snuggle closer to his warmth in the drafty room.

'Hi.' *Be cool, casual.* She stole a glance at him as he settled in. Still handsome. *Damn it.* 'How was your day?' she asked. Just a casual question for a new acquaintance. No crazy, ghost theories here.

'Uh . . . good.' He cleared his throat. 'Normal.'

Jeanie smiled. 'Normal is good.'

Logan nodded. 'If you like normal, you're going to hate this meeting.'

Jeanie smiled bigger. Was that a little joke from the serious farmer? 'Do things get wild at the Dream Harbor bi-monthly town meetings?'

'Just wait.' He'd leaned toward her and his low voice rumbled through her.

No time to dwell on that toe-curling sensation, though, because the meeting hall was filling in and Jeanie was busy taking in the sights.

People were starting to take their seats, the room warming significantly with the influx of bodies. A loud laugh drew Jeanie's attention to a few rows ahead of them. The owner of the laugh was a woman, maybe in her forties – though if she was, she looked great for her age further justifying Jeanie's small-town living plan. The people here aged so well! The woman laughed again, her sleek black bob brushing past her round face. She wedged herself in between an older woman with short, gray hair and a man in his twenties talking loudly, his hands punctuating every word.

'Book club,' Logan muttered in her ear.

'Book club,' Jeanie repeated faintly, watching as two other women, one with an infant strapped to her chest, joined the conversation from the next row. 'They look like fun.'

'Fun. Ha. They run this town.' Logan's ominous tone was completely at odds with the laughing, smiling group in front of them. Especially when the black-bobbed woman turned and gave him a big wave.

Logan groaned and waved back.

The rest of the group turned, and Jeanie could practically see their eyes light up, the whole group clearly pleased to see him.

'Logan! What a rare treat,' the older woman called.

'Hey, Nancy.'

'We miss you at our meetings,' the younger man said with a wink. A wink?

Logan grumbled. 'I never came to your meetings.'

The man laughed. 'Well, maybe not on purpose, but we liked roping you in. Especially when we read *Passion in the Fields – The Farmer and the Milkmaid*.' The man was talking so loudly that the entire room could hear. Several people giggled and turned to look at Logan.

'Oh, that was such a good one.' The woman with the baby clapped a hand to her chest and mimed a swoon in her chair.

Logan's face, when Jeanie sneaked a peek, was bright red above his beard. She bit down on a smile.

'Are you the new café owner?' The black-haired woman asked her. 'I'm Kaori.'

'Jeanie. And, yes, I'm the new owner.'

'Get that place up and running again!' the lady with the baby scolded with a laugh. 'I'm tired of meeting at Kaori's house. It's too cluttered in there. Cutesy vases and weird knick-knacks everywhere. It gives me hives.'

Kaori playfully smacked the woman's shoulder. 'Ignore Isabel. And welcome to Dream Harbor.'

The book club ladies then returned to talking amongst themselves.

'*Passion in the Fields,* huh?' Jeanie asked, unable to resist.

Logan cleared his throat and shifted in his seat, the chair creaking loudly in protest. 'I didn't read it.'

'Too bad. Sounds like a good one.' She stifled a laugh at the thought of Logan reading a book about a farmer and a milkmaid, and forced herself to stop casting herself in the role of said 'milkmaid'.

'I guess I need to get things opened up again. I don't want to anger the book club.' She'd meant it as a joke but even she could hear the uncertainty in her voice, the stress of not being ready to open creeping in.

'Don't worry about them. They're just looking for a place to peddle their pornography.'

Jeanie looked up just in time to catch the small smile on his face. Another joke.

'Well, we wouldn't want that. And we certainly wouldn't want to objectify farmers.'

Logan's smile hitched higher. Oh, damn, she might need to go check this book out later. Satisfy her new appreciation for farmers in a safe way.

'Did I miss anything?' A woman with curly brown hair dropped into the seat on the other side of Logan.

'Nope.'

'Actually, you missed a pretty interesting literary conversation,' Jeanie chimed in, reminding Logan of her presence.

'It was not interesting. Jeanie, this is Hazel. Hazel, Jeanie.'

Hazel extended her hand across Logan's lap and Jeanie took it. Hazel's fingers stuck out of her fingerless mittens, and they were cold in Jeanie's hand.

'Nice to meet you.'

Hazel's gaze flicked from Jeanie to Logan and back again. 'Nice to meet you, too. I run the bookstore next to your café.'

Jeanie's smile grew. 'Oh, it's so cute!'

Hazel's cheeks colored. 'Thanks.'

Jeanie was busy wondering if Hazel kept any farmer

romances stocked and nearly missed the woman's next question.

'And how do you two know each other?' she asked.

'Oh, the usual way,' Jeanie said. 'I nearly knocked his head off with a baseball bat because I thought he was an intruder on his way to murder me, but he was actually just dropping off adorable little pumpkins . . . er . . . gourds. And then I mentioned the café might be haunted so he suggested I come here for some . . . uh . . . help.'

Hazel's eyes widened behind her glasses. 'Uh . . . wow.'

Jeanie tried for a smile that made her seem slightly less unhinged, but she didn't think it landed. Hazel sat back in her seat with a small smile of her own. She whispered something to Logan, which made Logan give a fierce shake of his head. Jeanie didn't have time to overthink that before another woman landed in a chair in the row ahead of them.

'Do you see him over there? He's clearly plotting something,' she said, launching straight into a conversation Jeanie didn't know they were having.

'He looks like he's just talking,' mumbled Logan, and the new woman narrowed her eyes at him.

'Yeah, talking to the mayor. He's probably got more crazy plans to ruin this town.'

'It's just a trivia night, Annie.'

'A trivia night on the same night as my Baking for Beginners class! He planned it like that!' She glowered at the man across the room and Jeanie followed her gaze. The trivia-planning, town-ruining man in question was tall and handsome. Not like farmer handsome, but definitely attractive. Dark hair, bronze skin. His smile was more of a cocky smirk. What was in the water here? Were all the town's men sexy? Was that the dream of Dream Harbor? Jeanie couldn't say she was mad about it.

'You act as though we haven't known Mac since kindergarten,' said Logan.

Annie frowned. 'That's exactly the problem. You remember how mean he was. He stole your chocolate milk every day of second grade! You of all people should understand!'

Logan let out a low laugh, a soft puff of air. 'I'm over it.'

Annie crossed her arms over her chest. 'Well, I'm not.'

She finally glanced in Jeanie's direction, who smiled and gave a small wave.

'Oh, my gosh! You must be the mysterious new café owner! I'm Annie, owner of The Sugar Plum Bakery. Nice to finally meet you.'

'Am I mysterious?' Jeanie asked, sneaking a glance at Logan. His face was grim, but he didn't offer up an answer. 'Nice to meet you, too. Your bakery smells delicious every morning.'

'Then, come by! Oh, and also, I usually deliver scones to the café on weekend mornings. Spare me the greeting you gave Logan.'

Jeanie's cheeks heated in embarrassment, but Annie was laughing like it was all in good fun.

'It really wasn't personal—' she started to explain, but Annie waved a hand to cut her off.

'If I saw this big oaf skulking around the back alley and I didn't know him since birth, I'd probably try to hit him on the head, too.'

'I don't skulk.'

'You were a little skulk-y,' Jeanie added.

Annie jabbed a finger at Logan. 'See, you do skulk. I like her,' she said, pointing at Jeanie.

'When is this damn meeting going to start?' Logan's voice was an adorable mix of exasperation and despair.

Hazel patted his knee with her still-mittened hand. 'You know Mayor Kelly never starts on time.'

'Why do you call him that? Just call him Dad.'

Hazel shrugged. 'He's at work. I'm trying to be respectful.'

Logan rolled his eyes, but Jeanie couldn't help the smile on her face. She liked these people already. She liked this town. She liked this grumpy farmer. Was it too much to wish that she could fit in here? That Annie could actually like her, that the book club might ask her to join, that Hazel might introduce her to her dad, the mayor?

The pressure to make things at the café work was building. But if Jeanie had made sure Marvin was ready for his weekly meetings with billion-dollar investors, then surely she could run a small café. Right?

Chapter Four

Logan had always thought hell would have fire and brimstone, but it turned out hell was a town hall meeting sandwiched between the woman he had been trying to forget since this morning and one of his nosy best friends. Every time he glanced at Hazel, she waggled her eyebrows at him in a way that made him very uncomfortable – and every time he looked at Jeanie, she smiled up at him like she was having a wonderful time. What had he gotten himself into?

He didn't know why he'd told Jeanie about this damn meeting, or more importantly why he'd agreed to come. She'd just looked so flustered this morning, so confused. And tired. She was in over her head and, really, he was doing the town a favor. The Pumpkin Spice Café was the only decent coffee shop in town. If she didn't get it up and running soon, people might have to resort to drinking the watered-down, burnt stuff they served at the gas station near the highway. Or they might just go full zombie and start eating each other's brains for breakfast. If you thought about it that way, he was a hero.

Annie had taken over pointing out all the key players in the town as she unwound the world's longest scarf from her neck, her blonde hair flying wildly around her head.

'So, the guy up front with the hideous green tie is obviously the mayor.'

'Hey! I got him that tie.'

'Sorry, Haze, but that color is atrocious.' Annie shrugged. 'Anyway, the woman next to him in the power suit is the deputy mayor and our old principal. Her name is Mindy, but I will never not think of her as Principal Walsh.' Annie lowered her voice and leaned closer to Jeanie. 'She's terrifying.'

Jeanie giggled. Logan ignored the way the sound curled up inside him and settled in.

'And over there is my arch-nemesis, Macaulay Sullivan.'

'The trivia guy?'

'Don't be fooled by the trivia, Jeanie. He owns the pub next to your café. Watch out for him.'

Logan scoffed. The only trouble between Annie and

Mac was that they had the hots for each other, and neither would admit it. But he was not about to get into that now.

'Anyway, he's over there with Greg and Shawn, the owners of the pet store on the corner.'

Jeanie nodded, taking it all in, and Logan wouldn't be surprised if she pulled out a notebook and started making a cheat sheet. She seemed like the note-taking type. Not that he cared what type she was. He was here for the coffee, to help the town, and to avoid a zombie apocalypse. Not to think about what Jeanie's handwriting looked like, or if she would make little doodles in the margins.

She probably would.

'And over there is the Sharmas, who just opened a new restaurant further down Main. They have the best tandoori chicken,' Annie informed Jeanie.

Hazel jabbed Logan in the side, pulling his attention away from Annie's tour. 'Are you going to tell me how she managed to get you here? You never come to these things,' she whispered in his ear.

'Just being helpful. You know, neighborly.'

'Neighborly?' Her voice rose incredulously, like he'd never done a neighborly thing in his life.

'Yeah. I can be helpful.'

Hazel snorted. 'Helpful, sure. But coming to a town

meeting? That's way above helpful for you.' She pushed her glasses up her nose and gave him a thoroughly obnoxious grin. 'I think you have a crush.'

'I do not have a crush,' he hissed through clenched teeth, ridiculously worried that Jeanie would hear them. 'I am not a twelve-year-old girl. I just want a decent cup of coffee.'

His annoying little friend shrugged. 'Okay, sure. Just a helpful neighbor that wants coffee. Got it.'

He glowered at her but all she did was smile innocently. He didn't have a ton of friends; he probably shouldn't murder this one.

He settled back into his rickety old chair, arms across his chest. A crush. Absurd. He barely knew this woman. Other than the fact that she wore cutesy pajama pants, had the brightest smile he'd ever seen, and held a baseball bat like a major leaguer. Other than that, he knew nothing. And that's how he wanted to keep it.

The smoke had barely cleared from the last time he'd crashed and burned in front of the entire town. He wouldn't be repeating those mistakes anytime soon. Next time he dated someone, he would keep the whole thing far away from Dream Harbor. Maybe one of those nice long-distance relationships everyone was always talking about.

Not that he wanted to date Jeanie.

He just wanted coffee.

Mayor Kelly stepped up to the podium and cleared his throat. Logan groaned internally.

'Welcome, Dreamers,' the mayor said with his signature goofy smile.

Kill me now.

'First order of business.' He pushed his glasses up his nose in a manner so similar to Hazel's that Logan felt an involuntary softness for the man. 'Sullivan's Pub will now be hosting a trivia night on Tuesdays, starting at eight o'clock.'

Logan could feel the anger radiating off Annie. Or maybe repressed sexual desire. It was impossible to tell the difference. Her baking class started at six. People could do both baking and trivia, but he knew Annie would not accept that logic. Mac had infringed on her night.

Mayor Kelly waited for the excited whispering of the crowd to die down. People were already calling dibs on team members. Mac had the balls to turn around and wink at Annie. She started to rise, fists clenched at her sides. Logan grabbed her by the shoulders and pushed her back down into her seat. He held on an extra minute to make sure she didn't spring up and dive across the room to strangle Mac. Or kiss the smirk off his face. Either one would hold up the entire meeting.

'Okay, moving on. Next up on the agenda is the proposed stop sign on the corner of Mayberry and Cherry Lane.'

'Forget the stop sign, Pete! When are we getting our coffee back?' Leroy yelled from the front row.

Logan felt Jeanie tense beside him.

'Yeah! I can't drink my wife's weird herbal tea one more day!'

'Okay, okay, Tim. Settle down. No one is making you drink Tammy's tea.' The mayor held his hands up to quiet the crowd. Logan was right. They were on the verge of a zombie situation. 'I believe we have the PS Café's new owner with us tonight.' Pete smiled encouragingly at Jeanie. 'Maybe she can come up here and enlighten us on her plans.'

Jeanie drew in a breath and Logan thought maybe she wouldn't want to go up in front of everyone. In fact, he was ready to jump in and explain that she planned to open this weekend, but she was already up and walking toward the podium.

He had been trying so hard not to notice her tonight that he'd missed how her hair was swept into a neat twist at the back of her head, and instead of hedgehog pajamas she wore gray slacks and a sweater the color of fresh cream. Her tall, black heels tapped loudly on the old wood floor.

He blinked. This woman was not the one he met this morning. This woman didn't need rescuing. For the first time, he wondered who she had been before she moved here, what she'd done outside of Dream Harbor. He'd been so sure she needed him to help, to fix something for her. A bad habit of his.

She gave Pete one of her bright smiles and stood behind the podium. 'Hi, everyone. I'm Jeanie. Dot's niece.' She cleared her throat, her smile wobbling slightly. So, she was a little nervous. 'Sorry to have deprived you all of your caffeine for the week. I was ... uh ... just getting settled in, but the café will reopen this Saturday.'

Cheers went up from the crowd, and shouts of encouragement and welcome pulled Jeanie's smile even wider. Logan felt his own lips tip into a matching smile. For the coffee. He was happy about the coffee.

'I am having a little bit of an issue, though,' Jeanie went on. 'I've been hearing strange noises at night. It's ... um ... been very disruptive to my sleep and I was wondering if anyone had any thoughts on what it might be?'

'Murderous farmers?' Annie yelled out, and Logan kicked the back of her chair.

'It's probably just raccoons,' Mac suggested. 'I've seen a few fat ones digging out in the trash.'

Jeanie shook her head. 'I don't know. It really doesn't

sound like animals. And it's a bit different every night. Sometimes like a banging, sometimes like a scratching.'

Oh, the crowd liked this little tidbit. Suddenly the room was erupting in theories.

'Teenagers! Out causing trouble.'

'Just a little mischief. It is October, after all.'

'It's probably a stress dream. I do dream readings. Come see me!'

'It's been very windy lately.'

'You're just anxious, hon.'

Jeanie's head swiveled from person to person, listening to each crazy suggestion.

'Could be haunted.'

Jeanie's gaze snagged on Noah, captain of the *SS Ginger,* the town's one and only fishing tour company and Logan's other best friend. Lover of tall tales and beautiful women.

'Haunted?'

'Yeah.' Logan could see Noah's auburn-haired head bobbing in assent. 'Definitely. Those buildings on Main are crazy old. It'd be crazier if they weren't haunted, honestly.'

Logan would chuck something at the back of his friend's head if he thought he could hit him from here. He'd brought Jeanie here to find a more plausible explanation for her noise problem, not to further support her ghost theory. Although, looking around the room now, he did not know why he thought this crew would come up with a more reasonable answer.

'That's what I thought, too! But Logan thought that was a crazy idea.'

'Oh, did he?' Noah asked, one copper eyebrow raised as every head in the room turned to look at Logan. The question was written all over their faces. Not anything about noise or ghosts, but all about him and Jeanie. Mostly, how was he already acquainted with the cute new girl in town?

Nope, not cute.

Just a new neighbor.

He felt the heat creep up his neck.

'I think there could be something to this theory,' Mayor Kelly cut in before Logan had to answer any questions. And for a second, Logan was grateful. Until the next words left the mayor's mouth. 'Actually, now that you mention it, I had a dream about this.'

Dear God, save him. Not a Mayor Kelly dream. He really was in hell. This was officially the last time he'd try to save the town from caffeine-addicted zombies.

'A dream?' Jeanie asked, completely innocent of the insane way this town was run. Logan must have been groaning out loud because Hazel jabbed him in the ribs again.

He rubbed his side. Hazel's elbows were pointy as hell, and her glare was even sharper when he looked at her. But he kept his mouth shut. He had no desire to argue with her again about whether or not her father was clairvoyant. Another mistake he was learning from.

Never mind that, it was completely nuts to run an entire town based on your dreams. Even if it did happen to work out every now and then. And the town happened to be called Dream Harbor.

Mayor Kelly had stepped back toward the podium, ready to launch into the whole story of how he'd had a dream about becoming Mayor of Dream Harbor exactly one year before he was elected, and how he dreamt about that big ice storm before it happened, and the time he knew the nursery school had electrical issues and the electrician said he'd prevented a fire by calling him in time. Logan couldn't bear it.

'He has dreams,' Logan blurted out. 'Uses them to make decisions.'

Mayor Kelly beamed. 'That's right. Thank you, Logan.'

Jeanie glanced between him and the mayor, a bemused smile on her lips. She was having a good time. Damn it, if that didn't make it worth subjecting himself to this insanity.

'And your dream says that the café is haunted?' she asked.

Mayor Kelly shook his head like she was being silly. 'They're not always that clear. But I did have a dream two nights ago about a stranger. That must have been you.' He patted Jeanie on the back. 'Although we're nearly friends now!'

'Get on with it, Pete.' Some of the regular meeting-goers were getting antsy.

The mayor shrugged good-naturedly. 'Of course. Anyway, in the dream there was a stranger in need of help.' And then the mayor's eyes lit up in a way that Logan found very ominous. Even more so when he directed his delighted gaze at Logan.

What now?

'Oh, that's right,' Mayor Kelly went on. 'In the dream, our very own Logan Anders was the one to volunteer to assist our new neighbor.'

'Were there zombies involved?' Logan muttered under his breath.

'What's that?'

'Nothing.' Logan waved a hand. 'Never mind.'

The mayor had known him since he and Hazel became friends in ninth grade. He knew Logan as well as anyone, and there was no way in hell this was a real dream. This whole thing was yet another attempt at the town to get into his business. And after last time, he was determined not to let that happen.

'I vote for just the wind. Are we done here?' Logan asked, sounding like more of an ass than he meant to, but he refused to let Mayor Kelly interfere with his life. Dream or no dream. He also refused to notice the way Jeanie's smile had slipped at his harsh tone.

'You can't just ignore the mayor's dream, Logan,' Isabel piped up from the side of the room where she was swaying side to side to keep little Mateo asleep in his sling. 'You remember the nursery school.'

Logan pinched the bridge of his nose. 'Yes, I remember the nursery school.'

'And I didn't move my car before that ice storm and that huge limb came down right on top of it,' book-club Jacob added.

Half the room was nodding at him now and throwing out their own cautionary tales about ignoring the mayor's dreams. If he hadn't lived amongst these lunatics his whole life, Logan might be appalled. But instead, he was just weary.

'It's okay,' Jeanie's voice cut in through the commotion. 'Logan doesn't have to help. I'm sure I'll figure it out soon.' She still had a smile on her face, but it was the fake one. The one she'd given him this morning when she was trying to convince him she was fine. It was the lost one, the one that tugged on him.

Damn it.

'I'll do it.'

The crowd stopped talking, pleased with itself.

Jeanie smiled at him from across the room. Her real smile.

'I'd be happy to,' he added. And to his surprise, he meant it.

Chapter Five

'We come bearing gifts!'

Jeanie was wiping down the front counter for the twelfth time when the bell rang over the café door. Annie and Hazel pushed through it, their arms full of bakery boxes.

'Oh, my gosh, what is all this?' Jeanie asked as they piled them up in front of her. She had to peer over the top of the tower to see them.

'For your grand reopening tomorrow!' Annie organized the boxes in a steadier stack. 'The order isn't usually this big, but I figure you'll have a pretty big turnout for the first weekend back. People are very excited.'

Jeanie's stomach swooped with nerves. 'They are?'

'Definitely. Didn't you see them last night? They need their caffeine fix.'

Hazel opened a box and pulled out a scone. 'Are you ready?'

I ... uh ... I guess.' Jeanie grabbed a scone, too, and nibbled at the corner. 'Norman's been a big help. Thankfully, he knows all the ins and outs of the café.'

Annie shut the box. 'Save some for the paying customers!'

'Honestly, I'm surprised Norman is still here,' Hazel said, propping an elbow on the counter.

'Really, why?'

Hazel shrugged, her brown curls bouncing on her shoulders. 'I always thought there was something going on between him and your aunt.'

Annie laughed. 'Ignore Hazel. She likes to pair off everyone in the town.'

'Laugh all you want. I saw the way Norman looked at Dot. Something was going on there.'

'Well, I saw the way you were eyeing Noah at the town meeting last night. What's going on there?'

'Nothing,' Hazel mumbled, around her mouthful of scone. Her face had turned red up to her hair. Jeanie bit down on a smile. She'd thought the fisherman who supported her ghost theory was cute, too, but she didn't know these women well enough to join in on their teasing. She could picture it, though. She could imagine herself being friends with them, fitting in here. It was her new favorite fantasy when she couldn't sleep at night.

'So, why have we never seen you around town?' Annie asked, changing the subject. 'Dot used to talk about you and your brother all the time.'

'Oh, yeah...' Guilt, sharp and sudden, settled in her gut. She'd neglected a lot of things when she'd been so busy at work. Her Aunt Dot was one of them. 'We came to visit a few times as kids. I used to love it here, actually. Spending time in her café. But then, I don't know ... my brother moved to California and life got busy, I guess.'

Annie studied her like she was trying to piece things together, trying to figure her out. Jeanie wondered what she saw. Was she pulling it off? Cool, calm, café owner? Or could Annie tell she was a frazzled ball of nerves inside, totally afraid of failing the first time she'd done anything for herself? Running this café would be the first time she wasn't working her butt off to make things happen for another person. This was all for her. Which frankly made it that much more terrifying.

'What do you think of Logan?' Hazel blurted out, pulling Annie and Jeanie's gaze to her.

'Just dive right in, Haze,' Annie hissed, nudging her friend with her elbow.

'I think he's very ... uh ... nice.' Jeanie fidgeted under

their intense inspection. 'It's nice of him to help me figure out the noise problem.'

'How is he helping with that exactly?' Annie asked, her face a mask of innocence.

'He ... uh ... we ... decided to do a stakeout.'

'A stakeout?' Hazel's eyes widened behind her glasses.

'Yeah, like on police dramas. We'll stay up and try to catch whoever, or whatever, is making the noise.'

'And Logan agreed to this?' Annie asked.

'Yes, it was his idea. We're doing it Monday night.' In fact, Jeanie had waited until most of the meeting hall had emptied out before finding Logan waiting for her by the door. She'd intended to tell him he was off the hook, but instead, he'd told her his plan to come by on Monday to see if he could hear the noises for himself. Although if she was being honest, he'd never called it a 'stakeout'. That had been all her.

She warmed at the memory of his amused smile when she'd said it. She liked making the quiet farmer smile.

Hazel let out a small moan. 'Oh, no. It's worse than we thought.'

'What is?' Jeanie broke off another piece of scone and popped it into her mouth afraid of saying the wrong thing.

'Here's the thing, Jeanie,' Annie said, fiddling with the bakery boxes again. 'Logan tends to fall pretty hard and his last relationship—'

'No, no, no . . . it's nothing like that!' Jeanie interrupted, holding up her hands to stop Annie's explanation and in the process flinging a piece of scone across the café. 'He's just helping because of the mayor and because I sort of almost decapitated him and I just need to get some sleep. That's it. That's ... um ... that's all.'

Annie's eyebrows rose higher as Jeanie spoke. 'Hmm. Look, I've known Logan our whole lives so I'm immune to his particular charms, but I'm not blind, Jeanie. I know what he looks like. He's objectively hot, but he also has a good heart, and I just don't want him to get hurt again.'

Jeanie did not want to know how Logan got hurt before, not from Annie anyway. That was his story to tell.

'Really. It's just about getting a good night's sleep. I didn't come to town to seduce the local farmers.'

Hazel giggled at that and stooped down to pick up the piece of dropped scone. 'We're sorry to come and attack you like this,' she said. 'The town sort of has a soft spot for Logan. His dad left before he was born, and his mom died when we were kids. The whole town sort of adopted him after that.'

Oh, God, she did not need to think about an adorable little Logan losing his mother.

'I won't hurt him,' she croaked. She shook her head. What was she even saying? 'I mean, I won't do anything with him, to him.' Oh, this was coming out all wrong. 'I mean, I'm not here to date anyone at all. I just want a fresh start. That's it.'

Annie nodded. Satisfied. 'Great! Well, in that case, welcome to the neighborhood.'

'Thanks.'

Annie hustled out of the café, but Hazel hung back. 'He's a really good guy,' she said.

'I'm sure he is.'

'I don't think it would be the worst thing if you wanted to do something to him.' Hazel winked.

'I...' Jeanie's cheeks heated.

'Just don't run off back to the city and abandon him!' Hazel said cheerily as she turned to go. 'See you tomorrow, bright and early, for my pumpkin-spiced latte!'

'Bye,' Jeanie said faintly, but her head was spinning from that little visit. Did Logan's friends want her to date him or to stay far away from him?

It didn't matter, anyway. She was being honest with them. She didn't come here to seduce the local farmers or to date them.

She was just here to serve coffee and ideally not die of a stress-induced heart attack at the ripe old age of twenty-eight.

Several hours later, the bakery case was lined with scones, muffins, and pumpkin-shaped sugar cookies for the morning. Every surface was gleaming, and Logan's little pumpkins were on every table and counter, providing just the right amount of fall-y-ness. The café was ready, but Jeanie still felt a current of nerves running beneath her skin.

She slumped down on a stool behind the counter and surveyed her new domain. It was certainly different from her desk outside Marvin's office. No smudged computer screen to stare at, no incessantly ringing phone to answer, no dirty coffee mugs that she was always behind on bringing back to the break room.

Her feet didn't ache from running around in heels all day, but her back hurt from cleaning and organizing and preparing for tomorrow. Her mind wasn't swimming with Marvin's appointments, his wife's birthday, his mistress's new address, and his lunch order. But her stomach was rolling with anticipation for tomorrow's grand opening. What if it all went wrong?

What was she even doing here? She looked out the big front window at her view of Main Street. The street itself was quaint and tidy, with trees lining the road. The leaves were just starting to change, mixing yellow and reds in with the green. Gold and purple mums sat outside most doors along the way.

Note to self: Get mums.

The café was flanked by the Bluebell Bookstore and Sullivan's Pub. Annie's bakery sat on the other side of the bookstore. Add in a few other shops and restaurants, the pet store, and the post office, and that was Main Street.

It was, frankly, adorable. Autumnal, small-town New England at its best. Shouldn't she feel different here? Away from the frenetic energy of Boston, the traffic, and the crowds? Shouldn't she *be* different here?

She was damn well going to try.

She rubbed a hand down her face. Maybe she would also try to tuck in early and actually get some sleep before tomorrow. The café opened at seven sharp, she'd been told repeatedly by Norman. She couldn't shake the feeling that he didn't like her, but she decided to chalk his curt attitude up to general old-man curmudgeonly-ness. Her aunt had trusted him for years, so Jeanie did, too.

But grumpy or not, she was glad Norman had stuck

around. He knew all the ins and outs of the café and their two baristas had stayed on as well. Jeanie didn't know what she was worried about. This place could easily run itself without her. She probably hadn't even needed to close it for a week, but she'd been so overwhelmed when she arrived. The idea of people actually coming in and wanting their usual morning coffee had nearly sent her running back to Boston to look for her next assistant job.

She thought of the realtor she'd called from the bare floor of her new apartment above the café. Barbara Sanders. She'd insisted Jeanie call her Barb during their brief conversation. Barb's picture stared up at her from the business card Jeanie had found slipped beneath the front door. She was polished and coiffed, poised, with a wide perfect smile. Jeanie found herself wanting to put her faith in this Barb, wanting to let Barb solve her problems.

She'd nearly agreed to let her put the café up for sale, but then the image of Marvin's body slumped over his desk, his face resting on a stack of reports, popped into her head and she hastily told Barb she'd changed her mind; though she'd agreed to let Barb send over the comps for what other businesses in the area had sold for recently and then hung up the phone and ate an enormous salad for good measure.

But now as she sat here looking at the tidy little café,

her tidy little café, that she had zero business running, Jeanie thought she may have made a mistake.

The space was small, just big enough for a few round tables and chairs and Jeanie tried to imagine it filled with customers. Her heart squeezed with excitement and nerves.

The bay window in the front was the perfect nook for two cozy chairs, worn down with age and use. Jeanie's apartment above the shop shared the same original hardwood floors, something Barb Sanders had raved about. In the middle of the room stood the L-shaped counter with one side for the register and one side for a few more bar stools. The glass case next to the register was filled with Annie's treats. The walls were painted a creamy white and filled with paintings by local artists. Little torn bits of paper stuck on the wall beside them told the title and the price.

Jeanie stared at a particularly large painting across the room from her of a big purple cow. Did the artist get nervous about hanging it? Did she sit at home with a sick feeling in her belly that she wasn't actually a very good painter at all? Did she worry about what people would think about her colorful farm animals or did she just go for it?

The knock at the back door disrupted her existential crisis and her staring contest with the cow. She hopped down from her stool and went to the back, pulling off her apron as she went. She'd put it on this morning with the hopes that it would make her feel more official. No luck there.

Logan was the last person she expected to see at her door, but she'd be lying if she said she didn't feel a flutter of excitement at finding him there.

'Hi,' she said, opening the door wider.

'Here,' he said, not bothering with a greeting. He held out his hand and, in his palm, rested a small box.

'Um ... what...'

'Sorry. They're earplugs. I thought they might help ... uh...' Logan ran a hand down his beard, his cheeks above it pinkening, '... to help you sleep tonight. Before your big day.'

You are not here for the local farmers, Jeanie reminded herself, but the sweetness of the gift, paired with the slightly awkward delivery, was making it very hard to remember why she wasn't here for the farmers. Specifically, the large, handsome one currently darkening her doorstep.

'Thank you! That's very nice of you.' She took the little box from his hand, dutifully ignoring how big it was and how rough and warm his palm was against her fingers.

'I brought a new lock, too. Noticed the one on the back door doesn't work right.'

'You ... brought a new lock? For me? For uh ... for my door?' Had it just been a very long time since Jeanie had dated anyone, or was this the most romantic gesture she'd ever experienced?

'Yeah, well, I figured you wouldn't be able to sleep if your lock was bad.' He fidgeted with the chain lock he'd pulled out of his back pocket. 'Not that there's really anything to worry about around here. I just figured...' His voice faded away as his gaze snagged on Jeanie's smile. His cheeks darkened.

'That's perfect. Thank you, really. That's so kind of you. It would have made me nervous to not be able to hear, but with my new lock, I'm sure I'll sleep peacefully. Tomorrow's a big day and I need to be ready.'

He blinked. 'Right.'

Right. She was rambling. 'I'll take that, I guess. I'm sure I can figure out how to attach it to the door.'

'No need.' Logan was already grabbing the toolbox at his feet. 'I'll have it on in a few minutes.'

'Oh. Okay. Great.' Jeanie stepped back and let him in, and then she definitely didn't stand there and admire his forearms flexing as he screwed the lock into her door. She certainly didn't breathe deeper to get more of his fall-leaves-and-woodsmoke scent into her lungs. She wouldn't do that because Logan was just a friendly neighbor, and she was just here for a fresh start. And she was not a crazy person.

But as he finished up and Jeanie's immediate reaction was sadness to see him go, she couldn't help but think that Hazel was right.

Her feelings for the handsome farmer were worse than she thought.

'Will you be here in the morning? For coffee?' *Of course, for coffee, Jeanie. What else would he be here for? Don't answer that,* she admonished herself.

Logan straightened, dropping his screwdriver back into the toolbox. 'Wouldn't miss it.'

The coffee. He was talking about the coffee.

But something about the way he was looking at her, the small lift of his mouth at the corner, she thought maybe it wasn't just the coffee. And then Annie's words came back to her, Logan tends to fall hard, he had his heart broken. Jeanie was in no place to be responsible for someone's heart. Certainly not someone as sweet as Logan. Not when she didn't have a clue what she was doing here or who she even was anymore.

'Great,' she said, the word a bit too loud, too sharp as she nudged Logan toward the door. 'See you tomorrow, then. And thanks again.' She shut the door behind the bewildered farmer a bit too quickly, but she had to get him out before she did something she would regret, like bury her face in his soft flannel shirt and ask him to stay.

Logan was not responsible for helping her with the current messy state of her life. She needed to get that sorted out before she got anywhere near him, especially with his friends and the whole town watching.

Chapter Six

'Where you headed so late in the day?' Logan's grandmother caught him in the process of trying to slip out quietly.

'Going into town. Probably won't be back til morning.'

'Morning?' His grandmother's eyebrows rose to her curly white hairline. 'What's got you in town until morning? A new lady friend. Or a gentleman friend. You know it doesn't matter to me as long as you're happy dear,' she said with a smile, as she patted him on the arm and scooted past him into the kitchen. It would have been easier to confess that he was meeting someone in town instead of explaining that he was going on a ghost stakeout with the new owner of the PS Café, whom he'd been having a very hard time not thinking about all weekend.

He'd made it to the shop Saturday and Sunday, happy to have his usual coffee fix back in place. It had nothing to do with catching a glimpse of Jeanie behind the counter, beaming at each customer as she rang up their orders. Or the fact that she'd looked totally in her element even when every other townsperson wanted her whole life story and current business plan for the café. Or the fact that her rotation of fall sweaters hugged her curves in very distracting ways. He was just a man who liked coffee.

The reopening had a big turnout as expected, and Jeanie didn't have more than a word or two to spare for him both days, but she did manage to tell him that she'd slept much better with the earplugs. Which was good because the sooner she went back to sleeping at night, the sooner he was off the hook for helping her.

Which was definitely what he wanted.

'You want some dinner before you go? I got some stew in the crock pot,' Nana asked, and Logan waited until her back was turned before he grimaced. He loved his grandmother, but her cooking was atrocious. Her crock pot was where food dreams went to die.

'No, thanks. Already ate.'

She studied him as she scooped out a bowl of stew for

herself. Her light purple sweatshirt had a wolf on the front howling at the moon, and the fluorescent, athletic pants she wore underneath it meant she'd been at her aerobics class today. Logan bit back a smile. His nana had more energy than most thirty-year-old's he knew.

'So, you gonna tell me what you're up to, or you don't tell your grandmother things anymore?' She took a mouthful of stew and scowled, dropping the spoon back into the bowl. 'Something went wrong with that batch.'

Logan huffed a laugh as his grandmother pulled a carton of ice cream out of the fridge instead.

'There's not much to tell.' He leaned against the doorframe of the kitchen and the wood groaned. The old farmhouse was nearly 150 years old. There weren't many parts of it that didn't groan and creak like an old man's joints. He liked it that way. There was history in this house. It was worn in like the perfect pair of old jeans.

'You know I'm a cool grandma. One-night stands, friends with benefits, picking girls up at the bar. Nothing shocks me.' She took a big spoonful of ice cream and smiled. 'That's much better.'

Logan stepped into the kitchen and laid a kiss on her cheek. 'I know. You're very cool. It's just something Pete wrangled me into.'

'That man is nuttier than a squirrel in spring.'

Logan laughed. 'He sure is. I'll see you in the

morning.' He turned to go. The sun had already set, and he'd promised Jeanie he'd be there by eight.

'Well, I'm always here if you need to talk, my little loganberry pie.'

He never knew what the hell a loganberry was, but his nana had been calling him that as long as he could remember. At this point in his life, she was the only mother he knew; his own mother had slowly faded from his memory. Now all he had were bits and pieces, a flash of a song she used to sing, or the rose water scent she used to wear.

But Nana had always been there for him. He stooped down and gave her a hug, pressing a kiss to the top of her head. 'If anything worth mentioning happens, you'll be the first to know.'

She smiled. 'That's all I ask.'

He was greeted by the only ladies he ever understood as soon as he stepped outside. His little flock of silkie chickens were his pride and joy. He tossed them some leftover corn from his dinner as he walked to his truck, enjoying their contented clucks and coos. Chickens he could do. Chickens made sense. Chickens didn't pretend they loved you until you proposed in front of the whole damn town at the annual Christmas-tree lighting and then suddenly changed their mind.

Logan's body went cold and then hot at the memory. It wasn't just the devastation of losing Lucy or the absolute confusion at her answer. It was the utter humiliation of having it happen in front of everyone he ever knew. And then the damn pity in everyone's eyes afterward. It was bad enough growing up as the town orphan, adding 'pathetic, lonely man' to his resume was a real kick in the nuts.

Nearly a year later and he still wasn't over it. Not Lucy. Lucy, he was over. They never made sense anyway. They'd met while she was on some kind of girl's weekend. She'd caught his eye at Mac's, which wasn't hard since she was the prettiest girl in there and the only one he hadn't known since childhood.

Her girls' weekend turned into a hot and heavy weekend for the two of them and Logan thought that'd be it. But she kept coming back to visit and he took time away from the farm to go see her in Boston. For a while, he thought maybe it could work.

But in the end, Lucy wanted him to be something he wasn't. As it turned out, Dream Harbor was fun for a mini vacation, but not somewhere she wanted to stay. She didn't like small-town life. She hated the farm, thought it was too smelly, too dirty, too old.

He should have seen her answer coming from a mile away. But she'd said she loved him, and he believed her, idiot that he was. He knew a small, quiet proposal wouldn't have suited her. Lucy liked big and bold, loud and flashy. Everything Logan wasn't. Another giant red flag he dutifully ignored until it was too late.

And so there he stood, on the town's biggest night, in front of the giant tree in the middle of the town square. He'd planned it all out with Mayor Kelly. Right after the countdown, Logan would drop to his knee in front of everyone and propose.

The scene ran through his mind in horror-movie slow motion as he walked down the dusty drive to his truck. He had dropped to his knee, pulled out the ring and the entire crowd went eerily quiet. He should have noticed the alarmed look on Lucy's face. It wasn't the look of a woman about to say yes. It was the look of a woman ready to flee.

And that's just what she did. He barely had the words, 'Will you marry me?' out of his mouth before she was shaking her head and running from the square, leaving Logan to face the stunned crowd. She was on the first commuter train to Back Bay the next morning.

His stomach clenched at the memory.

Good, he thought. Hold on to that feeling. Because that was exactly what would happen again if he got involved with Jeanie. The town was already obsessed with her being here. One, because she was new. Two, because she was serving them their life-giving coffee. And three, because she was a beautiful ray of sunshine.

Nope. Cut it out. That's exactly the kind of nonsense that'd blinded him to reality last time. Jeanie just got here. Not to mention she had no experience running a small business. And she was used to living in Boston. Logan absolutely could not get involved with someone who had one foot out the door. Again.

No more dating flight risks. No more dating with the town watching.

Two simple rules to remember. Surely, even a man with a history of making horrible decisions regarding women could do that.

He stopped in front of the old fence that kept Harry Styles, his rescue alpaca, safely out of the driveway. Or attempted to. He was always finding the shaggy animal everywhere he shouldn't be, including with his head halfway in the kitchen window munching on the screen.

He gave the old boy a good scratch on his head, Harry giving him a flick of his ears in thanks. His grandmother had let the small group of girl scouts, that had dropped by with her cookie order one day, name him, but Logan had to admit, it suited him. There was something very confident about this alpaca, something that said he could sell out stadiums to thousands of screaming fans, too, if he wanted. He'd just rather be here, munching grass instead.

Logan scratched him a bit longer, letting his old memories drift away before heading to Jeanie's. It was a cool night even though it was only early October, and the wind rustled the dry leaves across the fields. The moon was full and bright overhead, with a stray cloud casting a shadow across it every now and then.

As good a night as any for a ghost hunt, he supposed.

He bid Harry goodbye and hopped in his truck. Might as well get this whole absurd night over with, he told himself, even as his stomach flipped with a new emotion he refused to identify as excitement to see Jeanie.

Chapter Seven

Jeanie reorganized the snacks for the fifth time since she'd laid them out. She might have overdone it. There were three kinds of potato chips, corn chips, and guac; pretzels in several shapes, a jumbo-sized bag of mini candy bars intended for trick-or-treaters; Twizzlers (which Jeanie hated, but thought Logan might like), fresh-baked cookies from Annie's bakery; and she had a pizza on the way.

Definitely too much. She straightened the avalanche of chip bags again. The only thing she knew about stakeouts was that they required snacks. Right? That seemed right. Also, she was nervous about spending the night with Logan, so she figured if she kept her mouth filled with snacks, nothing too bad could happen. That made sense. She had this totally under control.

The pack of Twizzlers slid off the table and landed with a slap on the floor.

Yep, totally under control.

She plopped into one of the overstuffed chairs by the front windows. She'd laid out the snacks on the coffee table in the little nook, figuring this would be the most comfortable spot for their stakeout. The rest of the café was filled with small round tables and wooden chairs, perfect for a quick cup of coffee but not great for sitting in all night.

For the past three days, those tables had been crowded with town locals from open to close. It had been hectic and busy and exhilarating. The café ran like a well-oiled machine and Jeanie spent a lot of the time greeting and chatting with people. She was even learning some of the regular orders for her customers. Having a customer come in and say, 'The usual, please,' and Jeanie knowing what that was seemed like the pinnacle of café ownership.

Everyone had been very welcoming, happy to share stories of her Aunt Dot and to ask her a million questions about herself. Jeanie had almost felt like she belonged here, or at least like maybe she could belong here.

The best part about opening weekend was she fell into bed exhausted each night and with the help of Logan's earplugs, and a newly installed lock keeping her safe and sound, Jeanie slept like a baby. And not one of those babies that's up all night. Like a really impressive sleeping baby.

She glanced at the snack mountain again. She probably should have called off this ridiculous stakeout. She was about to, and she would have, had she not come down the back stairs this morning, flying high on a full night of sleep, and heard it again. Scratching at her back door. But when Norman came in a few minutes later to help her open, he said he hadn't seen a thing back there.

It also didn't help matters that good old Norman had told her the history of this building and about the family that had died here. He said it was scarlet fever. Or maybe yellow fever? Some kind of colorful fever that had taken out the whole family.

Apparently, Aunt Dot had made peace with them over the years, but it was Norman's best guess that the family was not pleased with the change in ownership.

Jeanie grabbed a cookie and checked her watch again. 7.45pm. Logan should be here soon. He seemed like the type to be on time for things. Considerate of other people's time. Thoughtful enough to bring you earplugs when you couldn't sleep. Handsome enough to stop traffic. Things like that.

Why was she not supposed to date him?

Oh, right, she needed to get her life back on track

first. Figure out how to live in this tiny, odd town. Transform into the quintessential café owner. Calm and cool, maybe a little quirky. The kind of person who paints purple farm animals in her spare time. Like Aunt Dot. A free spirit just living her dream, following her bliss, or whatever. Then she could date the farmer. Maybe. If his friends said she could.

A firm knock at the back door startled her out of her thoughts. It wasn't the eerie scratching of a long-dead ghost, but the solid knock of the solid man on the other side. Jeanie got up and hurried across the café to the back door and undid her shiny new lock.

'Sorry, I'm late.'

Jeanie peeked at her watch. It was 8.02pm. She bit down on a smile. 'No problem. Come on in.'

Logan nodded and followed her across the small space.

'I thought we could set up here since it's more comfortable, but now I'm realizing I usually hear the noises out back, so maybe we should move toward the back of the café. I've never been on a stakeout before, so . . .'

Jeanie looked up from her rambling to see Logan staring at her snack pile.

'Oh, and I thought we might get hungry.'

She watched the corner of his mouth hitch up. 'We

might.' He ran a hand down his beard, his gaze still on the food. 'Not sure I've ever been this hungry though.'

Jeanie might have been embarrassed if she hadn't caught a glimpse of the other side of his mouth rising. She'd made him smile.

She grinned at him in return. 'Well, we have the whole night ahead of us. I haven't stayed up all night since middle school sleepovers, and we always had a lot of snacks for those.'

'Sure,' he said, the amused look still on his face as he tore open the pack of Twizzlers and pulled one out. Aha! She knew it.

'When's the last time you heard the noises?' he asked, lowering himself into the chair next to hers, getting right down to business. He tore off a piece of Twizzler with his teeth and chewed.

'This morning.' She sat down, too, taking a bag of sour cream and onion chips with her. 'You really like those things? They are objectively the worst candy.'

'Objectively, huh?' He studied the red licorice in his hand and then took another bite. 'There's been studies done on this?'

Jeanie laughed. 'Probably. It's common knowledge that they're the worst.'

Logan studied her a minute too long, causing the heat to rise in her cheeks. He took another bite. 'A woman with strong opinions.' He nodded, as if deciding something. 'I like that.'

Jeanie stuffed a handful of chips in her mouth before she could say that she liked his shirt and his face and his entire personality, even though she barely knew him. Instead, she just nodded between loud, crunchy bites.

'So, do you have strong opinions about ghosts, too?' he asked. 'You really think that's what's going on here?'

Jeanie shrugged. 'Maybe. It seems to be as good a theory as any.'

Logan raised an eyebrow as if to say, *really?* But he didn't voice his thoughts on that out loud.

'Plus, the mayor and everyone else seemed really convinced this was a good idea. I mean me and you ... I mean, you helping me with this.'

He huffed. 'Yeah. This town is full of great ideas.' Oh, no, she was afraid of this. He didn't want to have any part of this crazy stakeout thing. She should have known. She'd cornered him into it and then the whole town basically jumped on board.

'You don't like it here? Dream Harbor, I mean,' she asked, avoiding her real question for the moment.

'I love it here. It's my home.'

'Oh. It just seemed like you maybe didn't.'

Logan ran a hand down his beard. 'Do you have siblings, Jeanie?'

A bit of a left turn, but they were here all night. Good to keep the conversation going. 'I have a brother who lives out in California.' In fact, she'd been on the phone with Bennett an hour ago as she'd tried to pick out snack food. It had been his bad influence that convinced her to get way too much of everything.

'Okay, well you know that feeling that no one is allowed to say bad things about your brother except you? Like even if he bugs you, only you can say he's a pain.'

Jeanie smiled. 'Yeah, I get that.' In third grade, she'd uninvited two girls from her birthday party for accusing Ben of knocking down their snowman. And then she'd had to sit on him until he confessed when she realized he'd probably done it. It was a very confusing time for her.

He nodded and bit into another Twizzler. 'That's how I feel about this town.'

'So, you love them even though they make you crazy.'

'Exactly.'

'And you're here against your will because the mayor sent you to help the new girl?'

Please say no. Please say no.

He shook his head, his dark eyebrows pulling together. 'I'm not here against my will.' *Phew.*

'Okay...' She hadn't forced him into this insane evening of ghost hunting, but she couldn't help but feel like there was more to the story, like Logan had some other theory for why the town wanted him here.

Jeanie waited, munching on chips while Logan slowly chewed his way through the rest of the Twizzler. Finally, he met her gaze.

'This town, the people in it, they can be ... a lot. But they care about me.' He shrugged like it was no big deal to have an entire town of people care about you. Jeanie could count on one hand the people who cared about her.

She swallowed hard.

'But I don't believe in ghosts.'

She laughed. 'Ghosts or not, I'll be happy if we get to the bottom of this mystery. Although the earplugs helped a lot. And that new security system you installed – very helpful.' She smiled at him and watched the blush creep up his cheeks.

He cleared his throat. 'Glad it helped.' He shifted in his seat. 'Now tell me more about these noises.'

Chapter Eight

It was well past midnight when they rolled out the sleeping bags.

'Thanks for bringing these. I'm not much of a camper. You probably could have guessed that. Just imagine how I'd be in a tent with no lock and all manner of creepy noises outside.'

Jeanie smiled as she held onto the edge of the bag and shook it out. Logan was relieved to see only a few pine needles fall out. It had been a long time since he'd used these. He was glad she didn't shake out a family of mice.

'Although, I did camp with the girl scouts as a kid. But I was mostly in it for the s'mores. Once I learned you could make those in the microwave, that was the end of my camping days.'

Logan nodded. He'd already learned that most of

Jeanie's stories didn't require a response, and since she'd eaten half her weight in candy and washed it down with enough cups of coffee that he'd lost count, her stories had increased in quantity and speed. No time for a response, anyway.

'I could see you camping,' she went on, settling onto her sleeping bag. 'You're that type of guy.'

He sat across from her on his own sleeping bag. 'What type is that?' he asked, too curious about what kind of guy Jeanie thought he was to stop himself.

She tipped her head, studying him. Her thick black hair swung over her shoulder. 'You know...'

He shook his head. He absolutely did not know, but was now embarrassingly desperate to find out.

Jeanie blew out a sigh like he was being difficult. 'The rugged type, outdoorsy, flannel-y.'

'Flannel-y?'

'Yeah.' She gestured to the general area of his flannel-clad torso. 'You've got a very strong beardy, flannel-y vibe going on.'

Logan frowned. Was beardy bad? He ran a hand down his face self-consciously. Did Jeanie not like flannel? It was just so warm and cozy.

'Don't get me wrong,' she said, leaning closer. 'It's totally working for you.'

Oh. *Oh ... it was working for him.*

Her cheeks flushed pink in the warm light of the café. She blew out another breath and pushed her hair behind her ear. 'I just mean that flannel is very practical for your line of work, and the beard suits you. And I'm sure you're very good at camping.'

Practical. Right. That was him. Sturdy. Like a reliable piece of farming equipment.

You're a really good guy, Logan. The memory of Lucy's goodbye rang through him. *You've built yourself a nice, comfortable life here, but I just can't do it. I can't stay in this little town forever. I need more than this.*

He let his beard grow in after she left. Lucy hated a beard.

'I'll go grab us some pillows.' Jeanie jumped up and clambered up the backstairs to her apartment.

Damn it. He was probably scowling at her, all his Lucy-induced anger misdirected toward Jeanie. He glanced at his watch. 1.07am and still no weird sounds, no ghostly chill in the room, nothing out of the ordinary at all. This was absurd.

He toed off his boots and stretched out on the sleeping bag, his hands behind his head. He was positive at this point that these noises were nothing more than Jeanie's nerves about being in a new place. Which was totally understandable, but at some point she was going to have to get over it.

It might have been Nana's voice in his head, telling him he absolutely should not tell Jeanie to get over it. But even he wasn't that dumb. He would just hang out with her until she was feeling better. And he would not be a jerk. Even when her innocuous comments dredged up old insecurities.

The stairs creaked on Jeanie's way down, and she was standing over him with an armload of pillows before he could get up to help her.

'Here you go,' she said and dropped a pillow on his face.

He took it and stuffed it behind his head. 'Gee, thanks.'

Jeanie giggled and dropped the remaining pillows on her sleeping bag. Logan stared at the ceiling while Jeanie got herself settled, suddenly aware of the intimacy of lying next to someone in the middle of the night. Even if that was all it was.

They'd turned off the main lights in the café, leaving them in the soft glow of the night lights behind the counter. Moonlight streamed in through the big front window and the trees outside cast shadows on the ceiling. The room smelled like coffee and pastries.

'Now, we can't get too comfy,' she said. 'Or we might fall asleep and miss it.'

'Well, we wouldn't want that,' Logan murmured even

as he let himself relax into his pillow. It smelled like Jeanie, like her shampoo, and he resisted the urge to roll over and breathe in.

Jeanie's sleeping bag rustled as she rolled over to face him. He stayed on his back, feeling safer staring at the ceiling instead of looking into her dark brown eyes.

'I know you think I'm crazy.'

'I don't.'

Jeanie let out a little disbelieving 'harumph', her breath skating across the side of his face. Logan closed his eyes at the sensation, so soft, so warm.

'I'm fully aware of how crazy all this is. I just wanted everything to be ... perfect here, for this new ... endeavor. And I can't shake the feeling that something is wrong. Like something is trying to get rid of me.'

Logan rolled toward her, and she was so close, he could hear the hitch in her breath. His need to make her happy here rose to the surface before he could stop it, that same damn instinct that hurt him every time.

'You're doing great.'

Her eyes widened like she wasn't expecting that, and that hurt him too. Was she not used to hearing that she was doing a good job?

'I just had this vision of how it would be to live here and run my aunt's café.'

'And?'

She wriggled deeper into her pile of pillows, her eyes big and dark. 'And it's been different than I thought.'

And there it was. The reason he needed to stay away from this woman. She expected Dream Harbor to be something it wasn't, and she would expect the same from him.

'You need to settle in. It'll be fine.' His voice was gruffer than he intended, but her words reminded him of why he shouldn't be with her in this darkened café, smelling her pillow, wishing she was lying closer to him. It was like that first weekend with Lucy all over again, when he thought he could sell her Dream Harbor. And himself.

At least everyone still had their clothes on this time.

Jeanie's hair rustled against the pillow as she nodded, but she didn't look convinced.

'My boss died on his desk. And I found him,' she blurted out.

'What?' His feelings for her shifted violently again, and the little crease between her brows nearly killed him. 'Shit, Jeanie. That's awful.' No wonder she was so unsettled. Finding her dead boss. She wasn't just here for a little change of scenery. She was running scared.

'Yeah.' Tears pooled in her eyes. 'It was pretty awful.' Her voice was so small, so hurt. *Damn it, damn it, damn it.* He couldn't handle crying women. Every instinct in his body was clamoring at him to fix it, make it better.

He cleared his throat. 'What did you do there – at your old job, I mean.'

'Administrative assistant to the CEO.'

'Wow. Impressive.'

'Not really.' The slight change in subject kept the tears from falling. *Thank God.* 'I mostly ran around making sure everything went smoothly. Scheduled meetings, filed paperwork, got coffee. Things like that. But it ended up taking up my whole life. I never meant it to.'

She took a deep breath and rolled onto her back, so Logan did the same. Safe from her intense gaze again.

'I majored in business as an undergrad, but I never knew what I wanted to do with the degree. It just seemed like a safe bet, like I would figure it out afterward.'

'Where'd you go to school?' Logan asked. He'd keep the questions coming if it kept her from crying about her dead boss.

'B.U.'

'Go Terriers.'

She huffed a small laugh. 'The fiercest mascot around.'

'Hey, those little things can be ferocious when provoked.'

She laughed again and he let the sound roll over him.

God, she had a good laugh. The genuine kind that just kind of bursts out in a little spark of joy. He liked it, wanted to bottle it up and bring it home for when he was regretting this whole damn night and whatever came next that left him a broken mess again.

'Anyway, I took an assistant job and I guess I was good at it because I ended up at the top of the company by the end. But I'd never meant to do it for seven years.'

Their hands lay between them on the sleeping bags and Logan brushed her pinky with his own, encouragement to go on, but that small touch sent shivers through his body. It was late and the town was quiet around them. The only light was the soft yellow glow of the nightlights behind the counter. They were alone in their own little coffee-scented, candy-fueled bubble. And Logan liked it a little bit too much. Moments like this, nights like this didn't last. Eventually, reality hit and all you had left were two people with incompatible lives.

'Then one morning, I walked in with Marvin's usual latte in hand and there he was. It wasn't unusual for him to stay in the office all night. No one had checked on him. No one was even worried about him. He died completely alone.'

Jeanie sniffled next to him. Logan grabbed her hand

and twined his fingers with hers. Warm and soft and small. Perfect.

'Thanks.' She sniffed. 'The thing is, I realized that could be me. I'd let my job become everything. My boss worked all the time, so I did, too. I didn't have friends anymore. I saw my family a few times a year. I didn't even visit Dot and she only lived a short drive away!'

'Everyone gets busy.'

'I got the flu two years ago.'

Logan was getting whiplash from the turns in this conversation. 'The flu is very different from a heart attack.'

'I know, but I had it really bad. Multiple days of a high fever, throwing up, the whole nine yards.' She started sniffling again, her voice choked with tears and Logan gave her hand another reassuring squeeze. 'No one checked on me. There was no one *to* check on me. I threw up on my living room rug and couldn't clean it up until three days later. I had to throw the whole carpet away!'

She was fully crying now, sad little hiccupping sobs that twisted Logan's insides up so tight he couldn't breathe.

'Hey, hey, don't cry. Please. It's going to be alright.'

He unhooked their fingers and wrapped an arm around her instead, pulling her into him. She immediately buried her face in his side, and he could feel the warm, wet tears through his shirt.

'Shh ... everything's alright now.' He rubbed her back in slow circles, every bone in his body wanting to make the crying stop, wanting to make sure she never felt like this again. 'I promise, the next time you puke you can call me, okay? I'll clean it up. I deal with all sorts of gross farm emergencies every day. You haven't seen anything until you've had an alpaca spit on you.'

Jeanie's laugh was muffled in his shirt.

'This shirt is really nice,' she said. 'I told you being flannel-y is a good thing.'

He chuckled, pulling her closer, ignoring every warning bell ringing in alarm at how comfortable this felt. How right. She'd basically just confessed that the only reason she was here was because she was suffering from the shock and trauma of finding her dead boss. Once she was feeling better, what would keep her here then? It was only a matter of time before she realized this small-town life wasn't for her. Just like Lucy.

'Sorry about that,' she said, emerging from his shirt. 'I think I'm crashing from that sugar high.'

'Yeah, could be.'

Jeanie's hair hung into her tear-stained face. Logan tucked it behind her ear, letting his knuckles brush along her cheek. She closed her eyes, her wet lashes sticking together in black spikes. Her nose was pink from crying and her body was so warm next to his; she fit right into his side like a puzzle piece. And despite every reason not to, it seemed natural, obvious even that he would lean forward and kiss her, like they'd done it a million times before.

But before he could cross a line he couldn't uncross, Jeanie's eyes flew open.

'Did you hear that?' she asked, whispering so she wouldn't scare the alleged ghost away. Logan tried to hear over the racing beat of his heart, still not recovered from what he almost did, what he still wanted to do.

'I don't—'

And then he heard it. A distinct scratching sound. Followed by a shrill cry coming from the back alley.

Maybe they'd found a ghost after all.

Chapter Nine

Phew. That was close. Jeanie tiptoed behind Logan on their way to the back door to investigate. She was actually thankful to the ghost for interrupting what was sure to be a mistake. Logan had been about to kiss her, and she was totally about to let him. And then what?

Her imagination very helpfully filled in the 'then what?' with a pornographic slideshow of ideas. She shook her head free of the wildly inappropriate things she wanted to do to the grumpy farmer on her café floor. Now was not the time for that. She had an angry spirit at her back door.

'What do we do?' she whispered, nearly crashing into Logan's back when he stopped suddenly.

The scratching stopped and then started up again, like fingernails on wood. Oh God, oh God, oh God. Was there really an angry ghost at her back door? WHY HAD HER AUNT NOT MENTIONED THIS PLACE WAS HAUNTED?! She needed to call her up and have a very stern chat with her later.

An unearthly cry emanated from behind the door and Jeanie buried her face in the back of Logan's super-soft flannel shirt.

'I don't remember that yowling from last time. Do you think that means I've made them even angrier?' she asked, her voice muffled from the fabric.

'No, I don't.'

She could feel the vibration of his voice on her face and nearly giggled at the sensation. But then she remembered she was scared and continued her cowering. So much for her new low-stress lifestyle. Her laid back small-town persona had flown right out the window. She'd be lucky if she didn't die of a heart attack right here, right now.

Ugh, how embarrassing.

She heard the sound of metal on metal as Logan undid the chain lock on the door.

'Don't open it!' she yelled into the very firm space between his shoulder blades. 'We don't know what to do yet! We need a plan, a ghost-removal plan. Oh, God, we should have been figuring this out instead of me blubbering on and on about my problems,' she wailed, still speaking into Logan's back.

Something brushed against her leg.

'Gah!' She nearly climbed Logan's body – not the worst idea she'd ever had – until she realized the door was wide open and there was a pure white cat weaving its way in and out of Jeanie and Logan's legs.

'Well, there's your ghost.'

Jeanie stepped back. 'Wait. What?' She stared at the cat and the cat stared back. 'It's ... it's a cat.'

Logan chuckled. 'It's a cat.'

Jeanie's face flushed hot, and she covered her eyes with her hands. 'I am the world's biggest idiot,' she groaned, unable to look at the man she'd lured in here to help her. Her ghost was just a freaking cat! She would have preferred if an angry ghost was here to steal her immortal soul. At least then she would be vindicated in her concern.

'I'm so sorry I made you do this,' she said from behind her hands.

'Jeanie...'

'No, no, no. You don't need to be all nice about it. First, I almost take your head off, and then I force you to help me by taking me to that nutty town meeting, and then, oh, God, and then I get the freaking mayor involved!'

Logan peeled her hands away from her face. 'Hey. Stop that.'

Jeanie bit down on her bottom lip to prevent herself from more rambling.

'The only person that makes me do anything is my nana and that's only because she's put up with my crap since I was five years old. Got it?'

Jeanie nodded. 'I feel so dumb. It's just a cat.'

Said cat let out a plaintive cry at her feet. They both looked down and apparently realized at the same time that Logan was still holding her wrists. He dropped them like her hands were on fire and took a step back, nearly colliding with the wall behind him.

'We should probably get this guy something to eat. I've got cat food out in the truck.'

He was gone before Jeanie could ask why he kept cat food in his truck or what she should do with the cat in the meantime. She looked down at the scraggly white puffball.

'You kind of made me look bad, ya know.'

The cat stared at her, its turquoise eyes wide. It was eerie in its intensity, like it could see into her soul. Maybe this cat was a ghost?! Or maybe Jeanie needed to lay off the candy and get to bed before she totally lost her mind.

'Shouldn't you blink more?' she asked her new ghost-cat.

More staring, and then the cat stood and rubbed itself against Jeanie's leg. Well, now what? Jeanie had never had a pet. Never had time for one. Growing up, she wasn't allowed to have pets with fur or hair or feathers on account of her mother's allergies. So, other than a few short-lived goldfish, Jeanie had never cared for another living thing in her entire life.

Unless you counted Marvin, which maybe she should, although that turned out really badly in the end.

She glanced back down at the cat, now suddenly convinced she'd end up killing the darn thing if Logan didn't reappear very soon with that food. And then the cat started purring, the gentle vibration echoing up Jeanie's leg. Well, that was kinda nice.

She stooped down and gave the little beast a scratch between the ears and the purring intensified. 'Does this mean we're friends now?'

'It's certainly a good sign,' Logan's amused voice told her from the doorway.

Jeanie smiled up at him. 'We're getting to know each other.'

Logan gave her the nod that meant he'd heard and acknowledged her, but had nothing to add to the conversation, something she'd never personally experienced. She always had something to add. Maybe she should try more nodding instead.

Logan made his way around her and the cat and rummaged in the drawers behind the counter. He found the can opener, and as soon as the can was open, Jeanie's new friend suddenly had zero interest in head scratches. The cat beelined to the dish of food Logan set on the floor.

'Hungry. No tags. Probably a stray,' he said, leaning against the counter, arms across his wide chest.

'You keep cat food in your truck?'

'Of course.'

'Of course...'

Logan ran a hand down his beard, his gaze still on the cat. 'Never know when you might need it.'

'Right,' Jeanie said, biting down on a grin. This man was full of surprises. 'Do you have a lot of cats on your farm?'

'A few barn cats.'

'And?'

Logan's mouth hitched up in the corner. 'Two goats, an alpaca, and half a dozen chickens.'

'But I thought you were a produce farm?'

'They're rescues. They're not there to work. Well, except for the chickens. They lay an egg or two when they feel like it.'

Seriously? He rescued animals, too? This guy was sure hiding a lot behind that beard and scowl. It made her really question her instincts, considering she initially thought he was a serial killer.

The cat finished eating and Logan sank into a squat to pet it. He was still in his socked feet, with the sleeves of his flannel shirt rolled up. His hair was rumpled from laying down and he spoke softly to the cat while he scratched between its ears. The whole scene was so domestic, so intimate, Jeanie had to look away. This was how it would be if he slept over; if they woke up together and came down for a cup of coffee before the day started. Jeanie wanted it so badly in that moment it took her breath away. The fantasy washed over her so quickly, she forgot to stop it. Is this what she'd been missing?

Soft, quiet moments in the early morning hours.

She wanted to hold onto it, but she didn't know how. She'd never been able to before. Her life was fast and noisy, and she'd dived into it without really thinking. Life had just happened to her. For the past seven years, she'd managed to avoid thinking about what she wanted and now all she wanted was this man, petting this cat, and holding her against his strong body like he had before.

He'd almost kissed her. Her face flushed hot at the memory. He'd almost kissed her, and she'd wanted him to. Maybe he would try again...

'I can give you the number for the vet I use,' he said, interrupting her fantasy.

Huh? Vet for the cat. Her new cat. Right. Logan was not thinking about kissing her again, he was trying to help her with the stray animal that had apparently been tormenting her since she got here.

She cleared her throat, but her voice still came out strangely thick. 'That would be great, thanks.'

Logan stood to his full height and ran a hand through his messy hair. The cat stared up at him, clearly already missing his touch.

Same, cat. Same.

'I guess that settles that,' he said, and Jeanie searched her mind frantically for some other reason to get him to stay, for some other reason to get back in his comforting embrace. But she had nothing, and Logan looked exhausted.

What was she going to do? Hold him hostage? *Maybe?* No, definitely not the New Jeanie she was shooting for.

'Yep, all settled. Thank you for your help. I guess Mayor Kelly was right.'

Logan rolled his eyes. 'Don't encourage him.' He turned and grabbed the notepad she kept next to the register. It was full of her little notes about who was who and who liked what. The margins were full of hearts and swirls and flowers. Little doodles she made during the slow times, not that there were many.

She watched as Logan's eyes scanned the page. His lips tipped into a small smile before he turned the page and wrote the vet's name and number.

'She's the best. She'll get you all straightened out.' He added his cell number to the bottom of the paper. 'Just in case anyone throws up,' he said and then strode over to their little nest on the floor. He tossed the pillows onto the nearest chair and knelt to put away the sleeping bags.

Jeanie stood leaning against the counter, finding herself unable to move to help him. It was like her body was on strike against anything that would get him out of here quicker. 'Thanks again. I really appreciate it. All of it. Your help and being so nice to me and everything.'

He glanced over his shoulder at her, pausing in the middle of rolling up his sleeping bag. 'I think maybe you're not used to being treated right, Jeanie.'

His words landed hard. Damn.

Was it true? Had she gotten used to being treated poorly and taken advantage of? The nature of her job had been to make sure Marvin had everything he needed to do his job. But who made sure she had everything she needed?

She hadn't had anyone to lean on in so long. She hadn't slowed down long enough to lean, even if there had been someone there. When Jeanie looked back over the last seven years, her life was a blur of late nights at the office and early-morning coffee runs. Her last few relationships had been short-lived, and lately, few and far between, and her work friends were more acquaintances than friends. She certainly hadn't felt comfortable calling any of them when she couldn't even clean up her own vomit. Her mother probably would have driven the nine hours from Buffalo to Boston to help her, but that was insane, and Jeanie would never have asked her to.

Somehow in the frenzy of the last few years, Jeanie hadn't even had time to realize she was lonely.

Logan went back to rolling up the bags, his movements precise and efficient. He wasted no time in getting his boots back on and grabbed his coat from over the back of his chair.

She would call him if she threw up and was too weak to move afterward, and he would come. She already knew that, but she didn't know if she was comforted or terrified of this prospect. Logan was kind and sturdy and considerate. She could clearly see what he had to offer her. It was obvious.

But what did she have to offer in return? A pile of insecurities about running this café; an undercurrent of anxiety that she'd made the wrong choice moving here;

too much chatter, not enough listening – and a tendency to jump to the worst-case scenario in all scenarios.

It wasn't a great list.

And it also wasn't who she wanted to be anymore.

So, the New Jeanie plan had a new level, a final tier in which she gets the handsome farmer.

Her new cat meowed loudly at her feet. She wasn't there yet. First, she needed to get some sleep. Then she needed to figure out how to be a cat owner. Everything else would fall into place after that.

'I'm gonna get going.'

While she'd stood there daydreaming, Logan had cleaned up their snack mess and filled a bowl of water for the cat. Shoot. Not off to a great start.

'Okay, sounds good. Thanks again. And I'll see you later.' Jeanie winced. One of those goodbyes would have been sufficient.

'Get some sleep.' His voice was low as he brushed past her on his way to the back door.

Jeanie nodded. Much safer than saying what she was thinking and what she was thinking was that she would sleep much better if he stayed.

Chapter Ten

'I have a new theory,' Annie bustled in the front door, the brisk October wind following her in. Jeanie had known her for less than a week, but the woman always seemed to be in the middle of a conversation Jeanie had no idea they'd been having.

She liked it. It was something friends did.

It was late afternoon, so the café was fairly empty. Jeanie had insisted she would be fine on her own, and Norman had left early to take his niece to the zoo. Or was it to take his nephew to the aquarium? She hadn't been paying very close attention to Norman since most of her brain power was currently being used to daydream about Logan and his soft flannels and strong arms and his secret cat whisperer abilities.

'A new theory about what?' Jeanie asked from her

perch behind the counter. She'd brought a stool back here for when the café was slow, even though Norman had huffed and puffed about it. Customers don't want to see you sitting, he'd said.

'Customers want their coffee. They don't care if I'm standing on my head while I serve it,' she'd argued. He dropped it after that.

'A new theory about your ghost,' Annie said.

The butcher block counter between them was 'L' shaped, with a side for the register to place an order, and a side with stools for sitting. Annie pulled up a stool and sat with a sigh. The bakery closed at three so Annie was off for the day.

'Oh, right. Well, that problem is solved.'

'Solved? What, already?'

Jeanie slid Annie's usual chai latte across the counter, and Annie clutched it in her hands. She breathed in the spiced scent before continuing with her questions.

'Ghosts can be tricky. Are you sure it's gone?'

'Turns out it wasn't a ghost at all.'

Annie frowned into her mug. 'Did Logan convince you of that? He's the world's biggest skeptic, Jeanie. He only believes in things he can hold in his own two hands.'

'He did pet the cat that showed up last night with his own two hands, so I think it's settled.'

'A cat? No way.'

As if on cue, the cat who Jeanie had so cleverly named Casper, sauntered into the café. He walked to the square of sunshine on the floor coming in from the big front window, plopped down, threw a leg over his head, and began to lick himself.

If Norman was here, he would have a fit. He was less than pleased with the new Pumpkin Spice Café family member. But Jeanie had already taken him to the vet this morning, gotten him his shots, bought a litter box and a giant bag of vet-recommended cat food. This guy was here to stay.

Annie glanced at Casper and then back at Jeanie. Her skepticism was written across her round face.

'It's true. I was here last night with Logan and then we heard this scratching at the back door. It was the cat. It must have been what I'd been hearing all along.' Jeanie's face heated at the mention of Logan and being here all night with him and the memory of how his fingers had felt brushing across her cheek when he swept the hair away from her face.

Annie raised an eyebrow. 'Hmm.'

Oh, no, her farmer fantasies were clearly written across her face. She'd never had this problem at her old job. No one in her old life had evoked these feelings in her. She had never once wanted to burrow her face into the work shirt of any of her colleagues. It was the magic of the flannel.

'Well, if anything else strange happens, you let me know because I think Mac is up to something.'

It was Jeanie's turn to raise a skeptical eyebrow. 'You think Mac is haunting my café?'

'Not haunting.' Annie waved a hand, nearly knocking over her mug, and Jeanie slid it out of the way. 'I think he's trying to scare you off.'

'Why would he do that?' Jeanie had hardly met the man. A café owner and a pub owner basically worked opposite shifts. Other than a polite hello when she was closing up and he was opening, she hadn't interacted with Mac Sullivan at all.

'He wants your space. He's wanted to expand the pub since he bought it last year. I heard he made an offer to Dot for the café, but she turned him down.'

'Even still. Just because he wanted the café at some point doesn't mean he'd try to drive me out of here.'

'You don't know him like I do, Jeanie. Just be careful,' Annie added ominously, before sipping the latte Jeanie had slid back in front of her.

'Will do.'

The bell jingled over the café door and another cool breeze swept into the shop. Dry leaves swirled in its wake.

'Oh, aren't you a little darling!' Hazel stooped down to rub Casper's belly and he purred in delight. 'Where did he come from?'

'That's Jeanie's ghost.'

'Really?' Hazel looked up, her eyes wide behind her glasses. 'This little guy was making all that noise?'

'Apparently,' Annie said, still not sounding convinced. 'Jeanie and Logan were here all night before that cat showed up.'

'Oh?' Hazel stood and strolled toward the counter. 'And how did that go?'

'Fine. Good. Totally normal ghost stakeout.' Jeanie turned, suddenly finding it very urgent to wipe down the cappuccino machine. It was almost closing time, after all. Time to clean up for the day. Certainly not the time to face down Hazel's unnerving stare. It was nearly as unsettling as Casper's.

'Totally normal ghost stakeout, huh? Well, that's nice.'

Jeanie ignored the looks Annie and Hazel were exchanging and instead made Hazel her usual pumpkin-spiced latte.

'Yep. Very nice,' Jeanie mimicked, setting down Hazel's drink. 'And now it's all settled. The noises were just a cat.' She shrugged. No big deal. It was all over now. There was no reason for Logan to come bearing sweet little gifts like earplugs or to spend the night with her. No reason at all...

'Well, I just came by to give you a heads-up about tomorrow,' Hazel said, pulling off her fingerless mittens and laying them on the counter.

'Oh, lord,' Annie muttered.

'Heads-up about what?' Jeanie asked, perching on her stool again. She had been hoping to get a few hours of sleep after Logan left last night, but despite the lack of a ghost, the new earplugs, and the sturdy lock, she'd been too keyed up to sleep. After a full day of running the café, plus a lunch break of vet appointments and pet-supply shopping, she was exhausted. Again. So far, small-town life was kicking her butt.

'Wednesdays are book club days.'

'Okay...'

'They meet at the bookstore around noon, but they usually come in here after for coffee before some of them head back to work or have to get kids off the bus or whatever. I just figured I would warn you.' Hazel pushed her glasses up her nose, a faint blush creeping up her cheeks. 'They can be a bit ... rowdy.'

Annie snorted. 'Rowdy is an understatement.'

'It sounds like fun,' Jeanie said, remembering the laughing group from the town meeting.

'Oh sweet, sweet Jeanie,' Annie said, shaking her

head. 'They are going to come in here all hopped up on their latest smutty book, cackling like a coven of witches. And then they're going to want to know everything about you.'

Jeanie laughed. 'Aren't you being a little dramatic?'

Hazel picked up her mittens. 'They'll know your life story, your credit score, and your preferred dating app by the time they leave. Guaranteed.'

'I'm not scared.' Jeanie bit down on a smile at Hazel's grim tone.

Hazel shrugged. 'Just remember I warned you.' She hopped off her stool. 'I have to get back. We have preschool story time this afternoon. The author of *Black Cat Carves a Pumpkin* is coming with signed copies. It's going to be a madhouse.'

'Wait up. I have the cookies you wanted for the event. I'll go grab them.' Annie gulped down her now room-temperature latte, ready to follow Hazel out the door. 'Oh, Jeanie, are you setting up at the farmer's market on Sunday?'

'Farmer's market?'

'Yeah, Dot always sets up next to my tent. Your hot-cider-and-pumpkin-spiced everything goes great with my seasonal muffins and pies. You have to do it.'

'Oh ... uh ... of course. I'll ask Norman about it.'

'I'm surprised he didn't tell you.'

Jeanie frowned. Norman clearly didn't like her, but now it seemed the old man was hindering her from doing her job. She'd have to talk to him tomorrow.

'I'll be there.'

'Great!' Annie smiled at her from the door. 'Oh, and I wouldn't mention anything about Logan while the book club is here. They'll eat that gossip right up. It fuels them.'

Jeanie laughed, but inside her stomach swooped. The last thing she wanted was to become the topic of town gossip. Especially when there was nothing to gossip about. Nothing at all.

'Thanks. I have been thoroughly warned. Watch out for Mac, book clubs, and any mention of Logan. Got it.'

Annie saluted and walked out into the late afternoon chill.

Who knew small-town life was so treacherous?

Chapter Eleven

Logan's boots crunched over the dry leaves as he went out to check on the goats. He had to replace the sign next to their pen.

No donuts. The goats absolutely were not supposed to eat the apple-cider donuts he sold during apple-picking season, but that didn't stop every other kid from trying to feed them donuts. And these goats did not know what was good for them.

Kinda like him. Kinda like how he hadn't stopped thinking about Jeanie since he spent the night with her. For two damn days now, Jeanie had played on a loop in his head. Jeanie's delighted grin when he told a lame joke, Jeanie's enthusiasm for every type of snack food, Jeanie's rich dark-roast scent, Jeanie's soft body pressed against his.

He hammered the sign back to the fence post hard enough to rattle the slats all the way down, taking out his frustration on the wood. The sound reverberated through the quiet fields. A flock of crows flew to the treetops, their squawking disrupting the quiet even more.

He was being ridiculous, getting sucked in way too fast, just like last time. He barely knew this woman. Even if she had shared bits of herself in the dark of the café. Even if he *wanted* to know all about her.

Jeanie had barely been here for two weeks. She was starting a completely new job, in a new town, and this was all after she'd found her boss keeled over on his desk. Who knew if she'd even be here if it wasn't for that. Jeanie was running, and there was no guarantee that she would stop here. He'd be damned if he fell for another woman who was only passing through. He was done with people who used his town, his life, as some sort of pit stop on their soul-searching tour.

Hadn't Jeanie said she'd wanted things to be perfect here? That she had some kind of vision for how she wanted her life to be here? Well, there was no such thing as perfect, and he wasn't going to be the one caught trying to make Jeanie's life vision come true. He couldn't. It wouldn't work.

It never did.

The goats, Dylan and Marley, or the Bobs as his nana

liked to call them, stared at him forlornly like they knew the sign meant the end of their donut days.

'It's for your own good,' Logan muttered, and the Bobs bleated in response. They loved those damn donuts.

Logan trudged back to the farmhouse, wishing there was more to do today to take his mind off a certain someone. But it was a Wednesday morning in October; it was a quiet time for his little farm.

The orchard was only open Friday through Sunday for pick-your-own apples and pumpkins, with a hayride pulled by his grandfather atop his trusty tractor. It was the only real attraction. Logan refused to add all the nonsense some of the other farms around here did in the fall. No bounce houses, or corn mazes, or pony rides. Not that he had a pony. It was just the apples and pumpkins, donuts from Annie's, and the hayrides. Oh, and the Bobs. But the kids and families loved it. The money the farm made from pick-your-own apples kept the farm afloat for the whole winter.

But nearly halfway through October and the apples were almost done and even the pumpkin patch looked pretty picked over. The last big event of the season was the Fall Festival in town. Logan always supplied the pumpkins for the carving contest. He'd set dozens aside in the barn for the occasion.

Unfortunately, between his still competent

grandparents, his tendency to want to get ahead, and the diligent seasonal workers he'd hired, there wasn't much to do on this particular Wednesday when he really needed something to do. Fixing that sign hadn't taken nearly long enough.

He only made deliveries on Thursdays, and the farmer's market wasn't until Sunday afternoon. He could work on invoices for the seeds and supplies they'd need for spring, but he was feeling too antsy for that type of work today.

Maybe a cup of coffee would help.

He was dumber than the damn goats.

But he climbed in his truck and headed into town anyway.

Logan realized his mistake as soon as he stepped into the café.

It was Wednesday.

Book club day.

The bells over the door jingled as he stepped in, and five heads turned in his direction from their perches around the center table. Six, if you included Jeanie who stood next to the table, smiling her big Jeanie smile. His heart rode a roller coaster in his chest at the sight of her.

He should have stayed with the goats.

'Logan! Hey there!' Kaori's voice filled the small space and Nancy waved him over, as though he couldn't find them in the crowd of three other people hurrying out with their to-go cups.

'Come on over here and say hi to your old teacher,' Nancy said with a grin, seemingly oblivious to the fact that Logan didn't really want to know what kinks the woman who taught him to tie his shoes was into at the moment.

He sighed and ran a hand down his beard. There was no way around it. He made his way over to the table and nodded to the group.

It wasn't that he didn't like these people. They were perfectly fine, normal people. Well, normal by Dream Harbor standards anyway.

But he didn't want their pity or their sympathetic looks or their 'help' finding someone new, which seemed to be all they wanted to give him since the Christmas-tree-lighting debacle. It was like he was five years old again, suddenly without a mother but with an entire town of people wanting to check on him and bring him treats.

They were kind-hearted folk, all saddened by the loss of his mother and with no outlet for that pain other than to heap love on him, her baby, but he had his grandparents. He hadn't needed replacement parents at the time, and he certainly didn't need them twenty-five years later.

Not to mention that every time he saw them, he had to relive the memory of being down on one knee in the cold and the look on Lucy's horrified face. The humiliation, the failure was still too close to the surface, and seeing this group just dredged it all back up again.

'Hey, everyone. Jeanie.' He tipped his head in her direction and caught her gaze for a second too long. A slight flush broke out across the pale skin above the neckline of her sweater. It was a pale gray today, soft against her curves.

'Seeing you in town in the middle of a weekday feels like a Bigfoot sighting,' Jacob said with a laugh.

Logan managed to tear his gaze away from Jeanie to respond. 'Quiet day. Just came in for a coffee.'

'That was the nice thing about Lucy, she at least brought you into town more often.'

Well, damn. That didn't take long.

Nancy's wife, Linda, was oblivious to the horrified glances the rest of the book club were flashing in her direction. Linda was never big on social cues or not bringing up topics of conversation that no one wanted to discuss. He still remembered the Christmas party where she mentioned both his long-gone father and dead mother in one evening. Nana nearly kicked her out on her rear.

'Yep, that was nice, I guess,' he said, shifting on his feet. This was why he didn't come into town. The constant reminders of his failure. 'Not nice enough for her to stick around for in the end, though.' He nodded again and left the book club to their whispered admonishments of Linda's misstep. The last thing he wanted was to talk about Lucy in front of Jeanie, and especially not with the thoroughly unhelpful help of the book club.

Jeanie followed him to the counter to take his order, even though Crystal, who'd worked at the café since high school, was already standing there.

'The usual?' Jeanie asked, her tone light, even with the concerned crease in her brow. She obviously hadn't heard the full Lucy story yet or her dark eyes would be filled with pity, and he didn't want that; didn't want Jeanie filled in on his failed attempt at romance.

Or even worse than pity, she'd think Lucy was crazy for turning down his grand gesture. But if Jeanie was a grand-gesture fan, she was out of luck because Logan was all grand-gestured out. He shook his head; what was he even thinking? Jeanie didn't want anything from him except his damn coffee order.

'Yes, thanks.' He nodded hello to Crystal, who smiled

and went to refill the creamer bottles. Jeanie brought him his black coffee in a to-go cup. He'd left his reusable one in the truck in his rush to get in here. One mistake after another today.

'I figured you weren't staying.' She glanced over at the table of book clubbers. They'd clearly moved on from his sad tale and were back to cackling about their latest read. 'But I'm glad you came in. I mean ... it's nice to see you.' Jeanie's face flushed, and he wanted to tuck the escaped hairs behind her ear, to brush his fingers against her soft skin again, to hear the little intake of breath she'd made when he'd done it.

He shoved his hands into his pockets.

'Nice to see you, too.' The understatement of the year. Seeing her was far more complicated than 'nice' could ever communicate. He simultaneously wanted to jump the counter and give her the kiss he didn't get a chance to two nights ago and run the hell out of there and never look back.

Instead, he stood awkwardly in front of her hoping she'd chatter on about something so he could stay here looking at her for just a few more minutes.

Lucky for him, Jeanie always had something to chat about. 'Casper is settling in nicely. He sleeps at the end of my bed every night and it's helping me sleep better, too. Except for when he sits on my face around five every morning. Who needs an alarm clock anymore? Not me!' she finished with a laugh.

Logan laughed too, mostly to avoid making any comments about face-sitting. His composure was unraveling at a dangerous pace.

At some point during her story, Logan had leaned forward, resting his forearms on the counter between them. Jeanie's body bent towards his, as well, like they couldn't keep space between them. He sure as hell didn't want to.

'You named him Casper?' His voice was low so only she could hear it.

'Well, he was my ghost. And he turned out to be friendly, so just kinda fit...' She grinned, and his innards rearranged themselves.

'Makes sense,' he said, cursing the cat again for being found so soon, for ruining any excuse he had to see more of Jeanie, especially at night, especially side by side on her floor with moonlight streaming in the window. Damn cat.

Someone cleared their throat behind him, breaking the moment. He stood and apologized, stepping out of the way for Mr. Prescott, the mailman.

'I should go,' he told Jeanie over the hiss of the coffee machine.

'Okay, sure.' Her cheeks were flushed pink from

work, and loose tendrils of hair curled around her temples. She looked happy, like she belonged here in this cozy little shop, chatting it up with the people he'd known his whole life. She looked like she fit.

He wanted her to fit.

'Here you go, Mr. Prescott. Have a good day,' she said, handing the older man his drink. She turned back to Logan and knocked the wind out of him with her next words. 'Whoever Lucy was, I think she was a fool to leave.' She gave him a soft smile and then got started on the next customer's order without even missing a beat, leaving Logan to stumble back out into the sunshine wondering what to do next.

Because nothing about Jeanie was ever what he expected.

Chapter Twelve

There. She'd done it. She'd had a perfectly normal conversation with Logan that didn't involve a weapon, a ghost hunt, or her own tears. Success. She was well on her way to being the sunshine-y café owner she dreamed of being, instead of a big bag of anxiety and murder theories.

She watched him go before turning back to the next customers, a couple of college students from the next town over. The sight of them with their bags full of books and questionable piercings gave her the sudden urge to message her college roommate, Emily. Just one more person she'd neglected over the years.

She itched the spot on her nose where she'd let her piercing close up when she'd started interviewing for 'real jobs' and wondered if Emily still had hers.

'Jeanie, come back and join us!' Kaori called. 'We weren't done chatting with you.'

Jeanie bit down on a smile, remembering Hazel's warning. They'd probably ask for her blood type next.

The line at the counter was gone, and Crystal could handle it anyway, so Jeanie made her way back over to the book club table. The tiny surface was covered in empty mugs and well-loved paperbacks with half-naked men on the covers.

'Can I get you guys anything else?'

'Oh, no.' Nancy waved away her offer. 'We're just chatting a bit before Kaori has to be back at the office and Isabel has to pick up Jane from school.'

Mateo sat gurgling happily in Isabel's lap, munching on a shortbread cookie and Jacob tickled his chubby belly. The little boy giggled, showing his gummy smile. Isabel glanced at her watch. 'I still have some time,' she said with a knowing smile.

'Me, too. My next class isn't until three,' Jacob said, handing Mateo a fresh cookie after his landed on the floor.

'Linda and I are free as birds today, aren't we, love?'

'Every day since we retired.'

'So, pull over a chair, Jeanie.' Nancy gestured to the closest chair and Jeanie felt she really had no choice but to join them. She didn't want to be rude, and they were paying customers after all. And she also really liked them and wanted to join their fabulous little club.

'What did you read this week?' Jeanie asked, settling into her seat. She picked up one of the books from the table. A very impressive male torso filled the front cover with the title *Heat It Up* scrawled across the center. The author was Veronica Penrose which Jeanie very much doubted was a real name, but she liked it anyway.

'It's a male-male hockey romance,' Jacob told her, clearly excited about this week's pick. 'Enemies to lovers perfection. Highly recommend.'

'I'm not really into hockey,' Jeanie said, flipping through the pages slowly.

Kaori's laugh reverberated around the small space. 'Nobody cares about the hockey part, hun.'

Jeanie's gaze snagged on several interesting passages, confirming that this book was not at all about hockey. 'Right. Got it. Looks like a good one,' she said, her cheeks heating as she scanned a few more lines. It was possible Jeanie had been reading the wrong books her whole life.

'I just loved how vulnerable they were with each other,' Isabel said with a sigh.

'Yeah, and how freaking hot it was,' Nancy added. 'That thing they did in the car with the... '

'Okay, Nancy. Let's not scare Jeanie away just yet.' Kaori cut her off before Nancy could get into exactly what the rival hockey players did in their car, which was too bad because now Jeanie was curious. 'Anyway, we called Jeanie over because we weren't done getting to know her.'

Jeanie shifted in her seat as all eyes turned back to her. 'I think you know everything there is to know. Grew up in western New York, came this way for college, lived in Boston for the past ten years or so.' Jeanie shrugged, the truth of it hitting her again. That really was everything there was to know. She'd chosen Boston for college to escape the small town she'd grown up in and yet in the end, her life had become small, narrowed down to the frenetic energy of her work life and nothing else.

'You didn't leave behind anyone special in Boston?' Nancy asked.

'Nope.'

'And you plan to stay? Here in town,' Isabel asked, wiping the cookie crumbs from Mateo's face. 'I mean, you're serious about running the café?'

'Uh ... yeah. I mean, yes. Yes, staying to run the café is my very serious plan.' She had literally no other plan. No backup plan, no escape hatch, no run-back-to-the-city-and-find-a-new-assistant-job plan. Now that she was here, she was determined to make this work. It was just like she'd told Barb Sanders, the realtor, when she'd called again. Jeanie was the owner of the Pumpkin Spice Café, and she had no plans to sell.

Now she just had to convince herself, Barb Sanders, and the book club that that was true.

'Oh, we're so glad to hear it,' Kaori said with an encouraging smile.

'See, I told you she was different,' Linda said, giving Nancy a nudge with her shoulder. 'They're worried you're going to leave Logan in the lurch like Lucy,' she said, leaning toward Jeanie like she was telling her a secret. 'Poor Logan. She breezed into town and turned that boy inside out. Like I said, the only good part about her was she brought him into town more. I do like to see him, even all grown up as he is. I feel like I owe it to his mother to check in on him. Anyway, I still remember the look on his face when Lucy said no to his proposal at the Christmas-tree lighting— Ow! Who kicked me?' Linda reached down to rub her shin, leaving Jeanie in shocked silence.

Logan had proposed to this Lucy person. And she'd said no? Who was this woman and what was wrong with her?

'That's enough of that, my love,' Nancy said sweetly, even though Jeanie was sure the kick had come from her direction. 'Lucy never really fit in here. She wasn't a good match for Logan in the first place.'

Lucy never really fit in here. Jeanie glanced around the table. Did *she* fit in here? Maybe she needed ripped jeans like Jacob? Or more crystals like Isabel? Even little Mateo wore a string of amber beads around his neck. Chunky scarves that looked like a grandmother had knitted them seemed to be integral to the look of Dream Harbor as well. And Jeanie didn't own a single pair of fingerless mittens. They should hand them out when you cross into town.

Instead, Jeanie had been stuck with her business-casual wardrobe and hadn't had time to shop for anything different. In her slacks, sweater, and ballet flats with her hair in a low twist, she felt more ready for an afternoon business meeting than for a day running the town coffee shop. Kaori had a similar vibe, but she really was headed into the office for the afternoon – as some sort of lawyer, maybe? Accountant? Jeanie couldn't remember but she did know Kaori drank a large French roast with soy milk every morning.

If Jeanie wanted a new lifestyle here, maybe she needed to start dressing the part...

'You and Logan looked pretty cozy together at the counter,' Jacob said, derailing her wardrobe thoughts and diving directly into her Logan daydreams instead. 'He looked like he wanted to jump over it and—'

'Jacob,' Kaori snapped. 'You're making Jeanie blush.

Don't mind him, sweetie. He gets all kinds of crazy ideas in his head after we read these books.'

'If equal-opportunity orgasms and parity in relationships are crazy ideas, then I don't want to be sane!'

Kaori waved him off. 'Yes, yes, but let's not traumatize Jeanie at her first meeting.' Jeanie felt less traumatized and more horrified that Jacob was reading her mind, but she wasn't about to add that to the conversation.

'My first meeting? Does this count?' *Look at me, making grown-up friends and getting hobbies!* She could already feel years being added back onto her life.

'Of course, it does! And you're welcome to join us anytime. Give Jacob your number and he'll text you the book for the week. Now I have to go.' Kaori grabbed her purse and stuffed her book inside. 'I'll see you all later.'

'I should go, too. I want to get this monster down for a nap before his sister gets home,' Isabel said, collecting Mateo's pile of half-eaten cookies.

And with that, Jeanie's first unofficial meeting with the Dream Harbor book club ended in a flurry of goodbyes and promises to chat again soon.

Jacob stayed behind to get Jeanie's number.

'Thanks for including me,' she said as he typed.

'We're open to all,' he said with a smile. 'And...' he

leaned in conspiratorially, 'I know this town is like weirdly protective of Logan, but trust me, I saw the proposal and it was brutal. And the whole town witnessed it.' He winced, remembering it.

'We're just friends,' Jeanie said weakly. The thought of Logan having his heart torn out in front of everyone was making her feel dizzy and a little sick. Maybe she should sit down?

'Well, if you're thinking of becoming more than friends, which I don't blame you, that man is all the big broody handsomeness I could ask for, just make sure you're serious about it.' Jacob shrugged. 'Lucy hightailed it back to Boston after she dumped him, but if you really plan on staying ... things would be awkward, to say the least.'

'Right. Got it.'

Jacob smiled and slung his bag over one shoulder. 'K, well, see you later!'

'Bye.'

Jeanie dropped hard into the nearest chair as soon as Jacob was out the door. For the second time since she got here, she'd been warned to stay away from Logan. This town was not kidding about protecting their own. She rubbed her temples with her fingers, a full-blown stress headache coming on.

If she got involved with Logan, the whole town

would be watching. And then what happened when it inevitably ended? That was way too much pressure. Pressure she absolutely did not need. Pressure she left her old life behind to avoid.

She took a deep breath, inhaling and exhaling slowly, like she'd learned from the meditation app she'd downloaded shortly after Marvin's death. Not a problem. She would just steer clear of Logan from now on. Polite customer and barista chatter only. No flirting. No staring into his deep blue eyes. Definitely no breathing in his outdoorsy scent.

They were friends. Acquaintances, really. And that was just fine.

Jeanie was here to focus on herself, not to get tangled up in a town scandal, and she would just keep reminding herself of that until it stuck. She'd been silly to add Logan to her plan, anyway. Coming here was about finding New Jeanie, not about finding a man. Right?

Right.

It wasn't until she went back behind the counter that she noticed the book Jacob had left for her. *The Farmer and The Milkmaid*. The Post-it note on top read: to help you get it out of your system.

As Jeanie stared at the rugged man on the cover, his flannel shirt unbuttoned and flapping in the breeze, she knew it could never be as good as the real thing.

Chapter Thirteen

'Wait, I'm confused. Why does running Aunt Dot's café require a full personality makeover?'

Jeanie belly-flopped onto her bed with a groan, emerging from her pillows to find her brother's face staring at her from her phone.

'Because, Ben, I didn't just come here for the café. I came to ... to...'

Jeanie rolled onto her back, taking her phone and frowning brother with her. It was hard to explain now that Ben was looking at her like that, but she had her reasons, damn it.

'I came here for a new life. One that is slower paced, and you know, quainter ... or something.'

He huffed. 'You're looking for something that doesn't exist.'

'I will die if I stay in my old life, Bennett! Do you want me to end up like Marvin?'

'Okay, first of all, Marvin was at least thirty years older than you. Secondly, the man ate primarily bacon. And third, wasn't he balancing like a wife and two mistresses? That's a lot of undue stress, Jeanie. That's not your life.'

'My life was balancing his life!' Jeanie tried to erase the image of Marvin's lifeless eyes staring at her from atop his spreadsheets from her mind. 'And I can't go back to that.'

'So, don't. I think it's cool that you're a small-business owner now, but just because you moved to some small town doesn't mean you need to be a totally different person.'

Jeanie sighed. Her brother was so dense sometimes.

'Close your eyes,' she said. Time for a different tactic.

'Why?'

'Just do it.' She seriously needed friends that were not her younger brother. She waited for Ben to close his eyes before she continued. 'Okay, now picture the café, do you remember it? It looks the same. Old wood floors, lots of art on the walls, big ceramic mugs from the art school.'

'Yep, got it.'

'Now picture Aunt Dot.'

A small smile crept onto Ben's face. They'd always

loved their eccentric aunt, so different from their own strait-laced mother, with her long skirts and big colorful earrings, she just always seemed so interesting, so vibrant. So perfectly at home running her café, living her life on her terms.

'Okay, now picture me.'

Jeanie was still wearing her work clothes from the day. Gray on gray. She literally could not look any less like the woman she was trying to become.

Ben opened his eyes. 'You look fine, Jeanie. You don't have to be a hippie to run a coffee shop.'

'I'm not trying to be a hippie.' *I'm just trying to be as far from my old self, my old life as possible.* 'I just want to fit in around here.'

'Are those locals bullying you, Jean Marie? Because I'll come out there and...'

'And what?' she said with a laugh. 'You're going to fly here and beat up the townies?'

Ben's frown deepened. 'If necessary.'

'Well, I appreciate the sentiment, but actually everyone has been very nice so far.' Her thoughts immediately drifted to the deep blue of Logan's eyes and the way he'd leaned closer to her as she talked. Very nice.

'See, so everything's fine. The locals like you. You've got Norman helping you figure things out. And I just read that having a pet lowers blood pressure. You're well on your way to living forever.'

Jeanie glanced down at the cat that had taken up residence on her stomach. She supposed he had some calming qualities, like the gentle vibration currently emanating from him now. But that wasn't really the point. She wasn't so much afraid of dying as she was of forgetting to live her life.

Somewhere along the way, she'd forgotten to figure out who she was or what she wanted to be when she grew up. She'd graduated college all shiny and optimistic about her future with her nose ring intact, and then spent the next seven years having her soul sucked out one ten-hour day at a time.

And now here she was, grown up and without a single clue who she was without someone else demanding every second of her time. Without Marvin to manage, Jeanie didn't know what to do with herself.

Or who she even wanted to be.

But a new wardrobe seemed as good a place to start as any.

'I'm pretty sure Norman hates me,' she said, picking up the only part of Ben's comments she felt like dealing with at the moment.

'Why would he hate you?'

'I don't know, but he seems to always be annoyed

with me or something. And I'm apparently supposed to set up a tent at the farmers' market this weekend and he didn't even mention it.'

'Farmers' market? That's adorable.'

'Shut up. It's part of my new image.'

'I happen to like your old image.'

It was Jeanie's turn to frown. 'Don't get all sentimental on me now, Bennett.'

He stuck his tongue out, transforming into his seven-year-old self so perfectly that Jeanie couldn't help but laugh. 'I just don't see anything wrong with being the high-strung but cheerful, slightly paranoid café owner that almost took off the head of the local hottie farmer,' he said.

'I never should have told you that.'

'Honestly, I'm proud of you. A woman on her own needs self-defense skills.'

'Yes, so you've told me many times, which is probably at least partly to blame for my gross overreaction to a produce delivery. Also, I never said he was hot.'

Ben laughed. 'Pretend to be New Jeanie all you want, but I know you. As soon as you mentioned him, your face turned bright red.'

Jeanie rolled her eyes. Something about talking to her brother reverted her back to her childhood. Cozy and nostalgic, but terrible for having a serious conversation.

'Well, he's beloved here so the townsfolk probably would have come after me if I hurt him.'

Ben lifted a curious eyebrow. 'Beloved, you say? Tell me more.'

Jeanie shrugged, her hair rustling against her pile of pillows. 'They're just a really tight-knit community. They all grew up together and stuff. I think if you're born here, you're not allowed to leave.'

Ben laughed.

'Anyway, I need to steer clear of the hot farmer. The last thing I need is angry townspeople with pitchforks outside my door because I broke his heart at the town square dance or something.'

'Okay, you lost me. What the hell are you talking about, and is there really a town square dance?'

Jeanie sighed. All the conversations from the café today ran through her mind simultaneously accompanied by the memory of Logan's shocked face when she told him she thought Lucy was a fool. Shocked and hopeful.

'There's no square dance. At least not that I know of.' Although she would not be at all surprised if there was. 'It doesn't matter. Logan, the farmer that is, is off-limits. Way too much pressure there.'

'Right and you're all about that low-key life now,' Ben said, with a sarcastic smirk. But Jeanie didn't let that get her down.

'Exactly. Easy breezy Jeanie. That's me.'

'Well, I have to go. Some of us still have high-stress jobs we need to attend to.' Her brother worked in tech, and if she was honest, she still didn't really understand what he did. When people asked, she just said 'computers'.

'Okay, good luck. I'm going to go take up knitting or something. Maybe hiking? Hiking could be fun.'

'Not hiking. You have a horrible sense of direction.'

'Maybe New Jeanie has a great sense of direction.'

'She definitely doesn't. Stay out of the woods. Love you.'

'Love you, too. Bye.'

Ben's face disappeared from the screen, and she was alone with her ghost cat and her book about sexy farmers. She stared at the cover pretending to deliberate for only a minute before cracking it open.

Reading was probably safer than hiking, anyway.

Chapter Fourteen

'You sure you don't want me to stick around for the u-pick crowd today?'

Logan's grandfather flashed him an exasperated look. 'Positive.'

The older man pushed another crate of apples into the truck bed. A man of few words, Logan usually appreciated his grandfather's quiet nature, but at the moment he was looking for any excuse not to go to the farmers' market and possibly run into Jeanie. Not since he was certain he couldn't trust himself around her.

Her words from Wednesday had tattooed themselves on his brain. *Whoever Lucy was, I think she was a fool to leave.* What did she mean? That *she* had no plans to leave? Maybe all of Logan's worries were unfounded. And if that was true, then it meant he had no reason not to shoot for more with Jeanie.

Maybe they could keep it quiet for now. No need to alert the town gossip mill right away. But how would Jeanie feel about sneaking around? An image of him and Jeanie in a dark corner, her leg hitched up over his hip, his voice in her ear urging her to be quiet played through his mind with stark clarity.

'You gonna daydream all morning, or you gonna help me load this truck?' His grandfather's aggrieved voice broke through his highly inappropriate Sunday-morning thoughts.

He cleared his throat. 'Right. Sorry.' He grabbed another crate, happy for the distraction. This was how he'd been since Wednesday, all in his head about this woman he barely knew. It was too familiar. In the days after he spent that first weekend with Lucy, he'd nearly broken his thumb with a hammer, ordered three times as much fertilizer as they needed, left the gate open, and temporarily lost both Bobs. Nana was beside herself with worry.

Logan had a habit of letting women unravel him.

Which was why he shouldn't be going to the farmers' market today. The PS Café always set up a tent with hot cider and pumpkin-spiced lattes right next to Annie's bakery tent. And he was not ready to see Jeanie again. Not until he had a better grip on himself.

'Might be a big crowd today. Getting to the end of the season.' Logan leaned against the side of the truck, wiping the sweat from his brow. The sun was bright, and it was unseasonably warm today. There was a briny scent to the air, drifting in from the harbor, and it felt more like August than October. The weather was as unsettled as his insides.

His grandfather furrowed his bushy gray eyebrows, like two furry caterpillars under the brim of his old Red Sox cap. 'What's up with you?'

Logan sighed, running a hand down his face. 'Nothing at all. Just don't want to leave you here with a big crowd.'

'Me and your grandmother can manage. And those kids you hired to run the pick-your-own shack will be here.'

He was right, of course. There was plenty of staff to help his grandparents out, but his grandmother usually did farmers' market duty. Except for this weekend, when she decided she wanted to 'soak in all the autumnal excitement at the farm while it lasted.' Those were her exact words. Impossible to argue with.

His grandfather was still studying him, so he heaved in another crate to avoid the old man's gaze.

'You can't avoid town forever.'

'I'm not.'

Grandpa huffed. 'I don't like crowds much.'

That was an understatement. His grandpa avoided people nearly as much as he did.

'But I don't like the idea of you hiding out here just because of what happened.'

Logan made a noise that sounded eerily similar to his grandfather's huff, and then realized the two of them were standing the same: arms crossed, leaning against the truck bed. Okay, so he was a lot like the old man.

'Not hiding.'

'You hid after your mom passed, too.'

'I was five. And my mother died. I think hiding was warranted.'

'To a point.' Grandpa nodded. 'But eventually, we needed to push you a little. Convince you to play with your friends again. Nearly broke my heart when we had to force you back into school.'

Logan swallowed hard.

'Had to pull your little hands off my legs at the door. I hated it. Told your grandmother we should just keep you here with us.'

Grandpa took off his hat and ran a hand over his thinning hair. Logan didn't know that he had tried to keep him home, but he did remember crying every day at school for a month. Mrs. Pine – Nancy, as she made him call her now – let him sit on her lap at story time and carry around a special stuffed elephant she kept on her desk for emotional emergencies. The day Annie declared they were best friends was probably the day he stopped crying.

But that was completely different than this.

This was him trying to sort out his feelings before making a big mistake. Like last time. In front of the whole damn town.

'That's not what I'm doing.'

His grandfather finally looked away, giving him a slight nod. 'Alright. If you say so. Just don't let that woman keep you from trying again.'

That woman. Grandpa refused to say Lucy's name since she left, and insane as it was, Logan appreciated this show of solidarity.

'I won't,' he assured him, even though he knew that was exactly what he was doing. He was just tired of his pain being town business, however well-meaning they were. Maybe he just wanted to hurt in private this time. 'Better get going.'

His grandfather grunted in agreement, pushing away from the truck. 'Give whatever you don't sell to Annie. I want more of those pies.'

Logan smiled. Grandpa had a notoriously sweet tooth

and he'd been trading apples for pies ever since Annie opened the bakery.

'Will do.' He hopped into the cab and gave his grandfather a wave before pulling out, more confused than ever about what to do about Jeanie.

Unfortunately, catching a glimpse of Jeanie as he pulled into the town square where the market was held, did nothing to help him figure it out. She was laughing with Annie as they struggled to get her tent up, the wind catching the fabric and forcing the women to wrestle it into submission. Her hair was loose today, and it flew around her face with the wind as she laughed.

A few dark clouds crossed the sun, casting the square in shadow. The sunny day was quickly taking a turn, but the weather didn't usually stop people from shopping. If you waited for a perfect day in New England, you'd never do anything. The weather could swing from summer to fall in the course of a few hours, which seemed to be what it was doing right now.

Logan hopped down from his truck and strode over to where Jeanie was currently standing on her tent, a victorious look on her face.

'There, at least it won't blow away,' she said with a grin, still not noticing Logan coming up behind her. She looked different today, the work clothes he usually saw her in, were replaced with jeans and a colorful cardigan. She looked comfortable.

He decided not to take it as a sign that she was settling into her place here. A woman was allowed to change her clothes without it being some sort of declaration of her intentions.

'Might work better to keep the rain off, if it's over your head.'

Jeanie turned around with a start. 'Logan!' Her cheeks flushed pink. 'Hi.'

'Hi.'

He held her gaze, the air crackling between them. He hadn't imagined it. Every time he saw her, he felt it. This buzz under his skin. It was back, electric and real, like the storm brewing overhead.

'Hi, I'm here, too!' Annie cut in, waving a hand in his face. 'Your best friend since the dawn of time. Hi, there.' She grinned as he turned to look at her like she already knew exactly how he felt about Jeanie. Which also meant she'd know all about it when it fell apart. He prickled at the thought.

'Hey, Annie. Need some help?' He gestured toward the defeated tent.

Annie put her hands on her hips and stared down at the fabric beneath Jeanie's feet. 'I don't know if it's worth setting up.' She glanced at the sky. 'Do you think Pete will cancel?'

'I don't know. Maybe he should take a nap and see if anything comes up.'

Annie slapped his arm. 'Don't be mean.'

'The man makes decisions based on dreams, Annie. Don't pretend like it's normal.'

His best friend shrugged. 'It works out most of the time, Logan. I mean look at you and Jeanie and the ghost. Problem solved.' Another smirk.

'Yep. Problem solved.' He moved around to the side of the tent and helped Jeanie straighten out the side. The whole thing was really just a metal frame with a blue vinyl roof. It was literally called an 'easy-up' which at the moment seemed misleading, but it was standard farmers' market gear. Pete had spent some of the town budget one year to order these things in bulk.

In the current conditions, Logan was a little worried they might take flight. 'You got something to weigh this down with?' he asked, busying himself so he didn't have to look at either woman, Annie's knowing glances or Jeanie's bright smile. More storm clouds built inside him, hot air mixing with the cold off the water. Unsettled.

'We can use these.' Jeanie had the little sandbags that came with the tent to attach to each corner. It should hold if things didn't get too crazy out here. Annie's tent was already up and seemed to be doing okay shielding her pies and muffins from the elements.

'That should do.' He took the bags and worked his way around the tent, securing each post along the way. Annie and Jeanie chatted away like old friends while he worked. The sound coasted over him, warm and peaceful, in direct contrast to the weather and his churning insides.

'Let's put this here, and here are the little signs to label the drinks,' Jeanie was saying as she organized her table. Was it weird that his heart kicked with pride to see her using some of his gourds to decorate around the drink carafes? Yep, definitely weird.

'It looks perfect! So cute. People are going to be swarming around you for drinks today,' Annie said. 'Oh, and this is George. He works at the bakery. His cakes are to die for.'

'Nice to meet—'

The introduction was torn from Jeanie's mouth by the next gust of wind. Everything happened all at once after that.

Jeanie's easy-up easily lifted off the ground.

Annie shrieked, just as the clouds opened up and let loose a deluge of cold, fall rain.

Logan was soaked. Jeanie was soaked. Annie's pies were in grave danger of being soaked.

George sprang into action. 'We have to get these packed up!' He started reloading pies into plastic containers while Annie frantically threw muffins into Tupperware.

Jeanie stood watching her tent blow down the street, her perfectly set-up farmers' market table ruined by the downpour. She glanced at Logan, rain streaming down her face, plastering her hair to her head.

The look on her face wavered between laughter and tears, and he would be damned if tears won out.

'Let's go.' He grabbed her hand and they raced toward her tent. The wind whipped around them as they splashed through the rapidly forming puddles. Where had this damn storm come from, and what good was a clairvoyant mayor if he couldn't even predict the weather?

Logan was ready to drag Jeanie to the town hall next to give Pete a piece of his mind for endangering everyone with this farmers' market, when Jeanie's giggles cut through the sounds of the storm.

He glanced at her, and his breath caught. Her face was lit up, like the sun through the clouds. 'What are we doing?' she asked, her own breaths coming in gasps.

'We're going to catch that damn tent,' he told her, making her laugh even harder.

'Okay, but slow down!' She grinned at him as he

slowed his pace. 'You're fast when you have a tent to catch.'

'It's a safety hazard.' He tried to keep his tone serious, but he felt his mouth tipping up with hers. Her fingers were still entwined with his and they were running through the rain, and his heart was already storing these moments away for later, to obsess over when he couldn't sleep. Unsettled, but happy.

She fit here. She fit with him. His heart thumped the words over and over.

Her smile grew and she pushed the rain from her eyes. Those eyes, those dark-coffee eyes.

A crack of thunder overhead disrupted his thoughts of taking her face in his hands and pressing his mouth to hers.

'Let's go!' she cried and tugged him into a run again, racing down Main Street. Luckily the street was closed to traffic for the market, so they only had a few other people fleeing from the weather to contend with.

'There it is!' Jeanie's triumphant cry was quickly replaced with a dismayed gasp that cut through Logan's chest. The tent was tangled in a tree. Its big metal legs bent like a giant spider's; the blue tarp torn down the middle. 'Shoot.' Her face fell at the sight of the mess.

'I'll get it.' Logan tugged at one of the metal legs, determined to get the stupid tent out of the branches, as though this tent was the one thing keeping Jeanie here. He battled that piece of camping equipment as though it was the only thing preventing her from staying, as though her failed attempt at the farmers' market would send her crying back to Boston.

Would it?

'Hey.' She tugged at his arm. 'I think it's hopeless.'

'I can get it,' he growled, pulling harder until a branch cracked and the hole in the canvas tore open wider.

'Hey.' The hand on his arm grew more insistent until he turned to face her. She smiled. 'Let's go somewhere dry.'

He blinked. She was still here, smiling at him through the sheets of rain that continued to fall, her hand still on his arm, holding him tight. He swallowed hard.

'Okay.' He nodded. It was all he could manage. It was all he should say. Much better than the other words floating around in his head. Words about going with Jeanie wherever she wanted him to and all the things he wanted to do to her when they got there.

Instead, he just let her tug him toward the café.

Chapter Fifteen

They snuck in the back door and up the backstairs like teenagers creeping past parents. But it was really only Norman and a few customers stuck waiting out the storm in the café. Jeanie could feel the relief in Logan's body when she bypassed the front door, like he didn't want to be caught, either; like neither of them was ready to walk through the café holding hands.

This secretive thing was working for her anyway. Way less pressure.

She pushed open the door to her apartment and dragged Logan inside. 'We made it,' she said, her breath still coming out in little gasps.

'We did.' Logan's mouth tipped up at the corners.

She didn't know if they were talking about the storm or the people or their own reasons for staying away from each other. But whichever it was, they'd made it into her home. Together. Alone with no one watching.

They were both dripping on her hardwood floors and she should really get them some towels and she should really stop staring into Logan's blue eyes, but the rain was pounding against the windows and her chest was still heaving from their run here, and Logan had been so damn determined to save that tent for her, that something big and unstoppable was welling up in her chest and she couldn't help herself. She didn't want to help herself.

She wrapped her hands in Logan's soaking wet shirt and pulled him closer, relishing the surprised 'Oof' that left his lips.

That was as far as she got.

Pressed chest to chest with this sweet, grumpy man, wanting so much more but now afraid to go for it. This wasn't part of the plan. Was it? Was this New Jeanie? Did she accost men in her entryway? This had never been Jeanie's style in the past. The men she dated had been … fine. Just fine, perfectly nice, decent kissers, decent at everything else. But she'd never once felt the need to wrap herself up in them. She'd never wanted them to stick around very long, never really cared when things fizzled out.

But this, this was different.

This was new.

Logan's rough palm on her cheek stalled her thoughts. Her breath stuttered. He tilted her face up to his, his touch gentle but firm, his fingers digging into the hair at the base of her scalp.

A soft whimper, a deep groan, a rumble of thunder.

And then his lips were on hers, warm and soft and insistent, like he wanted to go slow, intended to, but once they touched, he couldn't quite manage it, couldn't quite stop himself from pressing harder, going deeper.

Jeanie wrapped her arms around his neck, molding her body against his, and his groan tumbled through her, rough and sweet at once. She could get lost in this. She could stay here forever.

His mouth moved down her neck and the sound of her moan would have been embarrassing if he hadn't matched it with his own. He burned a path down her damp skin with his lips and tongue and teeth.

He turned them both so that her back was against the door. He rocked into her, pressing her against the wood.

Oh, God, oh, God. He was so solid, so sturdy, so damn good at this. Every reason Jeanie had for staying away from Logan had blown out to sea with the storm, and she was about three seconds away from stripping off her wet clothes and skipping all the steps in between acquaintances and lovers, when the skies cracked, and the lights flickered out.

Shit.

'Logan,' she gasped as he licked the delicate skin of her neck.

'Mmmn.' His voice vibrated against her. His hands had wandered up her wet shirt, blazing hot against her cool skin.

'Wait.' She put one hand on his chest and Logan tore himself away, his hands dropping to his sides.

'Sorry. I—'

'No, don't apologize. That was ... I mean, I wanted to. I just...'

Logan ran a hand through his hair, sending rain droplets scattering. 'No need to explain. That was too much, too soon.' His voice was still rough, thick with need. 'I'll get out of your hair.'

'Wait.' This time when she said it, she tugged him close again. 'It's not that. The power just went out and I feel like I should go help Norman.'

He blinked. 'Oh.'

Jeanie smiled and waited for his mouth to hitch up in response. 'That was really nice.'

'Oh?' His smile hitched higher.

'Yeah. Really, really nice.'

Logan shifted against her, and she could feel how

really nice he also found the whole situation. She reached up and brushed another soft kiss against his lips, feeling the tickle of his beard against her chin.

'I think we should do it again sometime.' *Wow, New Jeanie was bold.* Maybe it was all that farmer smut she'd been reading; the way that milkmaid really chased her own pleasure. Or maybe it was the way Logan held her. Firm, tight, steady. It was nice feeling secure with someone when every other part of her life felt like it had been torn wide open and scattered to the wind. It was nice to lean against someone while she figured out where the pieces fit back together, while she rebuilt.

'You do?' Hesitance flashed in his blue eyes.

'We don't have to send out announcements to the book club or anything,' she said. 'This can be just for us.'

She felt him relax against her, bit by bit, as he considered her offer. What was she offering anyway? Secret make-out sessions. More than that? She wasn't sure, but after finding out about Lucy, Jeanie wouldn't blame him if he wasn't looking for another public spectacle. She could respect that.

New Jeanie was very understanding, apparently. New Jeanie also really wanted to kiss Logan again and was very willing to compromise.

'So, what would this be?' he asked, looking down at her.

She shrugged. 'We could figure it out as we go, I guess.' Easy breezy, casual. New Jeanie could figure things out as she went. With Logan holding her steady, she felt like she could figure out all kinds of things.

Logan still looked skeptical, the furrow between his brows deepening as she spoke.

'Or, we can go back to being friends,' she tossed out. 'Whatever you want.'

His eyes grew dark again, hungry, like the answer to whatever he wanted was definitely her. It was new, this feeling of wanting, of taking what she wanted, of being wanted in return. She liked it.

'We'll figure it out,' he said, pressing one more kiss to her lips before pulling away. 'Just us, though.' He ran a hand through his hair again. 'I don't want other people involved. Not even Annie. It's just once people find out about these things—'

'Of course. Don't worry about it.' She drew an invisible zipper over her lips and threw away the imaginary key. 'My lips are sealed. This is nobody's business but our own.'

'Thanks.'

They didn't talk about Lucy out loud, but Jeanie knew that's what he was thanking her for, for giving him the care he needed, and she felt a flare of protectiveness for this man. She wanted to give him what he needed, not what everyone else seemed to think he needed. And besides all that, she was happy to take some of the pressure off this whole thing, anyway. The last thing she wanted was the whole town watching them navigate this relationship.

The second-to-last thing she wanted to do was to leave Logan's arms, but alas, small-business owner duty called. Norman hated her enough. Leaving him alone in a power outage probably wouldn't help her case. 'I should get downstairs.'

'Right, of course.' Logan pulled back, letting his hands trace the edges of her hips before dropping them again. His rain-darkened hair hung over his forehead and the T-shirt under his flannel shirt stuck tight to his body. Maybe Norman would be fine?

'I'll grab a ladder from my truck and get that tent out of the tree once the storm settles down.'

Jeanie cleared her throat. 'Perfect, thanks,' she said, instead of 'you know what, forget Norman, forget the tent, forget everything except you and me and that flannel shirt on my bedroom floor.'

New Jeanie wasn't *that* bold.

Logan nodded and was out the door before Jeanie could change her mind.

'There you are!' Norman's disgruntled voice came from behind the counter as soon as Jeanie's foot hit the last step. She turned the corner into the café and his disapproving frown sent heat to her face. Had she been caught already? Were Logan's kisses somehow glowing on her skin? It certainly felt like they were.

You're the boss here, Jeanie. Not him.

She squared her shoulders. 'I got caught in the rain at the farmers' market. Just had to change my clothes.' The lingering imprint of Logan's fingers on the skin of her stomach warmed beneath her dry shirt.

Norman narrowed his eyes. 'Well, I've been here by myself, with this crowd and no power.' He huffed indignantly.

Jeanie looked around at the sparse, wet, and relatively calm crowd and nearly rolled her eyes. 'You seem to be managing it very well. Thank you for covering.'

Norman didn't have much to say to her compliment, so instead he said, 'We need to keep the refrigerator closed until the power comes back or we'll lose all the perishables.'

'Got it.' Jeanie gave him a thumbs up as she grabbed her apron off the hook near the register. 'Good call. We'll also have to go pick up the table and the carafes after the storm's died down. I kinda made a run for it and left everything.'

Another disgruntled frown.

'Anything else, Norman?' Jeanie asked cheerfully, finding it best to fight his grumpiness with positivity. It had always worked with Marvin, too. Jeanie was surprised to find a prickle of sadness in her heart at the thought of her old boss. For better or worse, they'd been together for a long time, and suddenly the thought of never seeing him again seemed impossible.

And then something strange happened to Norman's face. Was that a slight blush working its way up his cheeks? Was there an uncertainty in his eyes, a shyness?

'Have you spoken to your aunt?' he asked, diligently wiping down the counters and avoiding Jeanie's gaze.

She propped a hip against the counter. Well, this was interesting. Maybe Hazel was right about Norman. Maybe he did have a thing for her aunt. Maybe he was missing her. The thought softened her towards him immediately. Poor old guy.

Jeanie studied him as he cleaned. He wasn't a bad-looking man. She tilted her head. He might even be sort of cute in the button-up shirts and sweater vests he wore every day. His dark-framed glasses were quite distinguished, and he still had a full head of hair, graying at the temples. Aunt Dot could definitely do worse.

'I talked to her yesterday, actually.'

If Jeanie hadn't been staring at him trying to picture

him with her aunt on his arm, she would have missed the tiny change in his body language. The way he paused in his counter wiping, the way he leaned toward her just a little, as though wanting to get closer to any words about Aunt Dot.

Interesting, indeed.

'She asked how things were going so I filled her in. I told her you've been a really big help to me in getting settled.'

Norman did something entirely uncharacteristic then. He smiled. It was the first Jeanie had seen from the man since she got here, and she nearly fell over.

'She's having a great time in St. Thomas. Snorkeling, windsurfing. She even went zip lining the other day.' And just like that, the smile dropped from Norman's face. Aha! Even more proof he missed her aunt! His grumpiness toward Jeanie wasn't about her, at all! He just missed Dot. It was almost sorta sweet.

'Well, she should have trained you better before she ran off,' Norman said, with one last swipe at the counter before he marched off into the backroom, muttering something about taking his break.

Okay, so maybe Norman wasn't that sweet, after all.

Jeanie leaned her elbows on the counter, watching the rain pour down outside. A brave couple decided to leave the café and make a run for it to their car, and Jeanie watched them hurry out. That left her, an older man with giant headphones and the Sunday paper in his lap at the window seat, and a group of high school kids nursing the dregs of their lattes as they waited out the rain. The perfect crowd for a rainy afternoon.

The conversation with her aunt had been good. Jeanie was excited to fill Dot in on how things were going, and it was nice to see her aunt's tan face, with her dangly seashell earrings filling up the screen. Thinking back on it now, though, Dot had acted a bit odd when Jeanie mentioned Norman. She'd given Jeanie's comments about his helpfulness only a brief acknowledgment and then changed the subject to her latest snorkeling adventure.

Jeanie pulled out her book from under the register, running a hand over the half-naked farmer on the cover. It was possible she was getting too many ideas from this book, but she was suddenly convinced that something was going on between her aunt and Norman.

She flipped open to the next chapter, hoping the farmer would finally make his feelings for the milkmaid known. She didn't have time to worry about Norman and Dot.

She had her own secret relationship to think about.

Chapter Sixteen

It was Sullivan's Pub's first-ever trivia night and Noah had insisted they go. His exact words were, 'Come on, man. I need your big, beautiful brain to help me win!' To which Logan replied that his brain was neither big nor beautiful and they definitely weren't going to win, but here he was.

The problem was, he liked Noah. He especially liked that Noah hadn't grown up here and didn't really give a shit about Logan's lost father or his dead mother, had missed the Christmas-tree lighting debacle entirely, and just treated Logan like a regular guy. Plus, he talked so much that Logan rarely needed to when they went out, which suited him just fine.

He took another swig of his beer and checked out the crowd. It was a pretty big turnout, but he wasn't surprised. This town loved an event. Give them a festival, a club, a meeting, a class and they were on board.

Noah had snagged them a high-top table surrounded by three stools, one for each team member. He'd also recruited book club Jacob onto their team, but the man hadn't arrived yet.

'Hey, there's Hazel and the new café owner. What's her name? Jenny? June?'

'It's Jeanie,' Logan said, forcing himself to turn his head at a reasonable speed instead of whipping it around to get a glance at Jeanie.

'Jeanie, right,' Noah said, but his gaze was locked on Hazel, who nervously pushed up her glasses and glanced away.

Logan didn't have time to unpack the way his friend was staring at his other friend right now. He was too busy playing over the past few days in his mind. He'd only seen Jeanie briefly every morning, right in the middle of the morning commuter rush, when he came in for coffee. He was sure he'd been more awkward than ever, giving her his order and trying desperately not to make his feelings for her known to the whole town.

How did he stand normally? What did he usually do with his hands? Did he always talk this loudly? It had been a taxing few mornings, but Jeanie's bright smile and dark eyes were worth it. And now she was just a few tables over and he was paralyzed.

What was the protocol here? It'd be weird if he didn't go over, right? Why had he thought doing this, whatever this was, secretly would be easier than doing it out in the open?

He should have stayed home with his chickens.

This was why he didn't do things like this. This was why he didn't go to trivia nights or secretly date women (Date? Secretly make out with women?). He was a big, surly, awkward-as-hell guy who did better with animals than women. If Lucy hadn't come up to him at the bar that fateful night, he never would have had the nerve to talk to her.

He took another swig of beer, letting the bitter liquid wash away Lucy's name from his mind. He should have let Nana make him that dating profile, after all. He could be peacefully dating someone from Colorado or South Africa or the damn moon right now. Anyone other than the new girl in town that had captured everyone's attention.

Attention was the last thing he wanted. And yet he couldn't seem to stay away from her.

'We should go say hello,' Noah said, clapping Logan on the back and startling him out of his thoughts about dating moon women.

'Uh ... I should probably keep the table.'

'No worries about that.' Noah flashed him a grin, slapping a laminated card with a big number 4 on it in the middle of the table. 'It's reserved for us now. Go Team Four! We should probably come up with a catchier name, but first let's go say hello.'

Noah had already hopped down from his stool and was pleading with his eyes for Logan to join him. Was his loquacious friend nervous about talking to Hazel? Interesting.

Logan took one more gulp of beer for courage and followed Noah to Jeanie's table.

'Hello, ladies.'

'Hey, Noah, you remember Jeanie,' Hazel said, feigning casualness, but Logan watched her fidget in her chair.

'Are you guys ready to lose?' Jeanie asked with a grin, her eyes bright in the dim room.

'Wow, Jeanie. Coming in hot,' Noah laughed. 'I like it. And no, we are definitely going to win.'

'We'll see,' she said, crossing her arms over her chest. She let her gaze drift to Logan.

'Hey,' he said, his voice sticking in his throat.

'Hey.' Her gaze slipped to his mouth for just long enough to send heat through his body. She had ditched her usual sweater for a fitted tank top. In the heat of the crowded bar, the sight of all that bare skin short-circuited his brain. His thoughts were nothing more than static and the memory of how soft she'd been when he'd slipped his hand up her shirt.

'Um, hi everyone.' Annie's voice tore through the tension as she tossed her bakery bag onto the table. 'Weird energy here. What's up?'

Jeanie broke their stare first. 'Nothing's weird. Everything's great! Very excited to kick these guys' butts.'

Noah laughed. 'More fighting words. Okay, new café owner Jeanie. I like you.'

She beamed at the compliment and Logan wanted to punch Noah in the face for making her smile like that. He shook the irrational thought from his head.

'We should get back. I think it's starting soon,' Logan said.

'Good luck.' Noah flashed Hazel another smile and Logan didn't miss the flustered look on her face. He'd be sure to hassle her about that later. Especially after her 'crush' comments.

Jacob was waiting for them back at the table. 'Who wants a muffin?' he sang. 'They're from Annie's class and I think they came out pretty good.' He placed a misshapen muffin in front of Logan with a flourish. 'Ta-da!'

'Uh ... Is it supposed to be caved in like that?' Noah asked, and Logan nearly choked on his beer.

'Maybe I still need a little practice.' Jacob frowned.

'I don't think muffins go great with beer,' Logan added. Jacob's face fell. 'But I'll take one home for the morning.'

'Great! You'll have to tell me how it is. I think maybe I undercooked them a bit.'

'Alright, that's enough muffin talk,' Noah said, his attention fixed on Amber, the bartender and apparently the evening's MC, as she stepped up to the mic they'd set up in front of the bar. 'It's starting!'

Logan groaned into his beer. *Here we go.*

Unsurprisingly, they lost.

By a lot. Like, it wasn't even close. As it turned out, Hazel was a trivia master, which considering she spent her days surrounded by books, probably shouldn't have surprised Logan as much as it did. Her team won, although Nancy, Linda, and Tammy came in a close second.

Noah ate the rest of Jacob's muffins to console himself. Apparently, they weren't that bad, after all.

But Logan didn't really give a shit about muffins or

trivia, or the fact that – drunk on either margaritas or victory – Annie had turned trivia night into a dance off. All he could think of was Jeanie's flushed cheeks and her body in that tight tank top and her hair loose around her shoulders as she tipped her head back and laughed at something Hazel said.

Every once in a while, her gaze would snag on his and her smile would grow. His body tingled with awareness as he tracked her movements through the bar, so when she started gathering her things to leave, he didn't even have time to think before he was also moving toward the door.

He pushed it open, and they both tumbled out into the crisp, night air.

'Walk you home?' he nearly growled the words into her ear. Dry leaves blew past them on the sidewalk.

She laughed a little, her voice breathy when she spoke. 'Thanks, it's such a long way,' she teased. She smelled sweet like French vanilla spiked with vodka. He wanted to bury his face in her neck and get drunk on her.

He took her hand and nearly dragged her into the alley between the bar and the café. It was dark and he could barely make out the shape of her, but he could feel her, hear her surprised gasp when he took her face in his hands.

'I haven't stopped thinking about kissing you all week,' he rasped.

He could just make out her lips tipping up before she pressed them against his, soft and sure. 'Me, too,' she murmured between kisses. 'It's all I think about.'

'Damn,' he groaned as he ran his hands up her sides, bunching the fabric of her tank top in his fists. The cardigan she'd thrown on against the fall chill hung open in the front and he ran his hands inside over the dip of her waist, brushing against the underside of her breasts. 'I like this shirt.'

Jeanie giggled, burying her face in his neck. 'You like this plain white tank top?'

'So much,' he groaned when her breath ghosted across his skin. 'It's my favorite plain white tank top in the whole world.'

Her breath caught as he tugged her closer, her body pressed against his. Then her hands were in his hair, her mouth on his again and he was lost. Lost to sensation, to the taste of her, the feel of her in his arms. Lost to anything that made sense. Lost to Jeanie.

He grabbed her ass and hoisted her into his arms. She wrapped her legs around his waist, deepening the kiss. God, she was perfect, soft and warm, and just as keyed up as he was, her kisses wild, like getting to him was more important than anything else.

'I've wanted to do this since I met you,' she gasped. 'When I saw you carrying those big crates and your forearms were doing that sexy flex thing and I wondered if you could carry me.' She spoke the words in between kisses along his mouth and neck and along the shell of his ear.

'Sexy flex thing?' His voice was strained, husky and deep.

'Yeah, you know. The forearm thing.'

He didn't know the forearm thing, but the fact that Jeanie had pictured this from the start made him harder than anything else. He backed her against the wall, and she groaned into his mouth.

'Anytime you want to wrap these sweet thighs around me like this, I'd be happy to carry you,' he rasped.

She laughed, the joyful sound of it filling the dark alley. Suddenly everything came into focus.

The dark alley. The brick wall he had her trapped against.

Jesus, he was groping her in a dark alley. What the hell was wrong with him?

He pulled away, putting her gently on the ground. 'Sorry ... am I hurting you? This is ... we should...'

Jeanie blinked at him, desire still written across her beautiful face, clear even in the darkness. 'Go up to my apartment?'

Logan's heart stuttered.

Up to her apartment. Her apartment, where that tank top could end up on the floor, and that beautiful expanse of skin he'd gotten a peek at in the bar could grow until he saw everything, kissed everywhere.

Her apartment, where they'd wake up together tomorrow morning and he'd have to sneak out the back door like he was ashamed of her, when he definitely wasn't, but isn't that how it would seem?

Her apartment, as much as she seemed happy here, he still wasn't convinced she'd stay in for long, and then he'd be heartbroken all over again.

Up to her apartment. The words were fraught, the whole idea of getting in deeper with Jeanie was still too big a risk to him. Wasn't it?

The sudden crash from behind the buildings saved him from having to decide to follow his brain or other less helpful parts of his anatomy.

'What was that?' Jeanie's eyes grew wide in the dark, her grip on his arms tightening.

Logan cleared his throat, shaking the feel of Jeanie's body from his fingertips. 'Probably just raccoons. I'll go check.'

'I'm coming with you.' She grabbed his hand, letting him walk ahead as though she was afraid of what they might find.

They turned the corner to find the trash cans tipped, neatly tied garbage bags spilling out into the alley. Logan took out his phone and aimed the flashlight at the destruction. No raccoons.

'Must have run off.' He shrugged.

'I don't know...'

'You don't know what?'

Jeanie stepped around him, inspecting the trash bags. 'This is the third night in a row they've been tipped.'

'Okay, persistent raccoons.'

She shook her head. 'But the bags are never torn open. Wouldn't they tear open the bags to get to the food? Why would they just tip them over and then leave?'

Logan grabbed a bin and righted it. 'That is strange. Could be neighborhood kids. Halloween mischief or something.'

'It's only the nineteenth. Kinda early for mischief, isn't it?'

He tossed the garbage bags back in and slammed the lid. 'Maybe it's another ghost.'

Jeanie gave him a faint smile, but the worried crease lingered between her brows.

'You don't think Mac would do it, do you?' she whispered the question like the man might hear them through the brick wall of the pub and the noise of the crowd inside.

'Why the hell would Mac tip your trash bins?'

'Annie thought—'

'I'm gonna stop you right there. Any information about Mac from Annie is unreliable. Those two have had a weird vibe for years.'

'She just thought maybe he was trying to scare me off. So he could buy the café and expand. It kinda makes sense.' She looked small under the yellow light of the back door, defeated.

'I don't know what's going on, but I'm pretty confident it's not Mac. He wouldn't do something like that.'

She shrugged. 'Maybe not. I still just feel like...' She let the thought trail off, forcing a smile onto her face again. 'Never mind.'

'You feel like what? What's the matter?' *Let me fix it.* Those dangerous, tempting words tore through him. Those words got him into so much trouble before. *Let me fix it. Let me convince you to stay. Let me fool us both into thinking you belong here.*

'No, it's nothing.' She smiled bigger, faker. 'You're probably right about the raccoons.'

'Right, okay.' He shifted on his feet. The moment had passed, the moment that had him pressing Jeanie up against a brick wall, desperate to get closer; and now he didn't know what to do.

'I should probably get some sleep,' Jeanie said after another strained moment between them. 'Early day tomorrow.'

'Sure, of course.'

She reached up and planted a kiss on his cheek. 'Thanks for investigating the noise.'

'You gonna be okay tonight?' he asked, wanting to reach for her again, but not knowing if he should anymore. 'We can get Officer Dee to drive by tonight and keep an eye on things.'

'Not necessary.' She waved his idea away. 'I'll be fine. Don't worry about me and some silly raccoons or teens or whatever. No big deal.' Every word out of her mouth only served to convince him that she wasn't okay at all, but what else could he do? Demand she let him spend the night? Wasn't that the exact thing he'd just been trying to avoid?

'Call if you need me, okay?' His voice was gruffer than he planned, his frustration at himself coming out in his words.

Her gaze snagged on his, their dark-brown depths trapping him. 'Okay.'

'I'm serious, Jeanie. Weird noises, anything. Call.'

She nodded, her fake smile slowly transforming to genuine. 'I will call. I promise.'

'Okay. Good.'

'Thanks, Logan.'

'Goodnight, Jeanie.'

Chapter Seventeen

Holy crap, that man is a good kisser.

Jeanie leaned back against the door in the dark trying to catch her breath. But her breath would not cooperate because all her brain wanted to think about was Logan's mouth on hers and his hands raking across her body and his solid waist between her legs.

Oh God, had she actually confessed to wanting to jump into his arms since the day she met him? She could have been embarrassed about that, but then she remembered the way his groan had vibrated through her when she said it. Maybe it wasn't the worst thing she could have said.

But then whoever had been knocking over her damn trash cans had ruined the whole moment. It wasn't just the trash cans. She didn't want to tell Logan, but someone had been tipping over her new mums out front, too. Every damn night. Her flowers, her trash, she'd even found her mail strewn all over the sidewalk yesterday. Raccoons didn't go through your mail. She was pretty sure of it.

Maybe it was kids screwing around? But teenagers loved her pumpkin-spiced lattes! Why would they mess with their supplier? It didn't make sense.

She was determined not to be a hot mess every time she saw Logan, so she'd held back her theories about someone trying to get rid of her. Well, mostly held back. He was definitely skeptical of Annie's Mac theory, but it was making more and more sense to Jeanie. Who else would want her gone?

Casper padded down the stairs to greet her. Her original ghost. Maybe Logan was right. Maybe there was a rational explanation for all the rest of this, too. But she was determined to leave Logan out of it. If they were going to ... well, going to make out in dark alleys ... she wanted him to see her in the best possible light. Even if that light was the dim glow of the streetlamp.

And tonight, she felt like she'd nailed it.

She'd gone out with friends. She'd had some freaking fun for the first time in a long time. It was nice.

Making out with Logan was just the cherry on top.

New Jeanie liked cherries.

Jeanie bolted awake.

The sound of breaking glass tore through her sleep.

What the hell was that?

Her initial instinct was to hide under her covers but then she remembered she had a business to defend and a cat to protect. She peered out from her blankets and found Casper staring at her, wide-eyed in the dark.

'What was that?' she whispered but apparently the cat didn't know, either. Damn cat. She got out of bed and crept toward the window that overlooked the back of the café. A dark figure was back there with a baseball bat.

Oh, my God, oh, my God, oh, my God. This is it. See, people always think cities are dangerous, but small towns are where all the worst serial killers live!

Jeanie bit down on her bottom lip to keep all the crazy words from spilling out. Why? She didn't know. To appear perfectly stable in front of her cat, apparently. Which was a very stable thing to do.

She watched the figure. A man, probably. Men really had the market cornered on serial killing. He looked around, his movements a bit frantic but also kinda like he was confused and couldn't really figure out what to do next. Maybe he was a first-time serial killer, in which case, he was just a killer. She would be his first victim. How quaint.

Okay, think, Jeanie. Do something!

She ran back to her bed and dug through the covers for her phone, cursing herself for her terrible habit of watching old episodes of *Schitt's Creek* every night before bed. Inevitably she fell asleep holding her phone and it would get lost in the blankets. A few times she woke herself up when the phone fell directly onto her face.

Aha! Got it. Now what?

She should call 911, right? That's what you were supposed to do when your life was very clearly in danger. But was it, really, though? She didn't want to cause a whole big to-do if there wasn't anything going on. The whole town already knew about her almost decapitating Logan, she didn't really want to add fuel to the gossip fire.

She crept back to the window.

He was gone.

She pressed her forehead to the cool glass and peered left and then right down the alley. Nothing. Maybe someone was just cutting through.

She still held her phone clutched in her sweaty palm, Logan's words ringing in her ears. She could text him.

It was 2.23am. What was she going to say – 'Hey, sorry for waking you but there may have been someone walking through the alley?' No. No, nope. That was not the Jeanie she was shooting for these days.

Laid-back Jeanie would look for the perfectly reasonable explanation here. A law-abiding citizen of Dream Harbor was simply taking a shortcut through the alley on their way home from their respectable law-abiding job – probably as an ER nurse or something brave and noble like that.

She tossed her phone back on her bed to prevent herself from doing anything rash. She would not wake up the sexy farmer to alert him about nothing.

No one was trying to murder her.

Unfortunately, her racing heart did not want to hear about that. It wanted to keep her up for the rest of the night.

It was only 11.30pm in California. She fished her phone back out of the blankets and tucked herself in.

She texted Ben.

Hey, you up?

Her brother responded almost immediately. She could picture him tucked into his own bed; his California king-sized mattress half covered in his pack of rescue dogs. He had three, which Jeanie felt was far too many dogs, but Ben claimed there was no such thing.

I really don't want to receive 'u up?' texts from my sister.

Jeanie laughed out loud, startling the cat all over again. Casper jumped down from the bed with a long-suffering sigh. Or at least she imagined he sighed. It was impossible to tell with cats.

Shut up. I almost got murdered.
Again? Why is that always happening to you?
Don't know.
What happened this time?
I think I heard breaking glass and then I saw someone possibly but probably not lurking in the back alley.
Jesus, did you call the police?

Jeanie paused, her fingers hovering over the keys. She could lie, but then she would inevitably feel guilty about lying and confess to it at the most inopportune time, like in the middle of Thanksgiving dinner.

Um ... no.
WHY NOT?
I didn't want to seem hysterical.
Damn it, Jeanie. You need to stop with this crap. You are fine. A pain in the ass, but otherwise fine.

Nothing happened! And the person is gone now. I don't want to waste town resources.
And what about the broken glass?
I'll check in the morning. It was probably nothing.

It was definitely nothing. But she also was definitely not going to go downstairs by herself in the middle of the night and check. She was not lucky enough to have it be a sexy man two times in a row.

So, you texted me just to get us both worked up?
Yeah, basically. I can't sleep now.
How's the sexy farmer?
SHUT UP.
Hey if you can keep me up, I can harass you. So...
He's fine. A very nice man.
A very nice man?!! Wow, calm down.
Okay, fine. You really want to know? He's the best kisser in the entire world and his stomach has those lines and his forearms do the sexy flex thing...
Ok, ok! Stop! I surrender. Also, those lines are called abs.
Well, I wouldn't know. I've never had any.
Lol.
How's life in LA? You going to Mom's for Thanksgiving?
Probably not this year. Maybe for Christmas.

Oh, no! You have to come! Mom makes me sit with the little cousins at the kid's table when you're not there!
Hahaha why?
I don't know. It's like without you she bumps me down a level in the generations or something.
Well, good luck with that.

Jeanie wasn't ready to go to sleep yet. And if Ben got to ask her about Logan, then she wanted some details on her little brother's life, too.

How's that girl you were seeing?
Don't want to talk about it.
But I told you about the sexy farmer!
And now I deeply regret asking about him.
Bennnneeeettttt ... come on!
She didn't like dogs.
So you dumped her?
That's a deal breaker for me!
Ben...
I need to go to sleep.
Fine.

That little tidbit was actually more information than she usually got out of him about his love life. All she really knew was he dated but still hadn't found anyone worth keeping, or mentioning, or bringing home to meet the family. Not yet, anyway.

Are you in danger?
No, I'm fine. Go to sleep. I'll just rewatch season 4 again.
Schitt's Creek?
Of course.
David and Patrick forever.
Exactly. Nighty night, little brother.
Night, Jeanie. Don't get murdered.
Xo.

Jeanie then pulled up Netflix on her phone and pressed play. There was no way she was getting back to sleep tonight.

In fact, she was still awake at 5am when another text flashed on her screen, but this one wasn't from her brother.

Just wanted to check in. Everything okay?

Logan was checking in on her. Damn, that man was thoughtful.

Good morning! Everything is great. Will I see you for your usual this morning?

Yep. See you later.

See you later!

Jeanie's finger hovered over the kissy winky emoji. Nope. Too far. She would quit while she was ahead. This was good enough for now. Just right, actually. She could keep things with Logan casual and fun. No need to make things too intense, no need to demand things from Logan that he wasn't ready to give.

Chapter Eighteen

For the second night in a row, Logan found himself in town against his will. It was Nana's turn to go to the town meeting, but she pulled a muscle at her aqua aerobics for seniors class and had sent Logan in her place. He was hoping he could just confirm the farm's contribution to the Fall Festival – something he definitely could have done over email if the mayor didn't insist on doing it in person every year – and get out of there. But, of course, that's not how these things went in Dream Harbor.

'Order in the court,' Pete hollered from the front of the room. 'Only joking, folks,' he added with a chuckle. 'But if people could take their seats, that'd be great.'

The crowd was only half-listening. Everyone was too keyed up about the Fall Festival. It was Dream Harbor's second-largest event. Second only to the Christmas-tree lighting, which Logan refused to think about.

Logan sat in his usual seat in the back. His shoulders and arms hurt from lugging pumpkins around all day; moving them from one side of the barn to the other when Nana decided they looked better in the dappled sunlight. It had been a long day. After a long night of barely sleeping. He couldn't get Jeanie out of his head, everything they'd done in that alley. And everything he wished they'd done.

Maybe he should have kissed her again? Maybe he should have stayed?

But the moment had been broken and then he didn't know what to do. Before Lucy, Logan hadn't dated many women. Not surprisingly, his inability to strike up a casual conversation didn't help when trying to meet someone. It was why he thought Lucy was different. At least at first. She didn't seem to mind his quiet nature. Until she did.

Until she eventually found him and his life here lacking.

It hurt all the more because he thought he'd found someone who understood him. Showed how much he knew about reading women. So when Jeanie backed off last night, he wasn't about to initiate anything more.

He stretched his arms out in front of him, hands

clasped, and cracked his knuckles. He noticed the way his forearms looked with his sleeves rolled up. Then he thought about Jeanie noticing the way his forearms looked with his sleeves rolled up, and heat rushed to his face.

Quickly following that thought was a crowd of others including the taste of her mouth (spiked sweetness), the feel of her thighs around him (strong and warm), and the memory of her body pressed against his (perfection). He dropped his hands into his lap, changing his thoughts to aqua aerobics for seniors before he embarrassed himself.

Good old Logan, ruining town events with ill-fated marriage proposals and inappropriate erections.

He sighed and ran a hand down his beard, praying Pete would keep this meeting short. But so far, the mayor hadn't even gotten everyone to sit down and shut up so Logan wasn't holding out a lot of hope.

'Well, look who it is! Two meetings in a row!'

Annie came up behind him and planted a kiss on his cheek. Hazel followed her in and plopped down next to him. And, because apparently they were all friends now, and because the universe wanted to torture him, Jeanie hustled in after her.

'Are we late?' she whispered, sitting on his other side.

'Doesn't matter. Nothing's started yet anyway,' he said, avoiding her gaze. How on earth was he supposed to sit next to her like everything was normal, when all he wanted to do was kiss her again?

It was possible that a secret relationship was even more stressful than a public one.

'What are you doing here anyway?' Annie asked, unraveling her mile-long scarf. 'Isn't it Nana's turn?'

'She pulled a muscle.'

Annie frowned. 'Is she okay?'

'Fine. Just sore.'

'So, we get the pleasure of your company again,' she cooed, landing in the seat in front of him.

'Apparently.'

'Well, I'm glad you're here,' Jeanie said, and then Logan made a tactical error. He looked at her. He looked at her and she was smiling at him, and her eyes were bright chocolate-brown and a slow blush was creeping up her cheeks and he couldn't look away.

He couldn't look away until Annie snapped her fingers in front of his face, anyway.

'You two alright?' she asked, with a raised eyebrow.

'We're great,' Jeanie said at the same time he bit out a terse, 'Yep.'

'Did Jeanie tell you about her break-in?' Hazel asked.

'Break-in?'

'It wasn't a break-in really. More like a break-and-run away,' Jeanie said, attempting to reassure him with her smile, but all Logan heard was that *something bad* happened to Jeanie and he simply could not allow that.

'Well, what the hell happened?' He sounded like he was mad at everyone in the room when really, he was just mad at himself for not being there.

'Hey, hey. Calm down there, Hulk.' Annie's voice was teasing, but Logan wasn't in the mood. Jeanie knew something wasn't right last night and he blew her off. He'd tried to convince her it was a damn raccoon, while she had been in actual danger.

'Someone broke a window in the middle of the night. It's really not a big deal.' Jeanie waved a hand like it was nothing and Logan hated it. Why wasn't she going on about murder theories? Why no stakeout? Why no convoluted ideas about what happened?

Why the hell wasn't she letting him fix it?

'Why didn't you call me?' he ground out.

'I ... well...'

'Why would she call you?' Hazel asked, eyes round and innocent behind her glasses, but her knowing smile gave her away. 'She could have called me.'

Logan frowned. 'And what would you have done?'

'Same as you! Call the police.'

Right. Why hadn't Jeanie called the police?

He didn't have time to ask before Deputy Mayor Mindy's sharp whistle tore through the din of the crowd.

'Let's get started,' she said, her tone just as serious as it had been at school assemblies.

Logan squirmed in his seat. The quicker they started the sooner they would be done, but he had more questions for Jeanie.

'Why didn't you tell me about it?' he whispered, letting himself get close enough to brush his nose in her hair. She smelled like French roast today.

'I didn't want to bother you,' she whispered back. 'Hazel's making it sound worse than it was. It really isn't a big deal.'

'Yeah, but last night you were trying to tell me—'

'Logan.' The sound of his name, too loud in the quiet room, was an instant flashback to any time he'd gotten in trouble in class. Never for chatting with his neighbor, though; usually for staring out the window. 'You and Jeanie must be talking about how much you want to judge the costume contest, since that's what we're discussing right now.' Pete's cheerful tone covered up the sheer evil of his words.

'I ... we ... that's not...'

'Sounds fun.' Jeanie, sweet innocent Jeanie, did not know what she was saying. The costume contest was not fun. It was a cut-throat competition filled with die-hard Halloween fans and no one was ever happy with the outcome. Logan had seen fist fights break out over the results. He usually gave the costume contest a very wide berth, preferring to drop off the pumpkins to the decorating tables early, and then get suckered into trying fall-themed beers with Noah (they were always disgusting, but anything was better than breaking up a fight between Big Bird and Luke Skywalker).

'Wonderful!' Mayor Kelly beamed, and Logan felt his soul wither inside him. This was bound to be a disaster. 'Okay, next matter of business, bobbing for apples: good, clean fun, or ground zero for disease? Let's discuss.'

Jeanie nudged him with her shoulder. 'It'll be fun, right?' she reiterated in a whisper.

He nodded because he couldn't bear to tell her how inevitably not fun it would be, and because he was honestly terrified that if he said another word to her, Pete would have him signed up to inflate the bounce house with his mouth.

Instead, he settled in, trying to pay attention to the insanely long, meeting agenda and not think about the warmth of Jeanie's arm against his or the way she nodded along with what Pete was saying to show she was paying attention, or the fact that about halfway through the meeting, she pulled out her notebook and started taking notes accompanied by little pumpkins doodled in the margins.

How was a man supposed to concentrate on the pros

and cons of a pie-eating contest when the woman next to him insisted on being so adorable?

It was inconvenient really.

By the time the meeting was over Logan was nearly twitching with impatience. He needed to talk to Jeanie without becoming the next topic on the agenda. Mercifully, Annie rushed off to attack Mac for parking in her spot or something, and Hazel went with her, either as back-up or to make sure Annie didn't slug him. Logan wasn't sure which, but he really didn't care if a brawl broke out, as long as he was long gone with Jeanie by his side.

'Want a ride home?' he asked as Jeanie pulled on her coat.

'I'd love one.'

They made their way toward the door, and they were nearly free when Kaori and Jacob sprung from the shadows like freaking book-wielding ninjas.

'Jeanie, there you are!' Kaori greeted her with a big hug, acting as though she'd just been reunited with a long-lost relative.

'Hi!' Jeanie grinned at the woman. 'I just saw you this afternoon for your coffee break,' she said with a laugh.

'That was hours ago,' Kaori said with a wave of her hand. Jacob rolled his eyes and shoved a book in Jeanie's hands.

'Next week's read. It's a super steamy one so I hope we don't traumatize you too much.'

Jeanie laughed. 'I think I can handle it.'

Logan stared at his feet, trying very hard not to think about what Jeanie could handle. He could feel Jacob's gaze on him.

'How did you like that other book I gave you, Jeanie?' Jacob asked. His tonc implied some inside joke that Logan did not want any part of.

'I liked it. It was ... very inspiring.'

Jacob cackled in delight. 'Oh, good.' His gaze flicked from Jeanie to Logan. 'Is life imitating art?' He raised a perfectly groomed eyebrow.

Jeanie blushed to her hairline.

'What are you two talking about?' Kaori asked, but Logan had a very strong feeling he didn't want to know.

'Never mind,' Jacob sang, grabbing Kaori's hand. 'Let's go grab a drink before you turn into a pumpkin.'

'See you at the next meeting!' Kaori called with a wave as Jacob dragged her away.

Logan cleared his throat and Jeanie shifted uncomfortably, offering him an awkward smile. 'That was just ... you know ... book talk.'

'Sure.'

'Great, okay. Let's go.'

He followed Jeanie out the big double doors of the

meeting room into the foyer of the town hall. It was drafty out here, the old wheezing radiators doing their best and failing miserably in the face of the October wind, which swirled in through the door as people filed out.

They were stopped by at least five other small groups of neighbors on their way out, all wanting to tell Jeanie what a great job she was doing with the café. By the time they hit the sidewalk, she was grinning from ear to ear from the compliments.

They walked to his truck in amicable quiet, Jeanie humming a little tune under her breath as she waved to several more neighbors.

'Thanks for the ride,' she said hopping up into the cab. 'It's a lot colder than when I walked here.'

'Of course, anytime.'

'I guess I'll need to get a car. I never really needed one in Boston,' she said, smiling at him from the passenger seat.

'Do you miss it?' The question popped out of his mouth before he could think better of it.

'Miss what? Public transportation? A little.'

'No, Boston. I mean, I know it's really different here.'

Jeanie shrugged. 'I like it here.'

So simple. That one little sentence. But, God, did he want to believe it. She looked like she belonged here, tonight especially. She officially knew more people in this town than he did. He wanted her to belong here.

He wanted her 'I like it here' to mean: 'I like you and your smelly old farm and your slightly nutty grandparents. I like you and I'm sticking around.' He wanted her 'I like it here' to give him some kind of guarantee that of course, no one could really give him.

It was possible Lucy had messed him up more than he liked to admit. It was also possible that his grandfather was right, but Logan would never admit that.

He shook his head. 'Good. That's good.' Draping his arm over the back of Jeanie's seat, he backed out of the parking space and maneuvered slowly through the lot. There were plenty of people still hanging out and talking despite the chill of the night.

The drive was short; the town hall was only about a mile down Main Street from the café. The car hadn't even had time to warm up yet and the vent still blew cool air in his face. He pulled up in front of the café, under the yellow glow of a streetlamp. The wind was crisp and cold, shaking the colorful leaves from the trees. The sun had set hours ago, making it feel later than it was.

'Thanks again for the ride.'

'Why didn't you tell me about the broken window?'

he asked again, still hating that she hadn't called him last night when it happened.

'I told you; it wasn't a big deal.'

'Jeanie.'

She sighed. 'I just... I didn't want to overcomplicate this.'

'This?'

'This.' She gestured between them. 'Us. I didn't want you to feel ... I don't know ... responsible for me or something.'

'But I want to...' *Don't say you want to be responsible for her, for God's sake*. 'I want to help.'

She studied him, her brown eyes assessing him. Her lips twisted to the side as she thought. 'Okay, well how about this, I promise to let you know if I need help.'

'Promise?' he grunted.

'Yes. If I need anything, I will let you know.'

He didn't like that one bit, but he probably didn't have a choice. 'I think maybe you were right.'

'Oh?'

'Someone is messing with you.'

Jeanie's eyes went wide at his admission. 'You think so?'

'It's starting to seem like it.'

Jeanie opened her mouth and then slammed it shut again. What the hell was she keeping from him?

'What is it?' he asked, gruffly.

'Nothing.'

'Jeanie.'

She huffed. 'Nothing! I promise I'll tell you if there are any more developments in the case.'

'The case?'

'Yeah,' she said with a smile. 'The case of the Pumpkin Spice Mysteries.'

'Okay, Nancy Drew.'

She grinned. 'Logan?'

'Yeah?'

'Are you going to kiss me?' She leaned closer as she asked it and suddenly Logan didn't give a shit about broken windows.

'Do you *want* me to kiss you, Jeanie?' His voice was a low rumble and Jeanie's eyes fluttered closed.

'I think it would be very helpful if you did.'

He watched her lips tip into a teasing smile before he leaned forward and brushed his mouth against hers. She sighed and wrapped her hands in his shirt, pulling him toward her.

She belonged here, too, tucked against him, her lips on his, her little breathy sighs on his skin.

He deepened the kiss and Jeanie met him, her tongue sliding against his. Her hands were still in his shirt, tugging him like she couldn't get close enough. They were wearing too many layers of clothes and this cab was too cramped. He groaned in frustration as his hands ran over layers of coat and sweater. It was like making out in space suits.

'Hold on.' Jeanie pulled back, ripping off her coat and flinging it into the back seat. Her sweater followed, leaving her in the long-sleeved T-shirt she had been wearing underneath. She wasn't exactly naked, but at least he could see her shape, could run his hands over her curves, which was exactly what he was doing as Jeanie unbuttoned his shirt.

Once she had it opened, a frown crossed her face at the sight of the Henley he was wearing underneath.

'Damn it.'

Logan huffed a laugh. This was absurd. They should probably just cool it...

His thoughts stuttered as Jeanie's hands roved under his shirt, raking across the bare skin of his stomach.

'That's better,' she said against his neck as she kissed him on the rough stubble beneath his beard.

He grabbed her by the hips and pulled her round so that she was straddling him in the driver's seat.

'Even better.'

Jeanie grinned and he kissed her again. He couldn't get enough of her mouth, always smiling, always teasing him. So soft and willing.

Logan had one girlfriend in all of high school and their relationship lasted less than three months, but this moment, making out in his truck, still fully dressed but wishing he wasn't, took him right back to those torturous months. They grasped at each other, groped, and grabbed. No finesse, just need. Just like in those days, with some vague notion in the back of his head about why they shouldn't take it further, but the reasons disappeared with every drag of her tongue against his.

Jeanie's hands were everywhere, her fingers digging into his shoulders and then traveling up to tug at his hair. Their mouths were just as desperate, and when Jeanie rocked forward in his lap, he thought for sure he would die on the spot.

A choked groan escaped him, and she rocked again.

'Jeanie,' he rasped, his hands gripping tight to her hips.

He was in the middle of figuring out the complicated math that would get both of their pants off when Jeanie's ass hit the horn.

The blaring sound rang out through the quiet night.

Jeanie froze, her eyes comically wide, her breath coming fast and hard.

'Oops,' she whispered.

They both glanced around outside, emerging from the spell they'd been under to remember they were right in the middle of freaking Main Street, making out like they were seventeen.

Was this part of his plan to avoid town gossip? What the hell was he doing?

'We should probably...'

'Yeah, sorry. Definitely.' Jeanie untangled herself from his lap and flopped back into the passenger seat. 'I guess we got a little carried away.'

'I guess so.' He ran a hand through his hair, trying to get his breathing under control. Jeanie's face was flushed, her lips red and plush.

Don't look at her lips.

'Thanks again for the ride,' she said with a little laugh, rummaging around the back seat for her clothes.

'Sure.'

She opened the door and the cold October air helped cool his overheated skin. 'Call me if you need anything,' he reminded her.

She gave him an indulgent nod and closed the door, leaving him alone and more confused than ever about where he stood with her.

But already planning the next time he could see her.

Chapter Nineteen

'Can I get you a cup of tea while you wait, sweetie?'

'That'd be nice, thank you.'

Logan's grandmother, or Estelle as she insisted Jeanie call her, hustled back inside to make some tea. Jeanie was sitting on the steps outside the sprawling farmhouse Logan called home. It was beautiful. Old and for sure haunted, but beautiful. In front of her, a small flock of the funniest chickens she had ever seen pecked at the dirt. They each had a tuft of feathers on top of their head that gave them the look of having a very elaborate hairdo. They had the same tufts on their feet, which Jeanie imagined were like little fur-lined boots. Just looking at them made her smile.

This whole place made her smile. Until she remembered she hadn't been invited.

She'd just hopped in her new rental car and shown up.

And the longer she sat here, the more she thought maybe it had been a mistake. Maybe Logan wouldn't take kindly to her invading his home. But things had escalated in 'the Case' and she needed to get away from the café for a bit. Plus, she was nosy and really wanted to see where he lived and worked.

But maybe this was too much?

After their little make-out session a few days ago, Jeanie couldn't stop thinking about him, and not just because she still had stubble burn on her cheeks from kissing him. It was more about how upset he'd been about the broken window. It had her thinking that maybe he actually had wanted to help her figure things out.

Maybe she wasn't being too intense.

Then she'd decided to show up here and probably ruined the whole thing. Logan wanted to keep this thing between them quiet, and now she was ambushing him at home. She honestly wouldn't be surprised if Kaori or Nancy jumped out of the blueberry bushes and started asking her why she was here.

Not that she didn't love her new book club friends. But Logan was right: that club knew everything about everyone.

The old farmhouse door slammed shut behind her.

'Here you go. Nice to have someone else serve you a drink every once in a while, right?' Estelle leaned against one of the columns of the big wrap-around porch.

'Yes, very. Thank you so much, but I was just thinking I should probably go.'

'Go? But Logan should be back any minute.'

'That's okay. I don't want to bother him. I'll just talk to him some other time.'

Estelle raised a snow-white eyebrow, not at all convinced.

'I'm not like everyone else in this batty little town,' she said. 'If you and my grandson have something going on, I don't need to know about it.'

'I ... we...'

'Exactly. No need to discuss it.' Estelle wiped her hands on the frilly apron she'd put on over her tie-dyed sweatshirt and neon-pink leggings. 'But I do think you should stay. Logan's been shy ever since he was small. It always makes me happy to see him make a friend.'

Jeanie smiled at the older woman. She couldn't let this nice grandma down by running off now. Also, the thought of a shy little Logan was doing something mushy to her insides. She focused on the chickens.

'Do they have names?'

'I'm sure they do. That boy names everything, but I can't keep track.'

Thinking of big, sturdy, bearded Logan as 'that boy' nearly made her laugh out loud. 'Did he always like animals?'

'Oh, yes. He used to bring all sorts of critters home. Birds with broken wings, squirrel pups without mothers – don't need a psychology degree to figure that one out. Anyway, I had to draw the line the time he brought a bat into the house thinking it was injured. Turns out the damn thing was fine, just cold. Once it was nice and toasty in our house it shot out of the shoebox and started flying around the house shrieking like a, well, like a bat out of hell.'

Jeanie laughed, covering her face with her hand. 'Not a bat! Terrifying.'

Estelle nodded. 'Henry managed to chase him out, but from then on all rescues were relegated to the barn.'

'Makes sense to me.'

The sound of truck tires on the gravel driveway ended the conversation.

'There he is now. I'll let you two chat.' Estelle winked at her like she did not believe for one second that Jeanie was only here to chat. Great. Even Logan's nana was onto her farmer-seducing ways.

Jeanie didn't know if she should get up and meet Logan halfway down the drive or if she should sit here awkwardly and wait.

She went with sitting awkwardly.

A little fuzzy chicken hopped into her lap while she waited, making her feel a bit better. She patted its fluffy head, and it made a happy little coo-chirp sound. Meanwhile, Logan stepped out of the truck, not noticing her at all.

She watched him say hello to – what was, according to Estelle – an alpaca. Logan scratched the animal between the ears and Jeanie could swear the alpaca smiled. He made his way the rest of the way down the dirt path to the house, eyes on his boots until he was nearly to her.

By this time, she felt absurd for not calling out to him sooner, but she now had two chickens in her lap, and she was pretty sure one had climbed the steps and was looking for a way to perch on her head.

His gaze met hers and his eyes widened in surprise. He took her in, the whole ridiculous scene, Jeanie in her new, pre-torn jeans, her hair still tied back from work, with an assortment of birds twittering around her. One might have been drinking her tea. Was that bad for chickens? Oh, no. She did not want to be responsible for killing one of Logan's chickens. Jeanie tried to shoo it away.

'No, no. That's not for you little chicken. You don't want to get sick, do you?' The chicken cocked its head and stared at her with beady eyes. 'Shoo.' She waved her hand toward it and the chicken hopped up onto her arm like it was a perch. Well, damn it. She placed this chicken in her lap to join the others. Good thing these were weird tiny chickens, or she'd be out of room.

She looked back up; Logan was still staring at her.

He hadn't budged. He was just frozen, watching her. His mouth tugged up in the corner.

She grinned back. 'I think your chickens like me. These are chickens, right? They're weird.'

'Silkie chickens,' he said, striding toward her, a sort of shell-shocked look on his face.

'Ooh ... fancy,' she teased.

He ran a finger over one of the fluffy heads in her lap. 'Very fancy.'

'Do they have names?'

Logan's cheeks blazed red, and he ran a hand through his hair. 'Uh ... yeah.'

Jeanie waited. 'And?'

He sighed. 'Taylor, Rihanna, Lizzo.' He pointed to the three chickens in her lap. 'That's Lady Gaga and Britney over there. And this is Selena trying to climb on your head.'

'What?!' The laugh that burst out of her mouth startled the chickens and they flew up in a puff of feathers. Jeanie doubled over in a fit of giggles. 'You named your chickens after pop stars?' she wheezed.

Logan shrugged. 'It fits the theme.'

'Oh, my God, what theme?'

He let out a long sigh, but his lips kept tugging higher into a smile. Jeanie wanted to bite it. 'Well, the goats are Marley and Dylan.'

'As in Bob?'

'Yep.'

'And the alpaca?' she asked, unable to hide the mirth from her voice.

Logan grimaced. 'Harry Styles.'

'Harry Styles?' Jeanie shrieked with glee. 'Amazing.'

He had lost the fight with his smile and was now grinning at her. 'Can't stray from the theme now.'

'Oh, definitely not.'

Logan huffed a laugh. 'Everything okay?'

'Oh, yeah. Everything's fine. Sorry to just show up.' She stood to go, but Logan put a hand on her arm. He squeezed gently.

'You don't have to apologize. Is something wrong?'

'Well, I wanted to update you about the case.'

'Right. The case. Come with me. You can tell me all about it.'

He led her around the side of the house, past a beautiful garden of late-blooming dahlias, giving the trees a run for their money with their own golds and reds and burnt oranges. The black-eyed Susans had started to tip over on their long stems, but Jeanie could imagine how cheerful they must have been in the summer.

Jeanie breathed in the warm hay and dry-leaf smell of the farm. A hint of woodsmoke and over-ripe apples drifted through the air. The whole place smelled like Logan. Someone should bottle it. *Eau de Sexy Farmer*. She stifled a giggle and followed Logan to a door at the side of the house.

He let them in, and Jeanie blinked, allowing her eyes to adjust after the brightness of the day. She was standing in a tidy apartment. *Logan's* tidy apartment. His perfectly made bed was right next to her. Her mouth went dry.

'You want something to drink?' he asked, moving to the kitchenette along the far wall.

'Just some water would be nice.'

Jeanie looked around while he poured her a glass, trying to satisfy her nosiness without being too obvious. There was a small table next to the kitchenette, the bed that she was certainly not thinking about, which filled most of the space, and a door she assumed led to a bathroom. Two nightstands flanked the bed, but only one was covered in books. On top of the stack sat a pair of reading glasses. Dear God, did Logan wear reading glasses?! She did not stand a freaking chance with this man. She might as well just hand over her panties right now.

Logan cleared his throat and Jeanie's gaze snapped to his.

'It's not much,' he said at the same time she said 'I like your place.'

A small frown tipped his beautiful mouth down in the corners. 'My grandfather and I added this apartment onto the house about a year ago. He thought he and my grandmother would take it when I ... uh ... eventually moved into the big house. But there's not much reason for me to take that whole house for myself.' His cheeks were flushed red, a deep crease in his brow.

Jeanie flopped onto his bed and Logan's eyes widened. 'Well, I like it. Just the right amount of space.' She smiled up at him, hoping it conveyed everything she wanted to say but didn't feel like she should. Mainly that Lucy was the one who lost, the one who'd missed out on loving this sweet man and being loved by him in return. And that Jeanie wouldn't care if he lived in the damn root cellar at this point.

She was in deep.

Way deeper than she was expecting.

Way deeper than she could hide.

Logan continued to stare at her on his bed, his

expression transforming from sad to something hungrier, heavier. Jeanie could feel the weight of it in her belly.

'So, the case,' she blurted, breaking the moment.

'Right.' Logan ran a hand down his beard, leaning against the kitchen counter. 'What's going on?'

Jeanie sighed. *Here goes. Time to spill more nonsense into this man's lap.* But he asked for it . . .

Chapter Twenty

Jeanie was sitting on his bed. And it was scrambling whatever brain cells he had into a very ineffectual brain cell soup.

Seeing her on his front steps had nearly had the same effect. The way the late-day sun cut across her face, casting her in a golden glow. But it was her expression that had stopped him in his tracks, the wide smile, the spark in her eyes. She'd looked absurd, with his chickens using her as a perch, but she'd laughed through the whole thing, murmuring silly words to them, taking it all in stride.

And now here she was in his room, on his bed, smelling like sunshine and dark roast, and he didn't want to talk. He wanted to step into the cage of her legs and press her into his mattress. He wanted her breathy sighs against his neck. He wanted her moaning his name.

'Logan?'

Shit.

'Uh ... yeah. Sorry. What was that last part?'

Her cheeks were flushed, her lips a delicious apple-red. She looked like she knew exactly what he had been thinking about and like she was thinking about it, too.

She shook her head. Wisps of hair trailed down from her bun. 'I think the calls are coming from inside the house.'

Logan blinked. 'What are you talking about, Jeanie?'

'It's a horror-movie reference. Never mind.' She had slipped off her shoes and tucked her legs under her like she sat on his bed every day. Like this was how they always talked after a long day.

'I think whoever is trying to get rid of me actually works at the café.'

'Wait, really?'

She nodded, gearing up to explain her theory to him and Logan had to bite down on a smile. He was taking this seriously, but she was so damn cute when she got excited about something. Which was often. He loved that about her.

He *liked* that about her.

LIKED.

'So, there's been more strange stuff happening. The refrigerator was unplugged the other day. We almost lost all the milk! And then there was a whole morning when the cappuccino machine kept breaking, like over and over again even after we fixed it.'

'Okay. Definitely strange.'

Jeanie nodded, picking up steam. 'I know, right?! I even thought someone had stolen some of thc artwork from the walls, until I found it stashed in a supply closet. It's so strange. Who could have done it but someone who has access to the café during off hours?'

A prickle of unease settled in Logan's gut. Even if Jeanie wasn't in real danger, the fact that someone was screwing with her was unacceptable.

'So, who do you think it is?' he asked.

Jeanie gave him a small smile, a reward for taking her seriously.

'Well, there's only three people that have a key besides me: Norman, Crystal, and Joe.'

'Three suspects.'

Jeanie smiled bigger. 'Yes, exactly. So, Norman.'

Norman. Logan thought about the older man. He'd worked at the café for years alongside Dot. 'Why would Norman want to mess with the café? He loves that place.'

'That was my thought,' Jeanie said. 'He ran it with

Dot forever. Why would he want to ruin what they'd built, right?'

Logan nodded.

'Okay, so Crystal.' Jeanie shifted, tucking a wisp of hair behind her ear. 'I think she has a crush on you.'

Logan choked on his water. 'What? She doesn't.'

'She practically gets hearts in her eyes when you come in!'

'Absolutely not.'

There was no way Crystal had a thing for him. Crystal who was the prom queen of their high school, and a low-key local celebrity for her stint in a series of mattress commercials. No way. Last he heard Crystal was dating a semi-professional football player, although she refused to say which one. She definitely wasn't interested. 'Why would that matter, anyway?' he asked.

'Maybe she knows about us and she's mad and now she's out for revenge.' Jeanie's words ran together like she was almost too embarrassed to say them but needed to get them out.

'No one knows about us.' Even as he said it, he was thinking about the two of them the other night in his truck on the damn road. Anyone could have walked by and seen them. Yep. It was possible someone knew, but he still didn't think Crystal would care. 'I don't think that's it. What about Joe?'

Joe was young, barely nineteen with a lip ring and several neck tattoos. In a line-up, Joe looked like the criminal. But Logan knew Joe. Knew that he drove his own grandmother to aerobics class and had even given Nana a lift several times. It was hard to accuse a kid who took good care of the elderly.

Jeanie shrugged but she looked relieved to move on from her Crystal theory. 'Joe's a sweet kid. I don't know why he would do any of this. Plus, he really needs the job. It doesn't make sense.'

Logan blew out a breath, happy that Jeanie saw Joe the way he did.

'What do you think?' she asked, a furrow of worry between her brows.

'It is strange, but maybe this stuff happened by accident? Did someone kick the cord out of the refrigerator walking by? Maybe the cappuccino machine really is that temperamental?'

Jeanie twisted her lips to the side. 'Yeah ... maybe. It just feels off.' She shrugged.

The last time he'd brushed off Jeanie's concerns, she'd gotten her window broken in the middle of the night. He couldn't do that again.

'Maybe it's time for another stake-out.'

He caught the glimmer of excitement in Jeanie's eyes. 'You think?'

'Anytime you want me there, okay?'

'Thanks.' She stood up and his brain worked frantically to come up with a reason for her to stay. Stay today, stay forever.

The apartment was small. It took him three strides to be in front of her without a plan except to grab her by the hips and tug her toward him.

'If someone is screwing with you, we'll figure it out. Okay?'

She tipped her face up to his. 'Okay.'

He wanted to say more, wanted to ask her if she was happy here, if she liked running the café. If she harbored secret plans to run back to Boston as soon as he let himself fall for her.

She bit down on her bottom lip and held his gaze with her deep brown eyes.

Who the hell was he kidding? He'd fallen for her the first time he'd spotted those hedgehog pajamas.

And she was here now. He'd be a fool to waste it.

Logan's fingers dug into Jeanie's hips, a delicious pressure. Her hands rested on his chest, and she ran them over his shoulders and back again, just savoring the breadth of him, the solidness.

She realized this was why she'd come.

Not just to feel him up, although that was definitely part of it.

No, it was because in the short time she'd been here, Logan had become a grounding presence for her. Even when things felt like a mess at the café, or she wasn't sure she belonged here, or she wasn't sure how to be the Jeanie she was aiming for, being around Logan just made her feel ... right. Like she could figure all the rest out, but she wanted him around to talk to at the end of the day. To bounce ideas off. To tell her it was going to be okay.

He was comforting; safe.

But also sexy as hell. He reminded her by pulling her closer and dropping his mouth to the soft skin behind her ear. His lips trailed kisses along her jawline until he found her mouth.

'This mouth.' His voice was a low rumble. His hands skated up her sides, brushing over the curve of her hips, the dip of her waist, the side of her breasts. 'This body,' he groaned.

She kissed him, catching his groan, savoring the vibration of it coursing through her.

Jeanie was quickly learning that Logan didn't do anything halfway, including kissing her. He didn't rush. He took his time. He was *thorough*. Jeanie had never been kissed like that before. It was like he could kiss her all day; like he would never tire of it. Like kissing wasn't just a means to an end.

But Jeanie didn't want to kiss all night. She had other plans, or at least she did until the knock at the door.

The knock might as well have been gunshots for how quickly Logan reacted.

His hands pulled away from her body so fast she got whiplash. He took a step back and then another, putting as much space between them as he could. His face above his beard was a bright, embarrassed red. His blue eyes were wide with guilt or fear, or something else entirely; something like regret.

He tore away from her like they'd been caught holding the murder weapon while hovering suspiciously over the dead body and laying out their evil plan loud enough for everyone to hear.

He jumped away from her, like he might catch fire if he touched her.

He dropped his hands from her body, like he couldn't bear the thought of anyone knowing what they'd been up to these past few weeks.

And suddenly, this secret relationship was less fun.

She watched Logan run a hand through his hair as he walked to the door. She listened as he spoke to the person on the other side. Something about a shipment coming in early. And by the time he'd closed the door and turned back to her, the moment was thoroughly ruined.

Suddenly, the warnings from her new friends were ringing in her head. Warnings about Logan falling hard, about Logan having his heart broken. So many warnings about treading carefully around this man and trying not to hurt him. But for the first time since they started this secret thing between them, she wondered who was protecting *her* from getting hurt.

It had seemed like a good idea when they started, like a low-pressure way for them to have some fun, but now things were twisted in her gut. Things were less fun when she could see how this ended. When she could so clearly see how *not* over his ex he was. When she could feel how much she'd let herself *like* this man, to come to *depend* on this man. And she refused to let her feelings for Logan get all tangled up with her feelings about being here.

Whatever happened with Logan, Jeanie liked it here. She liked her new friends and her new book club. She was learning how to be a good owner and boss. She had a cat for goodness' sake! She couldn't let suddenly complicated feelings for Logan derail her plans.

'I should go.'

The crease between Logan's brow deepened. 'Jeanie, I—'

'No, no. It's fine.' She waved a hand, brushing off his impending apology. She didn't want it. She just wanted to go home and untangle her confused thoughts, to tend to her bruised feelings. 'It's just that I have some ... uh ... some inventory to do. And Casper needs dinner. You know how pet ownership can be.' She forced a laugh and tried to move toward the door, but Logan grabbed her hand and stopped her.

'I'm sorry about that. It was just a work thing, but you know how this town talks.'

'Right. I know. No big deal.' Her fake smile hurt her cheeks.

'Jeanie.' His voice was low, demanding she tell him what was going on inside her head.

'It's totally fine, Logan. This is what we agreed on from the beginning. It's just for us.'

He frowned, his expression darkening. 'You're not happy about it.'

'Says who?'

'Me. You're doing that awful fake smile.'

'What fake smile?'

'That one! The one you do when you're trying to convince me you're fine when I know you're not. Why do you do that?'

'I don't do that.' How dare he pretend he knew her so

well! 'I'm just starting to think maybe this isn't a good idea.'

He flinched at that, and Jeanie almost felt bad about it, but something about being tossed aside in the middle of a really great kiss had set something off inside her.

'We hardly know each other, and this has been really nice, and I really appreciate what you've done for me since I moved here, but maybe we should just cool it. For now, anyway.'

'Cool it?'

'Yeah.'

'That's what you want?'

Jeanie blew out a long, frustrated sigh. 'I don't know what I want, okay? That's kinda the problem. And every time I think I know what I want, you look at me like that and you kiss me, and I can't think when you kiss me!'

'You don't want me to kiss you anymore?' He'd stepped closer at some point, and he hadn't dropped her hand. He kept his fingers intertwined with hers.

'Well, I don't want you *not* to kiss me.'

'Jeanie.' He did it again, said her name in that stern, sexy way that made her want to spill her guts to him. He should have been an interrogator.

'Yes?'

'You're being very confusing right now.'

'I know. I'm sorry.'

'It's okay. I can wait until you figure it out.'

The tightening knot in her belly loosened. 'Okay.'

He nodded. 'Okay.'

'Logan?'

'Yeah?'

'What happened with Lucy?'

It was Logan's turn to blow out a long sigh. He ran a hand down his beard and shifted uncomfortably on his feet, like he'd rather run than have this conversation, and for a minute Jeanie thought he might not say anything at all.

'She wasn't happy here,' he said at last. 'She wasn't happy with me.'

'I'm sorry.'

He shrugged. 'It was going on for a while before I proposed, but I thought I could fix it. I thought I could change her mind about living here, but...' he hesitated, with another shrug of his broad shoulders, 'it didn't work.'

'It doesn't say anything about you that she left, you know.'

He huffed.

'I'm serious. Just because you weren't a good match doesn't mean it was your fault.' She held his gaze. He looked at her intently, like he was judging the sincerity of her words, like he wanted to believe her. 'Besides, she was clearly a fool to give up a chance to be co-owner of those hilarious chickens.'

A startled laugh escaped him. 'They are my biggest selling feature.'

Jeanie smiled, stepping toward him, already feeling herself pulled back by his gravitational pull. It must be because he was bigger than her. That was just science, right?

'I don't know,' she said. 'There are a few other things.'

'Oh, yeah?' A smile started at the corner of his mouth. A tentative, hopeful little thing.

'Well, I think you might have a future as a detective or maybe a locksmith.'

His smile tipped bigger.

'You're pretty cute.'

'Oh?' A blush crept up his cheeks.

'Yep. And not a bad kisser.' She stepped into him and planted a soft kiss on his lips. 'But I really am going to go.'

Her emotions were still way too all over the map to make staying here in this small space with this large man a good idea. She was bound to make decisions she would regret later.

'I like you, Jeanie,' he said, his voice low and rough.

'Okay, good.' It was good. A good start. But Jeanie still didn't know where that left them and this weird, secret limbo they were in. She didn't know if she was still willing to sneak around this town and pretend they weren't together when it turns out she really wanted them to be.

'Okay, good,' he agreed.

'I'm leaving now.'

He dipped his head and kissed her one more time, making her seriously reconsider her entire leaving plan, but then he let her go.

She hurried out of his apartment, still not sure who was protecting her heart in this whole mess of a situation.

Chapter Twenty-One

Logan was mucking out the goats' pen when Noah pulled up the drive. He technically had farmhands to do this type of manual labor, but they were all busy pulling in the last of the apple harvest along with all the squash in the back field. That, and Logan was punishing himself for his shitty behavior with Jeanie. He'd practically shoved her down when his grandfather had knocked on the door. He'd hurt her feelings, that much was painfully clear. Of course, he did. No one wanted to be treated like you were ashamed of them.

As much as Jeanie had been cool with their little arrangement in the beginning. She wasn't anymore. And now Logan had to decide if it was worth taking this thing public.

Was it worth failing, again, in front of everyone?

Was Jeanie worth it?

So, he was shoveling goat excrement to punish himself and to clear his mind. Who needed meditation when there was poop to clear?

Noah sauntered up to the pen and leaned against the fence, his forearms propped on the top of it while the Bobs nibbled at his shirt sleeves.

'Hey, aren't you the big boss man now? Your nana still making you clean out the animal pens?'

'The animals aren't technically part of the farm,' Logan said with a grunt, shoveling some fresh hay into the pen.

'Right. I forgot these are your babies.' Noah scratched Marley between the ears and the old goat bleated happily. Or grumpily. It was pretty much the same sound either way.

'What are you doing here?'

'Nice to see you, too, buddy,' Noah said with an easy-going grin.

'Hey, just because your season's done, doesn't mean the rest of us have all day to shoot the shit.' Noah had inherited his family's fishing boat, moved to Dream Harbor a few years ago, and set up a fishing tour company. But by this time of the year, tours were few and far between. He picked up bartending shifts in the winter to make ends meet, but as far as Logan could tell, Noah lived a pretty laid-back life until summer rolled around again.

'I came to check on you.'

'Check on me?'

'Yeah, of course. Check on you. Haven't seen you since trivia night when you bailed before the big dance contest, and I haven't heard from you since.'

'Been busy.'

'Sure, harvest and all. You could answer my texts, though. Kinda thought you might be dead.'

'Not dead.' Just not in the mood to talk to anyone. Not while his head was filled with thoughts of Jeanie and what the hell to do about her.

'How's Jeanie?' Noah asked as though reading Logan's mind. Sneaky bastard.

'How would I know?'

Noah gave him a knowing smile. 'I thought you were friends, that's all.'

Friends. Why did that word feel like a kick to the junk right now? 'Friends, right. Speaking of friends, I caught the way you were looking at Hazel.'

The redhead's cheeks blazed to match his hair. 'Don't know what you're talking about.'

Logan crossed his arms over his chest, leaning against the fence post. 'She's not like the girls you usually date.'

'What's that supposed to mean?'

'Hazel's smart.'

Noah scoffed. 'I date smart girls.'

Logan raised an eyebrow. 'What's the last book you read?'

'I don't know! Is reading a prerequisite for dating Hazel?'

'She runs a bookstore. Reading is her life. And I knew you wanted to date her.'

'Maybe I could show her other ways to have fun.' Noah waggled his eyebrows suggestively and Logan had the sudden urge to punch his overly handsome face.

He narrowed his eyes, something fierce and protective welling up in him.

'Hazel doesn't like that sort of fun.'

'Oh, really?'

'Stay away from her, Noah. She'll only end up getting hurt.' Logan knew how Noah went through women. He hadn't had a relationship last longer than the length of a summer vacation. The idea of sweet, shy Hazel getting mixed up with Noah had all sorts of brotherly instincts flaring up in him. Not that Hazel was his sister, but when you're friends with someone long enough it certainly starts to feel like it.

'Who says *I* won't be the one to get hurt?' The sun glinted off Noah's copper hair. The freckles dusted across his cheeks made him look younger, almost innocent, but then he flexed his forearm on the railing, and the half-naked mermaid he had tattooed there danced.

Logan huffed, kicking at the dirt in front of him. What the hell was he doing?

The absurdity of the whole conversation hit him smack in the face. He was worried about both his friends, not wanting them to get into something and then have it blow up in their faces. And it was turning him into a busybody like the rest of this town. He might as well join the book club at this point.

Suddenly, everyone's concern over him and Lucy felt a little less judgey. Like maybe they didn't see it as a failure, like maybe they just cared about him.

And maybe he was being a prickly recluse for the past year for no reason except his own damaged pride, and now he was going to risk a great thing with Jeanie because he was a damn coward.

Shit. That was inconvenient. Much messier than just being pissed at everyone including himself.

Logan shrugged, wishing he could shake off his revelation. 'Yeah, sorry. Do what you want.'

'So, I have your blessing then?' Noah said with an impish grin.

'Don't need it. Hazel's an adult.'

Noah nodded and Logan could already see the plans

he had brewing in those hazel eyes. But Noah's plans were none of his damn business.

He set his rake aside and wiped the sweat from his forehead. The late fall chill had set in but working in the afternoon sun still worked up a sweat. Noah watched him from his spot by the fence.

Logan didn't know if it was his friend's patience, or his new realization that maybe it was care motivating the people around him, or maybe it was just that he was tired of going over things in his own head, but he felt compelled to do something he never did.

He wanted to talk. About his problems. Out loud.

He took a deep breath. Noah raised an eyebrow.

'I think I screwed things up with Jeanie.'

A slow smile crept across Noah's face like he had been waiting for this moment. 'Feels like this conversation could use a beer.'

'Definitely,' Logan grunted, already regretting opening his big stupid mouth.

Noah followed Logan into the big house, down the hall, and into his grandmother's kitchen. He grabbed two beers from the fridge and handed one to Noah. He rummaged through the junk drawer for a bottle opener, but Noah had already popped the top on the edge of the counter.

'Don't let Nana see you doing that,' he muttered.

Noah grinned. 'Estelle loves me.'

'She loves her new countertops more.'

Noah laughed, settling into one of the chairs around the kitchen table. Logan stayed leaning against the counter, too restless to sit.

'So, what happened with Jeanie?' Noah asked, taking a swig of cold beer. Logan took one too to fortify himself.

'We've been ... uh ... I don't know, really, but I screwed it up. Hurt her feelings.'

Noah's eyes widened in delight. 'Oh, is that why you two scurried out of trivia night so fast? So you could...'

'It's not like that,' Logan snapped, even though it sorta was exactly like that. 'We were keeping it quiet, that's all. Didn't feel like having everyone know my business for once.'

Noah nodded. He hadn't been at the Christmas-tree lighting debacle, but Logan was sure he knew all about it. Noah definitely knew that one day Lucy was here and the next she was gone. When he'd asked Logan about it, Logan muttered something about it not working out, but he wouldn't be surprised if they'd hosted a town meeting about it at some point.

'This town does have a weird thing about you. Personally, I don't see it.'

Logan huffed a laugh. 'Yeah, well. I didn't feel like having this Jeanie thing on everyone's radar, but I think it's starting to upset her. The whole secrecy thing. I don't know.' He ran a hand down his beard, feeling like a complete idiot.

Noah's brow furrowed like he was thinking through a puzzle. 'So, maybe you just need to go public.' He must have seen the slightly queasy look on Logan's face because he went on, 'It doesn't have to be a big spectacle. Just, you know, date like regular people.'

Right. Date like regular people. That didn't sound so bad.

But that wasn't really all of it, was it?

'What did you think of Lucy?' Logan blurted out the question before he could think better of it.

Noah paused with his bottle poised at his lips, considering. 'She was beautiful. Nice girl. But I got a real 'eat, pray, love' vibe from her.'

'What the hell does that mean?'

Noah shrugged. 'Like she was trying to escape real life by coming here. Like she thought she could find herself or something.'

Everything that Jeanie told him about wanting to start over here, for things to be perfect, played over in his head. She was running from her old life, from her fears, wasn't she?

'And what do you think of Jeanie?' Logan asked, dreading the answer.

Noah's smile grew. 'Well, I've liked her since she kicked our butts at trivia. She's fun. Seems game for anything.'

Memories of Jeanie running through the rain with him, of Jeanie's mouth on his, of Jeanie quizzing him about snacks one minute and ready to catch a ghost the next, played through his mind. He thought of her chatting with every neighbor at the town meetings, of her becoming friends with his best friends. Had Lucy ever seemed settled here?

Would he ever stop comparing them?

He took another drink.

'Look, man, if you're worried about Jeanie ditching you, I don't see it happening any time soon. And as someone who has made a habit of only dating women who are here for the summer, that is my expert opinion.'

Noah finished off his beer. 'Anyway, this heart-to-heart has been fun! We should do it more often.' He grinned at Logan.

'Don't count on it.'

Noah clapped him on the shoulder. 'We'll see.'

Logan sighed, and his friend's laughter echoed down the hall as he showed himself out. 'See you around,' Noah yelled from the front door.

'See ya.'

Logan stayed leaning against the counter thinking

about their conversation long enough to watch the sun begin to dip in the sky. The sounds of the farm quieted; the distant hum of the tractor, the voices of his workers heading home, the bleating of disgruntled goats. He should get some dinner going so Nana wouldn't have to cook after her class. His grandfather was probably still out in the field, always the last to head in. He liked the quiet after a long day.

By the time Logan moved, he'd come to only one conclusion. He had no idea what the hell he was doing, but he was pretty sure Jeanie was worth it.

He just hoped he hadn't screwed things up completely.

Chapter Twenty-Two

Jeanie leafed through the papers that Barb Sanders, licensed realtor, had dropped off in person this morning. It was a list of comps for what other buildings in the area had sold for recently. Jeanie had thanked her and served her a large hazelnut latte with soy milk while insisting she really wasn't interested in selling.

Barb had smiled her bright-white saleswoman smile and told Jeanie to just think about it.

So now Jeanie was here at her little kitchen table, which doubled as her desk, in her apartment above the café in question, thinking about it.

If she was being honest, the amount of money she could sell this building for, café plus upstairs apartment, was staggering. She could easily pay off the last of her student loans and buy herself a cute little house somewhere. *Imagine that.*

She was definitely imagining that.

But is that what she wanted? She still didn't know. Plus, Aunt Dot had trusted her with the café. She couldn't just up and sell it, could she? She couldn't. Although, she had a feeling that if she told Dot she needed to sell so she could follow her bliss somewhere else, her aunt would have been all for it. Dot was very big on bliss-following. It was how she'd ended up with this café in the first place and why she was now cliff diving in the Caribbean.

It had been nearly a month since Jeanie had arrived in Dream Harbor, a bundle of nerves, running from her brush with mortality. Did she feel any different now? Had she become the calm café owner she wanted to be?

Casper jumped up onto the table and plopped down on the pile of papers, like it was a little bed laid out just for him.

'I was looking at those,' Jeanie told him. He stared at her with big round eyes. She scratched between his ears, savoring his contended purrs. 'It's okay. I'm not going to sell, anyway.' And somehow just saying it out loud to her cat made it true.

She wasn't going to sell. She didn't want that. She *liked* running the café. Even though she still hadn't solved the mystery of who was messing with her. And even though running her own business was just as stressful, if not more so, than being Marvin's assistant. At least now all her hard work was for her. For her dream. For her life. She wasn't ready to give up on that yet.

Whether or not it had made her a whole new person, she wasn't sure. But she did know that she'd made more friends this month than she had for the past seven years in her old life. She'd started reading again, she'd committed to more trivia nights – and she'd even signed up for Annie's beginner baker's class. She had a *life*.

Never mind her very life-affirming if not totally confusing feelings for the local sexy farmer. That was something she'd been trying and failing to untangle all week.

Her phone buzzed on the table, and she swiped to answer her brother's call.

'Are you already in your pajamas?' he asked, his face filling the screen. A dog howled somewhere in the background.

'I had a long day.' Jeanie glanced out the window. Already dark even though it was barely six o'clock. The wind whipped the nearly bare branches of the tree out front against her window. It was hibernating season. Pajamas were perfectly appropriate. Maybe she should have waited until spring to start over. Fall was a strange time for a reinvention. Fall was better for ... snuggling and eating food covered in gravy.

'Did you solve the mystery yet?'

Jeanie blew out a long sigh, disturbing the wisp of hair that had fallen in front of her face. 'No. And it's gotten worse. This morning I discovered the dishwasher was broken. The guy that came to fix it said someone had cut some wires in the back.'

'Shit, Jeanie. Have you reported any of this?'

'Yeah.' After the window-breaking incident, Jeanie had finally gone over to the police station and informed them about what had been going on. They'd started sending a patrol car by the café twice a night, which made her feel a bit better, but it didn't do anything to help if the person doing the damage was working for her.

'And what do your employees have to say for themselves?' Ben shushed a dog at his feet that Jeanie couldn't see, but could hear whining for attention.

'Well, Crystal immediately started to cry when I asked if she knew what was going on.'

'Hmm.'

'Joe assured me he'd keep an eye out for anything suspicious, and then told me what a great boss I was and how much he loves working for me.'

'Laying it on kinda thick,' Ben muttered.

'I *am* a good boss.'

'I'm sure.'

'And Norman got insulted. Said, how would he know about any of that? And then he floated the theory that some customer was doing it. How would that even be possible?'

'It doesn't make sense.'

'I know.'

'Maybe it *is* a ghost.'

'Shut up, Ben.'

'So, what are you going to do?'

Jeanie shrugged. She didn't know what she was going to do about it. Threaten her employees? Install security cameras? She didn't really love either of those options, but she had to do something. If she really did like running the café, if she wanted to keep her new life here, then she'd have to put an end to this nonsense.

'I'll figure it out.'

Ben looked skeptical but he didn't push her further. Instead, he admonished whatever dog continued to whine. 'No more treats for you. Not after you ate all that garbage yesterday.'

'Garbage?'

Ben rolled his eyes. 'Pudgy knocked over the trash can yesterday while I was at work and feasted on the garbage.'

'Gross.' Casper seemed to roll his eyes as if to say, *dogs, am I right?*

'And yet, today she's still acting like she's starving to death.'

'Well, name is destiny as they say.'

Ben smirked. 'How's the farmer?'

'His name is Logan.'

'And...'

Jeanie could feel her cheeks heating under her brother's assessing gaze.

'That good, huh?' he asked with a laugh.

'I don't know!' Jeanie shifted in her seat, bringing her knees up so she could prop her phone there. 'I thought things were good. They *were* good. But then, I don't know. I kinda freaked out.'

'Freaked out about what?'

Good question.

'I don't think he's over his ex.'

Ben grimaced.

'I know. Also, he's got this thing about people not finding out about us, which I thought I was cool with at first – less pressure you know? But now I'm not sure.'

'Wait a minute, this asshole doesn't want people to know about you?'

'It's not like that. It's just this town is really small, and everyone is in everyone else's business and I don't know, it was my idea. To keep it quiet.'

'Hmm.' Ben's deep frown almost made her laugh. Almost. 'Sounds like this guy wants to make it easier to cut and run.'

Jeanie's heart sank. 'It does?'

'Don't look at me like that, Jean Marie.'

'Like what?'

'With those big puppy-dog eyes. I don't know what this guy's deal is, but don't let him get away with hiding you, okay? Don't let him make you think you shouldn't be exactly you.'

'Thanks, Bennett.' Her voice was small, her throat clogged with tears. Stupid brother making her feel sappy emotions toward him.

Ben fidgeted, glancing down at the garbage eater at his feet and then back to meet her eye. 'He should feel lucky to be with you, that's all I'm saying.'

'Okay.'

'Okay.'

'I love you.'

'Ugh, damn it, Jeanie.'

She grinned at him, sniffling back the tears.

Ben sighed. 'Fine, love you too.'

'I knew it!'

Ben laughed. 'Goodnight.'

'Goodnight.'

Jeanie ended the call and rested her head on her knees, letting the pressure massage her forehead. Was Ben right? Was Logan trying to make it easier to end things with her by keeping their relationship a secret?

She could see where her oddly protective younger brother was coming from, but the explanation didn't sit right with her. It didn't feel like Logan. And, if she was honest with herself, it wasn't necessarily the secrecy that bothered Jeanie. It was the reason for the secrecy that snapped her back to reality the other day in his neat little apartment.

Logan had his heart broken in front of the whole town, and he clearly wasn't over it. Now Jeanie had to decide if she wanted to wait around until he was.

Chapter Twenty-Three

It was five in the morning on Fall Festival Day and Logan was in Nana's kitchen finishing his coffee.

'And you got all the pumpkins in the truck, right? Even the little ones from the back of the barn? Some of the kids just love those little ones.'

'Got 'em.'

Nana nodded, still ticking 'Fall Festival to-do items' off on her fingers. 'Okay, so you'll drop off the pumpkins, Grandpa and I will bring the last bushels of apples to set up at the farm tent. We already donated a bunch to the town hall a few days ago. They decided on a caramel apple station instead of bobbing for apples which seemed like a good call to me. All those kids spitting into a bucket of water is disgusting.'

Logan didn't bother to contribute more than the occasional grunt and nod. Nana was on a roll.

'Luis has the goats under control for the petting zoo. Mayor Kelly was so pleased you offered to bring the Bobs this year. The kids just love those goats.'

Logan didn't recall offering to do any such thing, but the wheels were fully in motion on this thing; there was no stopping it now.

Nana brushed her hands on her apple-patterned apron. 'And that should be about it, I think. All that's left is to enjoy the festival.'

'Yep, should be.'

Nana studied him with sharp eyes; clear blue, like his. 'Are you picking up that nice Jeanie who stopped by here the other day?'

Logan shrugged. He hadn't heard from Jeanie in over a week. He figured she was still upset with him, or maybe she'd just decided this thing wasn't worth the complications. Every time he picked up his phone to text her, he couldn't figure out what to say. And now he had to spend the day with her, judging the costume contest.

'I hadn't planned on it.'

Nana frowned. 'I thought you were working together today. Seems like it would be a nice gesture to offer her a lift.'

Logan decided not to point out that the town square,

where the festival was held, was just a few minutes walk from the café and he was sure Jeanie could manage it on her own. Nana had on her fighting face, as Grandpa called it. The face that meant she was not going to back down. And Logan glanced at the clock. He didn't have time for a fight.

'I'll swing by after I drop off the pumpkins.'

He had to get the pumpkins there early so the festival crew could set up the pumpkin-painting table before the crowds started arriving. People spent the full day at the festival, filling up on apple-cider donuts and Annie's hand pies for breakfast, and staying straight through until dark when they lit the square with hundreds of twinkle lights and a bonfire in the park.

'Very good. Well, I have to get ready!' Nana peeled off her apron and hurried out of the room to change into what Logan was sure would be one of her many Halloween-themed sweaters, probably accompanied by her classic, black witch's hat. She'd worn it to every Fall Festival for as long as he could remember. He smiled at the memory.

Before all large town events had been tainted for him, Logan used to love the Fall Festival. Especially as a kid. He would help his grandparents set up their stand and then he'd be off with Annie, and a whole crew of kids high on too much candy and donuts, in partial costumes they'd shed throughout the day. He loved how early it got dark, how high and hot the bonfire grew, how the whole night felt cozy and spooky at once. Like he was safe here with his grandparents and his friends, but there still might be danger lurking just beyond the glow of the fire.

Logan had always been a shy kid, but Annie made sure he kept up, that the other kids let him play. His grandparents always made sure he was loved even with his parents gone.

His whole damn life he'd been taken care of, loved, and protected. And somehow, he'd grown to resent it? He prickled at the idea of his family and friends knowing he'd failed, that he'd been hurting. It seemed absurd now. Especially if it meant losing Jeanie.

He was done hiding.

The shops were closed on Main Street. Everyone was at the festival. Logan was sure the café would have a tent set up selling coffee and hot cider all day, but he was hoping he hadn't missed Jeanie already. It was still early, the sun barely up over the horizon, casting the row of quaint shops in a golden glow. Logan peered in the front window, but the café was empty.

Shit. Maybe she'd left to set up already.

But talking to her before the festival suddenly seemed urgent, so Logan cut through the alley, memories of Jeanie's legs wrapped around him instantly filling his head, and went around to the back door.

He knocked, hoping she was just upstairs getting ready.

No answer.

He knocked again. Maybe he should text her?

'Jeanie?'

Or maybe he could yell her name in the alley like a deranged person. *Good call, Logan.*

He could see where she'd put cardboard over the broken window and his heartbeat ratcheted up. What if something was wrong? What if things had escalated and she hadn't told him? Would someone hurt her?

He knocked again, harder this time, feeling more frantic the longer he stood in this damn alley, staring at that damn broken window.

'It's open,' a small voice said from the other side of the door, and Logan didn't waste time. He shoved open the door and strode into the main café, his gaze scanning the room ... for what? A threat? A refrigerator unplugging. A window-breaking intruder? A disgruntled employee? A not-so-friendly ghost?

He didn't find any of those things. He found something a thousand times worse.

He found Jeanie sitting on the floor, her back against the bakery case, knees pulled up to her chest, tears streaming down her face. TEARS.

He dropped to his knees in front of her.

'What is it? Are you hurt?' His words were gruff, angry. Like he was mad at her tears.

She looked at him, her nose pink from crying and the highly offensive tears still streaking down her face and shook her head. 'Not hurt,' she sniffled.

'Well, then what is it? What happened?'

She dropped her head to her knees and let out the saddest little moan he'd ever heard in his life. It burrowed into his heart. It knocked the wind from his lungs. It destroyed him.

Why had he stayed away from her for a week? Why had he let Lucy continue to ruin shit for him? He liked Fall Festival. He liked this damn town.

And he really freaking liked this woman in front of him in the hedgehog pajama pants and ratty old cardigan.

'Jeanie,' he said, his voice firm now, serious. He had to know what the hell was going on so he could make sure it never happened again. 'Look at me.'

She sighed and lifted her head.

He couldn't take it. He gently took her face and brushed her tears away with his thumbs. Jeanie's eyes fluttered closed at his touch.

'Tell me what happened. Please, Jeanie. Maybe I can help? Or maybe not, but ... please let me be here for you. I know I screwed up the other day.'

She opened her eyes. 'That's not it.'

'Good.' Logan caressed her face one more time and then let his hands fall. He sat back on his heels in front of her, waiting.

Jeanie wiped her face with the back of her hand, blowing the wisps of hair from her face. 'It's stupid, really.'

'I'm sure it's not.'

She gave him a watery smile. 'Everything's just going wrong today, that's all. And it's the Fall Festival, and I know it's a really big deal and I just wanted everything to go right.' She took a deep breath. 'I'm trying hard, you know? To make this work.' She gestured around the café and maybe at him, too, like she was including him in whatever bullshit was making her life harder right now, and he hated that.

'You are. You're doing a great job running the café, Jeanie.'

She shrugged. 'Today's a disaster.'

'Tell me. What happened?'

'Crystal and I were supposed to run the festival tent for the first half of the day, until I had to judge the contest, and then Joe was going to take over. But Crystal's kid threw up last night so she called in sick and Joe can't get here until noon. And I can't get a hold of Norman at all, which is really weird.' She sighed again, but at least the tears had stopped. 'I think they hate me.'

'No one could hate you.'

She raised an eyebrow, an amused smile teasing him. 'I'm sure that's not true.'

'I'll help you run the table this morning.'

'You will?'

'Sure. As long as I get free coffee.'

She laughed. 'We'll see about that.'

'And once this festival is over, we're going to figure out what the hell is going on around here, once and for all. Okay?'

She sniffled again, but her smile was growing. 'Okay, thanks.'

He could leave it there, but he still felt shitty about how he'd acted. 'I am sorry about the other day.'

'You don't have to apologize for that. It's what we agreed. It was my idea.'

'I handled it poorly in the moment.' He shifted toward her. 'I gotta stop letting my past haunt me like that. I intend to, I mean.'

Jeanie gave a small nod, her body leaning toward his. He cupped her face in his hands again. 'It's really not about her anymore. It's my own stupid pride that got hurt. I don't want to screw things up with you, Jeanie.'

'We can take it slow,' she said, and he opened his mouth to argue, but she went on with a teasing smile. 'Maybe just don't throw me across the room next time.'

Logan huffed a laugh. 'Sorry about that.'

'Forgiven.' The word ghosted across his lips right before Jeanie covered them with her own. The knot that had been coiled in his gut for a week slowly untangled with every flick of Jeanie's tongue against his and every nibble of her teeth on his lower lip.

Logan lost track of time, lost track of everything until Jeanie pulled away and leaned her forehead against his.

'The festival awaits,' she said, her dark eyes glinting with excitement.

They had to go, but Logan had every intention of not getting interrupted the next time they were alone. A person could only take so many unfinished make-out sessions before they lost their damn mind.

Chapter Twenty-Four

True New Englanders love three things: the Red Sox, Dunkin's, and fall. Jeanie knew this, of course. She'd been one for the past decade, after all. But Dream Harbor's Fall Festival was a whole new level of autumnal worship.

The town square and surrounding streets were closed to traffic to accommodate the multitude of tents and tables and activities. There was pumpkin decorating, caramel apples, and cider donuts (that Jeanie could not stop eating, even though she'd already had three). Annie was selling pies and cookies, and anything made with apples or pumpkins, or cinnamon-spiced. There were tents selling all types of witchy wares: crystals and spell books and very authentic-looking witch brooms. Kids were lined up to get their faces painted, or for balloon animals, or to jump in the enormous bounce house set up on the lawn.

It was madness.

Delightful, apple-pie scented madness.

Jeanie couldn't help grinning from ear to ear as she sold cider and pumpkin-spiced lattes to the seemingly endless line of visitors. The day had started out cold, with a light frost on the grass, but the late fall sun had warmed things significantly by midday. Jeanie had even unwound her giant scarf and tossed aside her fingerless mittens.

Logan had worked beside her all morning, occasionally brushing his arm against hers or giving her a slow secret smile. It wasn't exactly a proclamation of his intentions in front of the whole town, but she didn't want that anyway. The fact that he was here beside her was enough. More than enough. It was doing all sorts of warm, swoopy things to her stomach, making the whole morning feel like it was cast in a glow of happiness. She wanted to curl up in the feeling, like Casper in a patch of sun.

'Happy Fall Festival!' Isabel stepped up to the table wearing an eerily accurate baby Yoda on her chest.

'Hi, Isabel! Hi, Mateo!'

Mateo-Yoda gurgled happily in return.

'Enjoying your first festival, Jeanie?' she asked, deftly

sipping from her coffee while keeping the hot cup out of Mateo's reach. 'Hi, Logan.'

'Isabel, hey.'

'I am. This is really pretty incredible. I like your hair.' Jeanie gestured toward Isabel's classic Princess Leia buns.

'Oh, thanks. It's a whole theme. There's a Mandalorian and a little stormtrooper walking around somewhere, but Mommy needs coffee if she's going to survive this day. I woke up to said stormtrooper leaning over my bed fully costumed at four this morning.'

'Yikes,' said Jeanie, with a grin.

Isabel smiled back, her gaze flitting between Jeanie and Logan. Heat crept up Jeanie's cheeks. Isabel *knew*. Somehow, with her secret mom and romance-reader powers, she knew exactly what was going on between Jeanie and Logan. Which was crazy because Jeanie wasn't even totally clear on it herself.

In fact, she half expected Logan to put distance between them, to find cups to stack, or the next customer to serve, but instead, he shifted closer. His broad shoulder brushed hers again, the back of his hand skimming her fingers.

It felt like a declaration.

Isabel smiled wider.

It *was* a declaration.

Quiet and sure and steady, just like Logan. He linked his fingers with hers and Jeanie's heart fluttered. Maybe he was serious about this thing between them, after all. Maybe New Jeanie was about to get the sexy farmer, even if he had seen her as a hot mess again this morning. Her heart kicked up its flutter into high gear.

'Well, I'll see you at the costume contest later,' Isabel said, excitement glinting in her eyes. She patted little Yoda on the head. 'Come on, Yoda, let's go find Mando.'

Jeanie waved goodbye and Logan slowly pulled his hand away, needing it to help the next customer, but not before he glanced down at her with another secret smile teasing the corner of his mouth.

'How long before everyone knows?' Jeanie asked quietly, smiling at the customers as she spoke.

She could sense his shrug without even looking at him. 'Not long.'

'And you're fine with that?' She handed Greg and Shawn their hot ciders. 'Have fun, guys!'

Greg raised his cup in a Fall Festival cheers gesture and the two walked away, leaving Jeanie and Logan alone for the moment.

'I'm fine with it. Are you?'

Jeanie swallowed hard, suddenly feeling the weight of what they were doing. Suddenly remembering that the eyes of the town on them meant that everyone would be looking at her, too. What if things didn't work out? What if she actually had no idea how to have a serious relationship? She never had before. Panic flashed hot in her gut.

Why was all of this occurring to her now, when this sweet, sweet man was trying so hard to make her happy? Had his kisses scrambled her brain that much?!

Damn it, Jeanie! Get it together.

She pushed a smile onto her face.

'Yep. Totally fine with it.'

Logan studied her a minute longer, his blue eyes searching hers until she had to glance away, afraid of what he'd find there.

'Okay.'

'Okay, great!' she said, putting as much sunny cheerfulness into it as she could. 'Joe should be here soon, and then we can go do our judging duties.'

'Uh-huh.' He glanced at her again, hesitant, a small frown creasing his brow.

She forced her smile bigger.

She'd wanted this, hadn't she? She'd wanted Logan to choose her for real. But somehow, she'd conveniently forgotten that she had to get her shit together, too. She shook her head like she could rid herself of these damn doubts.

It was fine. Everything was fine. Maybe Isabel

wouldn't tell everyone about the world's tiniest display of affection. Maybe everyone would be so swept up in the fall festivities that no one would care about her and Logan.

Maybe she was deluding herself.

Jeanie made a quick stop at Annie's tent before she had to take up her judging post with Logan. She just needed a minute of space. And another donut.

'Hey, George. Hey, Hazel.' Annie's baking partner stood behind the folding table turned makeshift counter. He greeted Jeanie with a friendly wave, while Hazel helped Annie unload more donuts from the fresh trays. How they'd managed to get warm donuts from the bakery to the tent was a mystery that Jeanie didn't have time to solve.

'Another donut?' Annie asked with a grin.

'Just one more.'

Hazel studied Jeanie with shrewd eyes as Annie handed her another sugar-covered delight. 'What's the matter?' Hazel asked, zeroing in immediately on Jeanie's turmoil. Did those glasses give her some kind of superpower?

Jeanie glanced around. Most people had moved

toward the costume-contest stage, so the bakery tent was empty. 'Well, it's Logan.'

Annie crossed her arms over her chest, the teasing smile dropping from her face. George muttered something about suddenly having an interest in buying some sage to clear the bad energy out of his apartment and scurried out of the tent.

'Of course, it's Logan,' Hazel said, leaning her elbows on the table. 'What happened?'

'Uh...' Jeanie fidgeted under Annie's stare. 'We ... well ... I think maybe he just held my hand in front of Isabel, so probably everyone will hear about that soon, and I really like him.' She swallowed hard. 'And he likes me. I'm pretty sure. And now I'm freaking out a little bit because I don't think I'm very good at this.'

'At what?' Hazel asked, while Annie's narrowed eyes did nothing to ease the tension in Jeanie's gut.

'At everything? Life, I think. Definitely dating. And you guys warned me, I know, and I just don't want to mess things up and I don't want the town to hate me if I do.'

She bit down on her lip and waited for their judgment or anger or support. She still wasn't sure which way it would go.

'No one's going to hate you, Jeanie,' Hazel said.

Jeanie glanced at Annie, whose mouth was set in a grim line. Not super convincing.

'And besides, everyone is bad at life in one way or another,' Hazel added.

Jeanie sighed. 'It just used to feel like maybe I was good at it. I had my job, and I did it well and I just ... I don't know, I did what I was supposed to do. And now, here ... it's not as clear.'

'There's no 'supposed to do' Jeanie,' Hazel said, her eyes earnest behind her glasses.

'I know. That's the problem, I guess. I feel a little lost.'

'Look,' Annie said, finally breaking her silence. 'All you can do is the best you can do.'

Jeanie nodded slowly, trying to take that in. 'Okaaay . . .'

Annie huffed. 'Stop trying to do it exactly right. You and Logan are both adults. If you want to be together, then you should be.'

'Really?'

'Of course.'

'You're not, like, mad at me or something?'

Hazel glanced at Annie's still rigid posture. 'You are kinda giving that impression.'

Annie shook out her arms. 'Sorry. It's just, there's a lot of history there. And when you first got here, we really didn't know if you'd stick around, and Lucy treated

Logan like he was a stop on her little self-exploration journey. I don't want to see that happen again.'

'Right.' Jeanie swallowed hard, thinking about the stack of real-estate papers currently sitting on her table, and the fact that at least one of her employees was working on some kind of quiet vendetta. And how she had no idea what to do about any of it.

'Anyway.' Annie shrugged. 'You should go for it. With Logan. It'll work out or it won't, but lucky for you the town can't live without its caffeine, so people will have to forgive you pretty quickly.' A smile finally crossed her face and Jeanie relaxed. A little bit.

Maybe they were right. She was overthinking this whole thing. And overthinking was not her style anymore. She blew out a long sigh. Right, time to go soak in all the fall goodness. She would figure out who was sabotaging her business tomorrow. Not today. Not on Fall Festival day!

Not when she had a sweet, sexy man waiting for her to judge some adorable Halloween costumes. Duty called.

'Okay, thanks.' She finished her donut. 'I'm off to judge the costume contest.'

'Oh, God, I forgot you got roped into that.' Hazel's face paled.

Annie grimaced. 'Yeah, good luck.'

Chapter Twenty-Five

Jeanie had worked in the sometimes cut-throat, always intense, high-stakes finance world for seven years of her life, but nothing had prepared her for Dream Harbor's Fall Festival costume contest.

Logan sat beside her at the judging table, his face set in an expression of grim determination.

She nudged his leg with hers. 'Isn't this supposed to be fun?' she whispered. Although, at this point even she was beginning to doubt it.

'According to who?'

Logan had already broken up one almost fist fight between two moms decked out in athleisure, each claiming their little zombie was the most terrifying. The pocket on his flannel hung limply from his chest from where one woman had clawed at him as he removed her from the stage. That little incident was followed by a debate over which version of Batman was the 'real one' and then a riot had nearly broken out when Nancy and Jacob took to the stage dressed as their favorite romance-novel cover. Their costumes were deemed 'too sexy' for a family event, which led to a rather keyed-up chant about First Amendment rights and a speech from Nancy about raising well-informed, sex-positive kids.

It had been quite the day.

But they'd made it to the end. On the makeshift stage in front of them stood the finalists. A toddler-sized bumblebee who looked to be about five seconds away from wetting their custom; a very convincing Wednesday Addams, made all the more impressive by the fact that Andy was actually a forty-five-year-old Black man; and Jeanie's personal favorite, Mindy Walsh, deputy mayor, dressed as a perfect Mayor Kelly, right down to the hideous tie and a dream bubble made of posterboard hovering above her head.

A gaggle of witches, Star Wars characters, a baby pumpkin or two, some adorably dressed-up dogs, and the full cast of *The Wizard of Oz* stood off to the side in the grass, having not made the cut. Jeanie could feel the vengeful looks being sent her way by several sore losers. At this point in the day, she was actually worried about what they might be plotting.

Tammy sat on her other side, acting as the third judge. Apparently, she did this every year and took her job very seriously.

'A bee won three years ago,' she whispered now, leaning in toward her fellow judges.

Logan blew out a long sigh on her other side.

'Does that matter?' Jeanie asked.

'It sure does, honey!' Tammy sounded utterly shocked at her ignorance. 'People wouldn't like it if the winner was always a bee.' Tammy was a transplant, born and raised in Louisiana. It was evident in everything she said.

'Uh ... right. Of course.'

Tammy scanned the stage again, like maybe she'd pick up on some detail that would make the winner suddenly obvious.

'Well, I think Andy put in a lot of effort,' Jeanie said.

Tammy scoffed. 'It's not about effort. It's about the best costume. Objectively speaking.'

Objectively speaking. Sure.

Jeanie could have sworn Logan groaned beside her. He seemed to be slumping further and further down in his chair like the thing was swallowing him alive.

'So, the winner should obviously be' Jeanie hesitated, hoping Tammy would fill in the answer for her. And Tammy was more than willing to oblige.

'Mindy as Mayor Kelly. Gotta be.'

Jeanie grinned. 'Yes. Gotta be. Agreed.'

'Logan, do you want to weigh in here?' Tammy leaned forward to see past Jeanie.

He shook his head so hard that Jeanie worried it would snap from his body and roll away. 'Nope. You nailed it again, Tammy. Mindy it is.'

Tammy smiled. 'Great. I will relay the results to Pete.'

'I hope she hurries,' Jeanie whispered to Logan. 'I think the bee is gonna lose it.'

Logan glanced at the stage, where the little bee now had her legs crossed, and then over to where Tammy and Pete were discussing the results. Pete seemed to be shaking his head as though he disagreed with the winner. Tammy glanced back at the judging table gesturing toward Jeanie and Logan.

'Oh, no, are we going to have to deliberate again? Is there some rule about not dressing up as a real person?' Jeanie asked. She officially never wanted to see another costumed town resident ever again.

'Hell, no,' Logan growled. He stood up from his seat at the judges' table and cupped his hands around his mouth. 'Mindy wins, little bee second place, Andy third. Collect your free donut coupon from Pete and clear the stage.'

Groans of dismay mingled with cheers of excitement

and if Jeanie wasn't mistaken, some rather loud 'boos' from the back of the crowd. Mindy pumped a fist in the air in a silent gesture of victory and the little bee ran off to the bathroom.

'Geez, you weren't kidding,' Jeanie said with a sigh. 'That was intense.' She was actually sweating.

Logan gave her a rueful smile. 'I told you; this town can be a lot.'

Jeanie twined her fingers with his and Logan's smile hitched higher. 'I like it.'

'How do you feel about haunted houses?' he asked, mischief glinting in his eyes as the sun sank below the trees. A pleasant thrill raced up Jeanie's spine.

'Nothing can be scarier than them.' Jeanie gestured toward where some of the contest losers gathered ominously. She wouldn't be surprised if they held pitchforks.

Logan huffed a laugh. 'Let's go.' He tugged her with him, keeping her close by his side as they made their way across the festival.

In fact, Logan kept her there even when they hurried past Kaori and her family; the book club president only had time to raise her eyebrows in surprise. Jeanie grinned back in return. He kept her right beside him as they stopped to say hi to Noah, even as the fisherman's grin grew bigger and he actually winked at Jeanie. Logan held her hand as they passed the bakery tent and waved to Annie and Hazel inside.

He even brushed a kiss on her cheek as they waited in line for Linda and Nancy to let them into the firehouse-turned-haunted house.

And with every little gesture, with every happy glance from the people around them, some of the nerves, the doubts, the worries eased in Jeanie's gut. This was her home now, her friends, her customers.

Her Logan.

She liked it.

She wanted to keep him, to keep this, to live in this perfect day for as long as she could.

'How scared should I be?' she asked, as they made their way through the spider web-covered entrance. Logan squeezed her hand.

'Well, the local scouts set this up every year. They tend to go pretty hard—'

Logan had barely finished his sentence before a deranged clown leaped out from the dark. Jeanie shrieked and buried her face in Logan's sleeve. The clown cackled maniacally and returned to his position to scare the living hell out of the next customers.

'You okay?' Logan asked, amusement clear in his voice.

'Yep, fine. Totally fine,' she said, her face still pressed

against him, her heart racing. He chuckled softly and led her around the next corner. A rather undersized witch stirred a smoking cauldron in the corner, but she recognized Logan and gave him a big grin before remembering her role and fixed her face back into a scowl.

Jeanie stifled a laugh.

Logan tugged her along, the smile clear on his own face even in the dark.

They wound their way through the maze-like interior of the house, with Jeanie clinging to Logan's hand. If she was honest, after the first scare from the clown she was fine, but any excuse to be this close to Logan was good with her. Maybe they weren't going to hide anymore, but it was fun to be away from the prying eyes of the town for a few minutes. Especially, when Logan pulled her into a corner, his mouth finding hers in the dark.

'Hi,' she whispered against his lips.

'Hi.' His voice was a low rumble. 'Are you enjoying the festival?' he asked, nipping her bottom lip.

'Very much.' His hands traced her hips. He squeezed her ass and tugged her closer. 'Even more so now.' She sounded out of breath like they had run through the haunted house.

Logan groaned, nuzzling against her neck. She gasped as he ran his teeth across the sensitive skin there.

'Hey! Who's that? I told you kids—'

A bright light flashed in Jeanie's eyes, and they froze, Logan's hands still clutching her backside, Jeanie's leg already hitched over his hip.

'Logan?'

He groaned and pulled away, and Jeanie knew that had it been light enough she would see the blush creeping up his cheeks. But he didn't shove her away this time. Just took her hand and faced Linda and her flashlight.

Linda laughed in delight. 'I thought it was those damn teenagers again! I've caught three different couples already making out in here. Guess we need to make it scarier next year.' She turned, laughing to herself, and made her way back through the maze.

Logan ran a hand down his face. 'Sorry about that. I shouldn't have—'

'Let's go back to my place.'

'This obviously isn't the time or the place, I just ... wait what?'

'Let's go. No interruptions this time,' she said.

Logan's eyes widened briefly before he dropped his mouth to her ear. 'No interruptions?' His breath was warm against her skin and Jeanie leaned into him further.

'Nope. Just you and me.'

His low groan vibrated through her.

'I mean, unless you wanted to go to the bonfire instead...'

'Absolutely not.' He grabbed her hand, and they raced through the rest of the haunted house leaving a very confused ax murderer and headless horseman in their wake.

Chapter Twenty-Six

He had Jeanie up against the wall as soon as they stepped into her apartment, his mouth on hers, devouring her, because he couldn't seem to help himself around Jeanie. Today was too good. She had been too good, too exactly what he wanted, too freaking close to perfect that it scared the crap out of him.

But he wanted it.

He wanted her.

He wanted to keep her.

Little moans and sighs escaped her lips as he kissed her and he wanted them all, her noises, her sweet body pressed against his. All of it. All of her.

Everything he had tried to hold back, to deny, to pretend wasn't happening was unraveling rapidly with every shift of her hips, with every scrape of her teeth on his neck, with every tug of her hands in his hair.

He'd been an idiot to try and act like he didn't want her, that he didn't want everyone in this damn town to know she was his.

Shit. He groaned, leaning his forehead against hers. He wanted Jeanie to be *his*.

She smiled up at him.

'Hey,' she whispered, already out of breath, her cheeks a delicious pink.

'Hey.' His voice was rough, his hands still tracing the curves of her body. He couldn't seem to stop mauling this woman every time he got the chance.

'My room's down the hall.'

'Right, sorry.' He backed up, unpinning her from the wall. *Slow down, Logan.*

She took him by the hand and started to lead him down the small hallway off the living room he just now realized they were standing in. He tugged her to a stop, and she glanced back at him.

'We don't have to,' he blurted.

She frowned.

'I mean ... I just didn't want you to think that we had to...'

'Logan,' she said, her smile growing into something warmer, heavier. 'I want to.'

'Okay.'

'Okay.' She pulled him with her to a room at the end of the hall, then flipped on a bedside lamp that cast the room in a cozy glow. 'It's a little messy.' She shrugged. 'Still getting settled.'

Logan forced himself to ignore the flash of anxiety he felt at the sight of the still-packed boxes in Jeanie's room. A mirror leaned against one wall, still not hung. The lamp by her bed sat on top of a large cardboard box. The bed was covered in a random assortment of pillows and blankets. The windows had blinds but no curtains. The walls had no pictures, no art.

Temporary.

Unsettled.

This room screamed impermanence.

Logan ran a hand through his hair, shoving down the panic rising in his throat. Had he gotten it so wrong again? Was he wrong about Jeanie wanting to stay? About her fitting in here?

She turned back to look at him where he stood frozen in the doorway. Her face fell. 'Oh, God, is messiness like a deal breaker for you? I should have tidied up a bit more.' She kicked a sweater under the bed and Logan tried not to wince.

He did like things to be neat, but that's not what was causing his heart to race haphazardly in his chest.

He cleared his throat.

'No, no. Sorry, that's not it.'

She waited, watching him. But he couldn't bring himself to say it. Couldn't bring himself to admit that he was afraid she would leave. That she would find him and his life and his town lacking just like Lucy did.

He refused to let Lucy have that power over him anymore.

Not with this adorable, nearly perfect, messy, funny person standing in front of him, with her cheeks still pink and her lips still red from kissing him. He crossed the room and took Jeanie's face in his hands.

'Just trying to take this slow. That's all.'

A relieved smile crossed her face. 'Oh, good. I've tried to be neater, but it never really sticks.'

Logan shrugged. 'I like you messy.'

She paused, her dark gaze meeting his, her smile even bigger now. Bigger and somehow more genuine. Happier. She hopped up into his arms and he caught her with a gruff laugh.

'Thank you.'

'What are you thanking me for, Jeanie?'

She shrugged and buried her face in his neck, her lips warm on the skin above his collar. 'Thank you for saying that, for being here.'

He gave her ass a squeeze. 'I wouldn't be anywhere else.'

She made a little purring sound against him, and he shoved down the wish that she'd say it back, that she'd assure him there was nowhere she'd rather be either. She was here now, in his arms and he'd be an idiot if he didn't take this chance to be with her.

He backed her up toward the bed and lowered her onto the mattress and seeing her there with her big brown eyes and her pink cheeks, watching her teeth dig into her bottom lip, snapped any control he had.

Taking things slow flew right out the damn window along with any fear that they shouldn't do this.

Jeanie was already kneeling on the bed, unbuttoning his shirt, sliding her hands inside, tugging it off his shoulders.

'This too,' she said, lifting his undershirt and running her hands across his abs with wicked fascination. He pulled the shirt over his head, and she kissed his stomach eliciting a sharp gasp from his lips.

She grinned up at him. 'These are really good abs,' she said. 'Like, I honestly didn't know these were a real thing on real people.'

He huffed another surprised laugh, feeling his face heat under her appraising stare. Would he ever be able to predict what was going to come out of her mouth next?

She ran more kisses from his stomach up his chest to his neck, her fingers tracing their own path. Logan clenched his fists at his sides, wanting to grab her but not wanting to stop her, her light, soft touches along his body like torture.

By the time her hands were in his hair, tugging him closer and her mouth was on his, her tongue flicking against his lips, Logan had lost all sense of time and place.

His only thoughts were of Jeanie.

Jeanie's lips on his.

Jeanie's cinnamon-sugar taste.

Jeanie's soft body pressed against his own.

These clothes had to go. He was tired of barriers between them. He didn't want another frustrating make-out session. He didn't want to be scared of this anymore.

He wanted skin, warm and bare against his.

He ran his fingers beneath the hem of Jeanie's sweater, skimming the top of her jeans. Her stomach was hot and soft. He ran a hand up her back, tracing the dip of her spine.

She shivered when he touched her around the band of her ribs, letting his thumbs drag along the underside of her breasts. She broke their kiss to pull the sweater over her head and then her mouth was on his hot and wet and demanding.

Her torso when she pressed it against his was scalding.

Damn, how was she so perfect? So, everything he wanted?

His fingers dug into her flesh, wanting her closer, needing everything. He found the clasp for her bra, undid it, and tossed it aside. He cupped her breast in one hand, running his thumb over the peak. Jeanie's half sigh, half whimper at the contact nearly undid him. He lowered his head and took her nipple in his mouth. Jeanie arched into him as he swirled his tongue around her. She gasped, his name a broken whisper on her lips.

More. He wanted more.

He sucked and licked until Jeanie was quivering and then broke away for long enough to lay her back on the bed and peel the jeans from her body. More skin. More Jeanie.

With every layer he tore away, he could feel himself falling deeper, faster, more irreversibly in love with this woman.

Love.

Damn it. He'd done it again, but he couldn't stop, didn't want to. Not now. Not with Jeanie spread out in front of him, her skin golden in the soft light of the lamp, her dark hair tangled on the pillow.

She looked at him with dark, hungry eyes, but he was frozen.

Something was necessary here, wasn't it? A declaration? A discussion about what he wanted from her, about what she wanted from him.

Weren't they doing this all wrong?

But what did he expect her to say? That she loved him, too? Already. After so short a time. She hadn't even unpacked all her clothes yet. How could she have possibly decided to love him?

'Logan?'

He blinked.

A furrow appeared between Jeanie's brows, and she went to cover herself with a blanket. Logan stopped her with a hand on hers.

'Don't. I want to see you.' His voice was low and rough. He didn't recognize it.

Jeanie dropped her hand, her gaze steady on his. He took her in, all of her. He'd take her for however long he could have her. He was a fool if he'd thought he could turn back now.

'Logan.' Jeanie's voice was a soft whimper that obliterated Logan's doubts completely.

He covered her body with his and took what he wanted.

Whatever Logan had been about to say as he knelt over her, he never said it. Jeanie only had a few seconds to wonder about it before his mouth was everywhere. His lips, warm and firm and insistent on her body, the coarse hair of his beard tickling the skin on her chest, her stomach, her thighs.

She tried not to think about the look she kept catching on his face tonight. The look that said exactly how he felt about her. Like he wanted to keep her. Like maybe this was more than an attraction. Like he wanted to do more than just be a helpful neighbor.

Logan's head dipped between her thighs and Jeanie's thoughts scattered like fall leaves, impossible to hold onto while Logan kissed her there.

There in the center of her, building her pleasure until the sheets were fisted in her hands and she couldn't stop the low, keening moan from escaping her lips. Logan licked her with the persistent determination of a man used to doing a job right. His tongue was fast and firm and just freaking perfect. So perfect Jeanie thought she might cry.

She nearly did cry when he slipped a finger inside her, his groan vibrating against her sensitive flesh. He added another finger and crooked them, touching something inside her she previously thought was myth. The pleasure was deep and aching, now, but he didn't relent with his tongue or his fingers. Logan, steady and reliable, kept going until the pressure was too much, until her back bowed from the bed, her feet digging into the mattress. Until she came apart under his tongue and his hands. Until she couldn't remember for the life of her why she shouldn't be with this man.

There was no reason at all.

He was good and kind, and the abs, dear God, the abs.

Why was she standing in her own way?

He grinned up at her, a little sheepishly. 'Good?'

Jeanie let out a disbelieving laugh. 'Very, very good.'

He shifted from his position between her legs and shucked off his pants. He moved his way up her body, letting the length of him slide against her. He rained a path of kisses across her clavicle to her shoulder and buried his face in her hair.

'You're beautiful,' he whispered, and she thought that might actually be true, with the way he squeezed her thigh in his hand and rocked against her with his hips like he couldn't help himself.

She wanted more of him. She wanted all of him, in fact.

Words bubbled up in her throat, trying to push their

way out. Words about how she felt about him. Words that were way too strong and way too soon and way too intense for how she should actually feel about him.

And Jeanie didn't want to scare this one away.

She didn't want to be the intense girl. Or the woman who was a bit too much. She didn't want to overthink this or overdo it.

She just wanted to be here with Logan in this one perfect moment on this one perfect day. So, the words that came out of her mouth weren't big and emotional and important.

Instead, they were practical.

'Condoms are in the bathroom.'

Logan stilled. 'Right.' He pushed off of her and made his way into the bathroom that Jeanie knew was also a mess, but maybe it didn't matter. Maybe he could actually overlook her too muchness, her messiness. Maybe he wasn't lying when he said he liked her messy.

At least for now.

'In the medicine cabinet,' she called, and he came back a second later with the packet in hand, wasting no time to slide one on and rejoin her in bed.

'You're sure?' he asked, even as she wrapped her legs around him, even as her whole body called for his.

'Yes.' The word had barely left her lips before he was in her, filling her, his arms holding her, and it was so much. It was everything. And Jeanie didn't know how they'd gotten here so soon, or where they went next.

But for tonight she was going to let Logan hold her.

He paused, his forehead pressed against hers, letting her adjust. Or by the look on his face, his pupils blown wide, letting himself adjust.

'Jeanie.' His voice was as awed as she felt. 'I—'

She kissed him. Afraid of what he might say. Of what she might say in return.

This thing between them wasn't what she expected. But, damn it was good, and she wasn't ready to let words mess it up. So, she held him tight, her legs wrapped around his back, and deepened the kiss.

His restraint snapped.

He moved, his hips thrusting forward again and again until Jeanie was a whimpering mess beneath him. The pleasure built again, a deep ache in her core, and Logan shifted the position of his hips. He kept his gaze on hers, watching her reactions.

'Like that,' she gasped and his mouth tipped into a sexy smile as he did the same motion again. Sparks shot to her toes.

'Touch yourself, Jeanie,' he said, still thrusting into her in long slow strokes. He dipped his head and whispered the next words into her ear almost like he was too shy to say them to her face despite everything they were doing. 'Make yourself come.'

How could this man be so unbelievably sexy and adorably sweet at the same time? Jeanie wasn't about to question it. Logan shifted his hips again, giving her more space and she slipped her hand between her legs.

Logan watched her with hungry eyes. His hands dug into her thighs as he held her at just the right angle. Her fingers worked faster, moving in conjunction with Logan's thrusts. It didn't take long. Her orgasm hit her hard and sudden, and so unexpectedly good, like this whole damn thing. Jeanie gasped out Logan's name as he shuddered and groaned above her, following her right into the surprising pleasure of it all.

He carefully rolled off her and laid beside her. 'That was...' she panted, her forehead against his shoulder.

'Yeah,' he rasped, his own breath still coming in short spurts. 'Damn, Jeanie.'

She giggled, happiness burbling up behind the release. Logan planted a kiss on her head, and then got up to clean up the condom. When he returned and wrapped himself around her, nothing had ever felt more right.

Chapter Twenty-Seven

Logan woke up to the sound of the shower running and the sun streaking through Jeanie's blinds. He groaned and stretched, letting her scent and everything they'd done last night wash over him.

It had been...

It had been... perfect. Perfect despite the unpacked boxes and the words left unsaid. Today he would say them.

He rooted around in the tangle of blankets for his boxers and found his shirt tossed over a chair. His blood heated at the memory of Jeanie yanking it off of him. Maybe he should join her in the shower.

The idea of a soaped-up Jeanie was very tempting, but they had things to talk about first. Things he should have told her last night, but had still been too chicken to say. Today he would tell her that he wanted her. That he had fallen head over heels in love with her and he had been a fool to try and deny it, and he had been an even bigger fool to try and hide it. And that if she wanted him to shout it from the freaking café counter during the morning rush, he would.

But first, coffee.

He strolled out to the kitchen and started the coffee maker. He found mugs in the cabinet, placed neatly beside the sugar and honey. In fact, most of the kitchen was tidy with no partially packed boxes in sight. Jeanie was just taking her time settling in. He couldn't fault her for that.

The small kitchen led out to the living room, where Logan found a table and two chairs. Jeanie must use it as a desk, as well, because the surface was covered in papers. Logan cleared some out of the way and stacked them in a pile.

A business card slipped from the stack and floated slowly to the floor.

Barb Sanders, the realtor who had once tried to convince him to sell his grandparents' farm, stared up at him from the floor. He stared back at her, her too-bright smile mocking him.

Casper sauntered over and sat his big fluffy body on

the card, as though to save Logan from the panic currently stirring in his veins. Or to cover his owner's tracks. Logan tore his gaze away from the cat and the card and turned his attention back to the pile of papers. He hadn't intended on looking at them. He hadn't intended on snooping.

But he'd seen the card.

And now he saw the real-estate listings. The comps for other business properties in the area. He saw where Jeanie had circled some of the numbers. He saw her little enthusiastic exclamation points in the margins.

He saw the astronomical amount of money Jeanie could sell this building for. She could do so much with that amount of money. Reinvent her life entirely. Find her own dream instead of recycling her aunt's.

She could leave and never look back.

His gaze roamed over the living room, taking in details he'd been too distracted to see last night. The kitchen might have been organized, but the living room was just as unsettled as the bedroom. A large box labeled 'photos' sat menacingly next to the couch.

Jeanie had no intention of staying.

And he'd fallen for it, again.

He'd fallen for her.

His blood flashed hot then cold as the realization set in. He'd been nothing more than a stop on her trip. And he'd paraded all over the damn festival with her yesterday. Everyone in town had seen them together.

He'd given everyone yet another reason to look at him with those 'poor Logan' looks.

Shit.

He had to get out of here.

He was about to head back to the bedroom to grab the rest of his clothes when the shower stopped. He froze next to the table and the incriminating pile of papers. Maybe he could run out of here in his underwear. That would really top his failed-proposal story.

No, he couldn't run. He had to face her. And then get the hell out of here.

He waited, listening to the sounds of Jeanie padding around her bedroom. She hummed a little tune to herself, and Logan wanted to cry. Or scream. Or tear something apart. He wasn't sure which. Maybe all three.

Jeanie emerged from the bedroom wearing nothing but his discarded flannel shirt from the night before. The sight nearly brought him to his knees.

Why was she doing this to him?

'Morning,' she said cheerily, her cheeks rosy from her shower. Damp tendrils of hair curled around her ears. Logan's fingers twitched with the need to touch her. 'Thanks for making coffee.' She smiled, and Logan's heart lurched like it could escape him and go live with her instead.

'Yeah ... uh ... I have to get going.' He couldn't meet her eyes. Not now. Not anymore. Not since he'd so fundamentally misunderstood this entire situation.

'Oh. You do?' The disappointment was clear in her voice, but she pushed through it. 'I guess I should give you your shirt back.'

'Keep it.' His voice was gruff, rude, and sharp, but he couldn't help it. There was no way in hell he could take that shirt back now. Not with Jeanie's freshly showered smell all over it.

'Logan, is something wrong?'

He sighed and ran a hand down his face. 'No, everything's fine. Just need to get home.'

'Okay.' She moved toward him, her warmth overtaking him, crowding him. 'It just seems like you're upset about something.' She glanced toward the table, her stare lingering on the papers before realization dawned on her face.

'Didn't realize you were planning on selling,' he said. 'Surprised me, that's all.'

'I'm not.'

Logan shook his head. 'I think maybe you are, Jeanie. Maybe that's what you want.'

'It isn't.' Her mouth turned down into a frown, and

Logan hated it. Wanted to kiss it right off her face, but that kind of thinking had only gotten him into trouble.

'Maybe you should.'

'What? Why would you say that?' Her gaze snapped to his, hurt simmering in her eyes.

He shrugged, feigning a casualness he didn't feel, not a bit. His body buzzed with hurt and anger that he'd fallen for the wrong woman again. That his heart had led him right down this same path.

'Look around.' He gestured to the living room and Jeanie's gaze skittered over the boxes and empty walls. 'You haven't even moved all the way in.'

'I... It's just that I've been busy.'

Busy, maybe. Or maybe this wasn't what she wanted at all. 'We don't know each other all that well ...' She flinched at that, and considering everything they did last night he knew it was a real asshole thing to say, but if he didn't push her away, he'd take her in his arms and be even more devastated when she left. 'But it seems to me you ran away from your old life. Your boss died and you got scared. But maybe this isn't really where you want to be.'

Her hands were on her hips now, her eyes narrowed. His flannel shirt rose up, exposing more of her thighs. He tore his gaze away. He was suddenly wishing they were both wearing pants for this conversation.

'For someone that doesn't know me, you sure have a lot of opinions about what I want.'

'I think we should just cool things off for a while,' he said, echoing the words Jeanie had said to him a week ago. He should have listened.

He would not look at the tears pooling in her eyes. *He would not.* He'd been down this road before, and he knew what happened when you tried to make someone live a life they didn't want. Unhappiness for everyone.

'Fine.' She sniffled and swiped her tears away with the back of her hand. 'You have some shit to sort out, anyway,' she said and spun on her heel back toward the bedroom. The door slammed behind her.

Damn it.

He'd woken up this morning planning on telling Jeanie he was in love with her and instead, he'd suggested they 'cool things off.' What a mess.

He glanced back at the table and Jeanie's exclamation points mocked him from the listings. If Jeanie didn't want to stay in Dream Harbor, he sure as hell wasn't going to be the one to convince her otherwise. Despite what his stupid heart was telling him.

The bedroom door opened again, and his completely misguided hopes rose.

Jeanie tossed his jeans into the hallway and slammed the door again.

Right.

There was no fixing this.

He grabbed his pants, tugging them on as he hopped toward the door. His boots still sat toppled over next to Jeanie's where he'd tossed them the night before. He'd been so frantic, so eager to get to her, he hadn't cared where anything ended up.

Now, he stepped into them, not bothering to tie them, grabbed his coat off the back of the chair, and left Jeanie's temporary apartment behind.

Chapter Twenty-Eight

Sometimes life punched you in the face and then kicked you while you were down.

That's how Jeanie felt when she caught Norman tampering with the thermostat in the break room the day after Logan left her apartment; the day after he'd suggested she shouldn't be here at all. It was like life was beating the crap out of her just for funsies.

'Norman, what are you doing?' she asked, even as the sinking feeling in her gut told her she already knew. She probably should have figured this whole mystery out much sooner, but maybe she'd been afraid of confronting her aunt's most loyal employee. Not to mention the disapproving look Norman gave her when he turned around, which was enough to make her feel like she was the one in trouble. Maybe she was misreading the situation.

'It's freezing in here. The customers have started to complain,' she went on as though she needed to explain why he shouldn't be messing with the thermostat after she had set it for the day.

Norman met her eye, and a flash of regret crossed his face, but he quickly covered it with his usual scowl. He tilted his chin up and squared his shoulders. 'I quit.'

The words were so unexpected, Jeanie couldn't process them. Her short-circuiting brain refused to comprehend them.

'What do you mean, you quit?' she asked, her voice going all high-pitched and panicked. 'I need your help.' Whatever Norman had been doing with the thermostat or anything else in this café – Jeanie refused to think about his long list of possible crimes – she couldn't run this café without him. He was the one who knew how to do everything!

Norman shook his head. 'You really don't.' He turned away from her and opened his employee locker.

'I really do.' She put a hand on his arm to stop him from clearing out his things. Surely, they could work this out. It was obviously one big, giant misunderstanding.

The midday rush had already started, and she'd left Crystal completely alone at the register. She needed to get back out there, but she also needed her most experienced employee not to quit on the day after she'd been dumped.

Dumped? Can you be dumped by someone you hadn't really been dating?

She wasn't sure, but she sure as hell felt dumped. And she'd had absolutely no time to process that before Norman dropped this bomb in her lap.

'I do need you, Norman. You know how everything works around here. You're Aunt Dot's most valuable employee.'

Norman scoffed, shrugging out of her grasp. He pulled a cardigan, several paperbacks, and a Tupperware box filled with homemade granola bars from his locker. 'Apparently, I'm not.'

'Have I not been treating you well? I'm sorry, Norman. I really am. This is my first time being in charge and I'm doing my best. What can I do? How can I fix it?' She was bordering on hysterical now, but the lunch rush was getting louder, and she could hear Crystal's flustered voice over the din of the crowd. They normally had three people working this time of day.

Norman blew out a long-suffering sigh. 'It's not you. Not really.' He pushed the glasses up on his nose and faced her for the first time in this conversation. 'It's me. I've been tampering with the business.'

Of course he had. She'd known it as soon as she saw him turning the thermostat down after she'd already adjusted it three times this morning, but what she didn't understand was why her aunt's long-time manager had been screwing with her. What the actual hell was going on?

'Why? Why would you do that?'

'I'm not proud of myself. And I understand if you want to press charges.' He folded his hands primly in front of him, and the idea of Norman in his argyle sweater vest and tortoiseshell glasses in a police mug shot was enough to almost make Jeanie laugh. Or cry. Or both.

She pinched the bridge of her nose, feeling a stress headache coming on. 'I'm not going to press charges. But why on earth would you do it? I thought you loved the café?'

'I do.' He winced. 'I do love it and I wanted to buy it, but your aunt wouldn't sell it to me.'

Wait, what? Norman wanted to buy the café. 'Really?'

'Yes. She said you needed it more.'

'Oh.'

'And I thought if I could make it a bit too difficult for you, you wouldn't want it. Maybe you would sell it to me.'

Jeanie sunk down onto the bench beside the lockers.

'Oh.'

Norman ran a hand down his sweater vest, straightening himself out. 'The whole thing was beneath me and I apologize. It got quite out of hand. I never intended for windows to get broken. Or to scare you in the middle of the night.' He winced. 'Jim went too far with that. Obviously, I will pay for any damage done. And I quit.'

'You don't have to quit,' Jeanie said weakly. Everything Norman had just told her swirled ominously in her head. She might throw up. 'Wait, who's Jim?'

Norman cleared his throat. 'My ... uh ... associate.'

Jeanie's eyes widened. 'You hired someone to break my window?'

'Not specifically. I just thought he could make things a little ... *untidy* around here.'

'Oh.' The syllable was quiet, defeated.

'Again, I apologize.' And with that, he picked up his home-made snacks and other belongings and left Jeanie sitting with her head in her hands.

The way she saw it, she had two choices. One, she could curl up in a ball on the perpetually sticky floor of the break room and stay there for the rest of forever. Or, two, she could get up and go to work in her café.

She groaned into her hands. Choice one was tempting. Rolling up in a ball sure seemed like the right call. A ball was cozy, protective. She could live happily on the floor, scrounging for crumbs, never facing another adult responsibility – or sexy farmer who turned out to be a complete jerk – ever again. Tempting, indeed. However, there were downsides. The main one being the sticky floor. No matter how many times she mopped back here the floor remained sticky and she didn't know why. It was not knowing the source of the stickiness that really grossed her out. She didn't want to be sticky. Also, she would be quitting on Crystal and Aunt Dot, and herself. Which she didn't particularly want to do.

Despite what Logan said. The big dummy.

So that left her with one option. She tied on her apron and got her butt in gear.

'Hey Crystal, sorry about that.'

Crystal glanced over her shoulder as Jeanie emerged from the back room. She blew out a sigh of relief. 'Oh, thank God,' she said with a flustered smile. 'You're here.'

Yes, she was here, damn it. This was her damn café. And despite Norman's efforts and Logan's fears, she wasn't going anywhere.

She stepped up to the counter. 'Hey, Marco. The usual?'

The man gave her a friendly smile. 'Hey, Jeanie. That would be perfect.'

Jeanie nodded and got to work.

Chapter Twenty-Nine

'All right, where is he?' Annie's voice filled the house before she did.

'Kitchen.' His grandmother didn't even hesitate before she threw him under the bus.

'How bad is it?' Another voice. Hazel was here, too. Wonderful.

'Pretty bad. He's cleaned the house from top to bottom and rebuilt the chicken coop.'

Logan frowned. Was it so bad that he cleaned when he was upset? There were worse things he could do. And he'd been meaning to fix that coop. He just happened to have time now that the Fall Festival was over. And he had no beautiful new café owners to help.

His stomach turned like it did every time he thought

about the festival and Jeanie and everything that happened after it. It had been a week since he'd seen her.

And since he'd had a decent cup of coffee.

It was killing him.

But he knew it would hurt worse if he let himself get in any deeper with her, only for her to decide she was done with her little experiment here. He couldn't do it.

'Okay, Mr. Clean. Drop the rag,' Annie said, coming into the kitchen with a basket of muffins in her hands.

'Actually, he has more of a Bounty Man vibe going on,' Hazel added, cocking her head to the side and taking in his signature beard and flannel shirt.

'Ha. Ha.'

Annie didn't waste time making herself at home – this was her second home, after all; had been since they were kids. Annie was one of six and she fell somewhere in the middle. In a family so big, it was hard not to get lost in the mix. Annie loved the attention of Nana and Grandpa, and Logan liked having an occasional pretend sister around.

Not that he would admit that right now when she was hustling around his kitchen making tea and sticking her nose in his business.

Hazel sat at the table and grabbed a muffin, but Logan caught her stealing sad glances at him out of the corner of her eye. The exact type of look he'd been trying to avoid. Annie set down a cup of tea in front of Hazel and slid into a seat at the table. She grabbed a muffin and slowly peeled the wrapper, staring at him with that damn disappointed look on her face. He couldn't take it.

'Jesus, Annie. Just get on with it.'

She pursed her lips in displeasure. 'What did you do?'

'Why do you assume I did something?' He tossed the dirty rag in the sink and crossed his arms over his chest.

Hazel's gaze tracked his movements. His body language was defensive. That's what she'd say if she wasn't letting Annie do all the talking. For now.

'Well, for one thing, you and Jeanie were all cute and cozy at the festival, and then, *poof,* you disappeared.'

'I didn't disappear. I'm right here.'

Annie frowned. 'And for another thing, Jeanie has been significantly less perky than usual, but she won't talk about it.'

His heart twisted. 'What do you mean?'

She blew out a sigh, like it was difficult to talk to someone so stupid, which was probably true. 'I mean, that Jeanie has been working her butt off this past week since Norman left but she—'

'Wait a sec, Norman left?'

'He quit,' Hazel piped in.

'Why would Norman quit?'

Hazel shrugged. 'All Jeanie would say is that he decided to explore other options. It was weird.'

Logan shook his head, sinking into a seat at the table. Annie slid him a banana chocolate-chip muffin. His favorite. At least she brought snacks on this harassment mission.

'I don't get it. Why would Norman quit and leave Jeanie in the lurch like that?'

'Seems obvious to me,' Annie said. 'He didn't like the new management.'

'Everyone likes her,' Logan growled, hearing exactly how unhinged he sounded but not able to stop it.

Annie raised an eyebrow. 'Some more than others.'

'She's not gonna stay, Annie. I didn't feel like dragging it out this time.'

'What makes you so sure?' Annie looked like she might snatch his muffin back to punish him. He pulled it closer.

'She's considering selling. She could make a lot of money, too.' He shrugged. 'This whole thing was just an experiment for her. Eventually, she'll get tired of it and go back to her real life.'

For a small bookish woman, Hazel moved like a

freaking ninja. He didn't see the slap to the side of his head coming until her hand made contact with his skull.

'Ow! Haze, what the hell!'

Annie stifled a laugh.

'This is her real life! Why would she be killing herself to keep the café open all week – even though they're crazy short-staffed – if she was leaving? Why would she be joining the book club and signing up for baking classes, if she didn't like it here? Why would she be falling in love with you, if she didn't plan on staying?'

Logan choked on the muffin he had been shoving in his mouth while Hazel delivered her gut punch of a speech. Muffin crumbs spewed out of his mouth. Annie brushed them off the table onto his newly swept floor.

'She doesn't love me,' he rasped between coughs.

'Maybe not yet,' Hazel said with a shrug. 'But I've seen the way she looks at you – and the way *you* look at her, by the way – and it's not nothing. It's not the way someone looks at a passing fling.'

He swallowed hard.

'At some point, you're going to have to try again,' Annie added. 'Take the risk. Jeanie's worth it.'

'You need to deal with your abandonment issues,' Hazel added, sipping her tea.

'My what?' Logan sputtered, and Annie smacked him

hard on the back, causing more muffin crumbs to spray across the table.

'Logan, your dad left when you were a baby, your mother died when you were a child, and your one serious, adult relationship ended when she left you. I think it's pretty clear what's going on here.' Hazel pushed her glasses up her nose while Logan stared at her in disbelief.

'That sounds right,' Annie piped in. 'Been reading a lot in the self-help section again, Haze?'

Hazel shrugged. 'I thought we all already knew this.'

Logan ran a hand down his beard. 'Jeez, Hazel. You're not pulling any punches today.'

'Just trying to be helpful.'

He nearly laughed. Hazel's version of helpful was to lay all his bullshit out on the table and show him no mercy. But she wasn't wrong. Seeing those still-packed boxes and realtor listings shouldn't have pushed him over the edge like they had. He should have at least talked to Jeanie before bolting from her apartment. Abandonment issues. It sounded complicated, but it was simple. He was afraid. Afraid of Jeanie leaving. Afraid of failing again. Afraid of getting hurt.

And he'd let that fear guide every interaction he'd had with Jeanie. It made him want to deny his attraction to her. It made him want to hide what was going on between them. And it made him freak out and jump to conclusions instead of talking to her.

To top it off, he'd retreated to the safety of the farm and had been hiding out ever since. Just like his grandfather had warned him about.

And with that string of unsettling realizations, his friends stood from their seats to leave. Annie put their mugs in the sink and Hazel planted a kiss on the top of his head.

'Good luck,' she said with a surprisingly hard pat on the arm. When the hell had Hazel gotten so strong? 'I'm sure you can fix things with her. And at the very least, you should stop in for a cup of coffee. There are rumors around town that you left on either some kind of meditation retreat or mountain climbing in Peru.'

Logan shook his head. 'Why?'

'My dad had a dream about you and a llama on some sort of high peak or something. He wasn't totally clear.'

'This damn town.'

Annie grinned on her way out of the kitchen. 'You love it. See you soon!'

He was sure his groan followed them down the hall, but they didn't look back. They'd said their piece and left their muffins. Nothing left to do now but let him stew in the information they'd laid at his feet.

Norman had quit.

Jeanie was still fighting for the café.

He apparently had abandonment issues.

And what the hell was he doing? Running scared. Giving up on something good before it even started? All because of, what? One failed relationship with the wrong person?

It was time to finally let that shit go.

Chapter Thirty

Jeanie peeled open the fresh pack of Oreos and inhaled their familiar scent. They smelled like childhood and home, and like she could totally survive this day if she just shoved about four of them in her mouth really quick before she had to get back to the café to cover the register for Joe's break.

She checked her phone while she chewed. A new voicemail from her mom that she was sure was about Thanksgiving and that she would deal with later. A text from Jacob with the title of the next book club book. And a string of texts from Ben.

Still alive?

Haven't heard from you in a few days.

Did the sexy farmer chop you up into bits and bury you in the pumpkin patch?!!

The last one was sent twenty minutes ago.

Jeanie, seriously. You okay?

Oops. Apparently, she hadn't talked to Ben in a few days, but she'd been so busy interviewing people to replace Norman and working any hours that Crystal and Joe couldn't fill in. Things had been so crazy that Hazel and Annie had each taken shifts, which was so nice and made Jeanie almost cry any time she thought about how she had real friends now.

She shot off a few quick texts to confirm she was in fact not chopped up in a field.

I'm alive.
Sorry!
Super busy.
Love you.

She waited for a response as she ate one more cookie, wiping the crumbs on her apron. Her phone pinged.

Phew! Call me later. I want updates on the thriving business.

Jeanie smiled. Thriving? Maybe. She certainly had enough customers. She'd solved the mystery of who was causing all the problems; or rather, the mystery had anticlimactically solved itself. Now if she could just find some responsible college students to hire, she'd be all set.

Oh, and she probably needed to find a new produce source for her smoothies because she had no desire to see Logan ever again.

He could stay on that damn farm and hide away forever for all she cared. He could just go—

'Where's Jeanie?' A voice boomed from the café and Jeanie froze where she stood in the breakroom, her mouth still stuffed with cookies. Did she somehow summon him with her thoughts?!

'She's on her break.' *Good job, Joe,* Jeanie thought, chewing frantically.

'I need to see her.' Logan's voice was loud enough that the entire breakfast rush must be able to hear every word. Especially since the bustling café had gone quiet as soon as he came in. She hadn't told anyone what had happened between them, but the fact that they'd traipsed around the festival together and then Logan had completely disappeared from town for a week, had been enough to crank out some very strange rumors from the mill.

Last Jeanie heard he was riding a llama and meditating.

'She ... uh...'

Oh, no, Joe was faltering. *Stay strong, Joe! Don't let the giant farmer intimidate you!*

'Jeanie.' Logan's voice was louder, like he had bypassed talking to Joe and was now just calling her name and was going to keep doing it until she came out of the breakroom. She glanced up at the one, small window but didn't think she could fit through. *Damn it.*

'Jeanie, please. I need to talk to you and if you don't come out here, I'm going to say everything I need to say in front of every one of these nosy people out here.'

There were a few murmurs from the crowd – some disagreement about being nosy – until the dissenters were shushed by everyone else trying to hear what would happen next.

She hesitated.

'Okay, I guess that's my answer,' Logan went on. 'Jeanie, I've been a real ass.'

Someone in the crowd let out a little cheer at that.

Oh, my God, what is he doing?

She couldn't let him do this. Not in front of everyone. Not with everything she knew about him. She wasn't a monster.

She burst out of the break room. 'Don't!' Logan's gaze

locked on hers. *Shit*. She forgot the way those blue eyes sucked her right in, like a damn magnet. 'Just come here, for God's sake.' She came around the counter, grabbed him by his soft, flannel sleeve and pulled him into the break room to the great dismay of the crowd.

There were actual 'boos' as they left the room. These people really needed to get a hobby.

Getting away from the prying eyes of what felt like the entire town had seemed like a good idea until Jeanie was alone with Logan in the tiny break room. Why was he so big? And why did he smell so damn good?

His blue gaze roved over her like he was drinking her in after the drought of not seeing her for a week. She hated that she felt the same way, taking in every detail – from his trimmed beard to the dark smudges under his eyes. Maybe he hadn't been sleeping well. Maybe he'd been thinking about her as much as she'd been thinking about him.

No, Jeanie. No. You will not fall prey to the sexy farmer again. He'd been a complete jerk. He'd slept with her and then had the audacity to tell her what she wanted, that she'd be better off leaving altogether! And then ... and then! He'd disappeared for a week while she was left here to solve mysteries and run a café by herself!

If there was one thing Jeanie had figured out over the last week, it was that she belonged here in Dream

Harbor. She liked being here and she liked herself here. She still hadn't figured out exactly who New Jeanie was, but she knew she didn't allow men, not even the sexy-farmer variety, to toss her aside like that.

Having gotten herself sufficiently keyed up inside her own head, Jeanie opened her mouth to let Logan have it. But he was already talking. Apologizing.

'I'm sorry. I should have talked to you sooner.'

Jeanie crossed her arms over her chest. *Well, that was true.*

'And I never should have left like that.' He ran a shaking hand down his beard. 'I've got shit to work through, I know that. The stuff with Lucy affected me more than I wanted to admit, and I was scared to repeat it.'

Lucy. Right, one more reason this thing with Logan wouldn't work.

'Look, Logan. I can't be what you want.'

He flinched.

'I tried. I thought I wanted to be this new person, that I could be this new person. And I am a little bit, but I'm also still the old me. I'm kind of a mess, and it'll probably take me several months to unpack; and I overreact and overthink. I tried to be a sunshine-y ball of quirky calmness, some archetype of the perfect small-town café owner. I tried to be like Dot. But I'm not. I'm just me, and

I like running this café. *My* café. I don't know what Lucy was like, but I'm not her. I'm—'

'I don't want her.' His answer was sharp, fierce.

'Then what do you want, Logan? Because I sure as hell can't figure it out.'

'You. I want you.'

Jeanie sighed, her emotions ricocheting between anger and hurt and hope. 'I can't—'

'I want you exactly as you are.' He stepped toward her, surrounding her with his outdoorsy scent and she almost caved. She almost buried her face in his sun-warmed flannel shirt and gave into his words.

He kept going, further weakening her resolve. 'I want the Jeanie that almost decapitated me, I want the one who believes in ghosts, the one who talks to my chickens and runs through the rain to chase a farmers' market tent. I meant it the other night, I like you messy, Jeanie.' He stepped closer. 'I like you every way. I like you in your buttoned-up blouses talking at town meetings. I like you when your hair is spilling down around you and you're wearing that ratty old cardigan. I like wiping away your tears; and your laugh is my favorite sound.'

Jeanie swallowed the burn of emotions in her throat. 'But you don't trust me to stay.'

He blew out a ragged breath. 'I'm working on that. But I trust you to tell me the truth and I'm ready to listen.

If you love it here, then I want you to stay.' He glanced away, giving Jeanie the chance to breathe away from the intensity of his stare.

Her heart was racing. Did she want Logan as a part of her new life here?

He brought his gaze back to hers and her breath caught. Of course, she wanted him, but she wasn't letting him off the hook that easily.

'Well, I'm staying.'

He nodded, his eyes wary like he didn't want to assume her staying meant anything about them being together.

'I solved the mystery without you.'

'I heard.'

'Norman wanted to buy the café.'

Logan's eyebrows rose at that tidbit. 'Really?'

'He was upset that Dot didn't sell it to him. That's why he was trying to scare me away.'

Logan huffed, shaking his head. 'I'm sorry you've been dealing with that alone.'

Jeanie shrugged. 'Annie and Hazel have been helping out. I'm in the process of hiring some new people.'

'I'm glad. Did you tell Dot?'

'Not yet.'

Logan nodded again and shifted uncomfortably on his feet in front of her. She could see his patience cracking. She could see him cracking wide open for her. 'Jeanie.' His voice was sandpaper, gravel under truck tires.

The sound of her name in that tone dragged the words from her lips. She couldn't help it. 'I want you too,' she said, unable to hold it in anymore.

His lips tipped in the corner as he stepped toward her, crowding her in the small space. 'You do?'

She nodded, suddenly unable to form words. He took her face in his hands and tilted it up. 'I'm in love with you, Jeanie.' The words coasted over her skin, warm and sweet.

'You are?'

'Yeah. Have been for a while.'

'Since when?' she asked, with a teasing smile. Logan traced her cheek with his thumb.

'Probably since I saw your hedgehog pajama pants.'

'Oh, no,' she groaned.

His smile tipped higher. 'Or it could have been since you enlightened me about the best snack foods.'

She laughed. 'Well, I've loved you since I saw how many tiny pumpkins you could carry at once.'

He blew out a long sigh, relief and happiness dancing in his eyes. 'Does pumpkin carrying rank high on a man's attributes for you?'

'Apparently,' Jeanie said with a grin, and he kissed

her smile. 'It's good training for this—' She launched herself into his arms and Logan caught her with an 'oof' escaping his lips. His back hit the lockers, rattling them, and Jeanie laughed against his neck.

He squeezed her waist and held her close. 'Warn me next time.'

She kissed him. 'Deal.'

Logan kissed her back, his tongue found hers, his relieved groan vibrating through her.

'I heard a crash. Everything okay—' Joe's words died as soon as he saw the scene in the break room. 'Uh ... sorry.'

Jeanie gave him a thumbs up from her perch in Logan's arms. He buried his face in her hair, hiding or breathing her in, she wasn't sure which.

'All good,' she told Joe as he scurried back out to the café.

Logan grumbled against her neck. 'Missed you,' he said, before trailing kisses down her skin. Jeanie was about to tell him the same when a cheer broke out in the café.

'Joe is not known for his discretion,' Jeanie said, hoping this wouldn't send Logan running again.

'Good.' Logan kissed her again; and then, still holding her, he walked back out to the café.

'What are you doing?' she squeaked.

He held her thighs tight as every head in the café turned toward them. Jeanie spotted the entire book club in the corner. Kaori's eyes were wide as she nudged Isabel. Jacob gave Jeanie an enthusiastic thumbs up. Hazel had popped in for her usual latte, Tim and Tammy were here in their athletic wear on the way to the gym; and even Mayor Kelly stood frozen by the door, Noah just in front of him.

Good lord, what was Logan doing?

'I love this woman,' he announced gruffly, like he was expecting someone to fight him on it.

The café went silent.

Here it comes. The heart attack that I'd been running from, Jeanie thought. At least she would die in a beautiful man's arms instead of alone at her desk. That was something.

'We already knew that!' Linda yelled from the back, breaking the silence. Laughter and cheers and a few whistles rose up in the café.

'Not everything is about you, man,' Noah told him, coming up to the counter. He slapped Logan on the back. 'But congrats.'

Logan blew out a frustrated sigh. 'This damn town,' he muttered, and Jeanie giggled. 'Noah, can you cover Jeanie for the afternoon?'

The fisherman grinned. 'Of course.' He hopped over the counter and landed beside a surprised Joe.

'You're taking the afternoon off,' Logan whispered in Jeanie's ear.

'Sounds good to me.'

Jeanie waved over Logan's shoulder to The Pumpkin Spice Café customers, who had already gone back to sipping their drinks and chatting about the weather, as though declarations of love happened in the middle of their morning coffee every day.

Chapter Thirty-One

Jeanie was back in Logan's arms as soon as the door to his apartment slammed behind them; her mouth on his, her hands in his hair.

Jeanie tugged at his shirt, pulling it from his arms.

'This has to go, this all has to go,' she said, yanking her own shirt over her head. Then, she stood in front of him and unhooked her bra.

'Damn, Jeanie,' he rasped, his voice thick and deep.

She gave him a little smirk and pushed her jeans down over her hips. It was the smirk that did him in, that little knowing smile. There was no hiding it anymore. She knew just how much he wanted her. *Good.* He didn't want her to ever doubt it.

She stepped toward him and undid the button of his jeans. The brush of her fingers against his bare stomach sent sparks across his skin. The sound of his zipper being pulled down was added to their rapid breathing, and the rain that had just started coming down on the roof.

Logan groaned as Jeanie pushed his jeans over his hips, her hand grazing his erection on the way down. She flicked her gaze up to his, deep brown and happy. Trusting.

'I missed you,' she said and his heart broke a little for the week he had lost.

'I missed you, too.' He pulled her close, grabbing her full ass and delighting in her little moans when he squeezed. 'Wrap those sweet thighs around me, Jeanie.'

She met his eye again and gave him a smile filled with so much love and so much desire his heart kicked hard against his ribs. He had to have her now. Now and always.

She launched into his arms, and he held her up easily, turning so that her body was now between him and the wall. When his mouth landed on hers, it wasn't gentle, but he couldn't help it. He'd thought he lost her and now that she was here, he couldn't hold back. Not anymore.

By the way she was kissing him, she felt the same way.

'Logan,' she moaned as he rocked his hips into her. She arched against him, and he kissed down her neck. He dipped his head lower and found her nipple with his mouth. He sucked and licked until Jeanie was writhing against him.

'Logan, please. I need you now.'

He groaned and pulled himself away from her breast. He pinned her against the wall, holding her with one hand, using his other hand to pull her underwear to the side.

'You want it like this, Jeanie? Against the wall?' The question came out rough, gruffer than he meant it. He'd only wanted to know she was sure about this, that she was comfortable. But it came out like a filthy threat.

Jeanie moaned. 'Yes, like this. Please,' she panted, and Logan got impossibly harder.

He took himself out of his boxer briefs and slid against Jeanie's soaking wet entrance. 'Condom?' he asked, his voice barely recognizable, his body shaking with restraint.

'I went back on the pill.'

'Thank God,' he sighed.

Jeanie let out a breathy laugh, even as her body trembled against him. She met his gaze. 'Please, Logan.'

He pushed into her, slowly, so slowly, until she squirmed against him, until his body was flush against hers. He leaned his forehead against hers and they breathed out together.

'Good thing you lifted all those heavy pumpkin crates, huh?' she asked with a sly grin.

He huffed a laugh. A laugh that became a groan when she clenched around him. So perfect, his Jeanie.

And then he moved. He thrust into her, holding her steady, her thighs squeezing around his hips. He thrust into her again and again until she whimpered in his arms.

He froze. 'Am I hurting you?' His breath was ragged.

'No, not hurting me.' Jeanie clung to him, her arms wrapped around his neck. 'Keep going. So good.'

He kissed her deep and demanding and she took him in, all of him. He changed the angle of his hips and she gasped against his lips. He did it again and he knew she was close, panting and groaning. Again and again, until Jeanie broke around him. Her nails dug into his shoulders, and her heels dug into his back, anchoring him in this perfect moment.

He stayed buried deep, with Jeanie pinned to the wall, and came hard inside her. He held her, their ragged breathing the only sound between them. Jeanie's thighs were shaking when he eventually lowered her to the ground, and she kept her arms wrapped around his neck.

She placed a kiss on his chest before peering up at him. 'That was quite the reunion.'

He couldn't help his smile. 'I told you; I missed you.'

Jeanie grinned. 'Well, now you don't have to.'

Logan blew out a long sigh.

'But' Jeanie went on, 'We can definitely do that again.'

He laughed. 'Deal.'

Jeanie in his bed and the cold, fall rain hitting the windows, was Logan's new favorite thing. She was wearing one of his old worn flannel shirts and nothing else, her hair spread across his pillow. A slow smile curved the corners of her mouth.

He was propped up on one elbow looking down at her and he could only imagine the idiotic look on his face, but he couldn't help it. He was too damn happy to worry about his face. Somehow, he was lucky enough to get a second chance with this woman and he wasn't about to take that for granted.

Jeanie traced an idle finger across his bare chest. The light touch made him want to dive back between her legs where he'd already spent most of the afternoon. Her cheeks flushed like she'd had the same thought at the same time.

'Thanks for kidnapping me,' she said with a smile. 'I needed a day off.'

'Happy to help.' He dropped his lips to her exposed

collarbones and kissed along the ridge, finding her fluttering pulse with his lips. Jeanie's giggles turned into little sighs as he tugged her closer.

'I might need another day off to recover from today,' she said, her voice breathy and raw.

He loved this Jeanie, too. The one that wrapped her legs around him and pulled him close, the one that wanted him as much as he wanted her.

He chuckled. 'Me, too.'

Her smile imprinted itself on his skin as she buried her face in his neck. He was ready to ensure they'd both need a few days off when Jeanie's stomach gave a loud rumble. When was the last time she'd eaten? Probably not since this morning. They'd been distracted to say the least.

He eased back. 'Hungry?'

Jeanie untangled her legs from his. 'Yeah. Suddenly starving.'

'I've been a horrible captor—. Uh, host.'

Jeanie laughed, the happy sound fizzing all around him. 'The worst.' She let her gaze rake over his bare chest. 'Although, you have been very accommodating in other ways.'

He narrowed his gaze and then dove forward, capturing Jeanie in his arms. She squealed in surprise, laughing as he pinned her to the bed again. 'So glad you think so,' he growled as he kissed her neck, his hands finding her curves beneath his oversized shirt.

She squirmed against him, and he nearly forgot his intentions to feed her until her stomach growled again.

'Damn,' she muttered.

He laughed, pushing up off of her. 'I'd never forgive myself if I let you waste away.' He found sweatpants and pulled them on, enjoying the way Jeanie watched him from the bed.

'I don't keep a ton of food in here, but I'm sure we can scrounge up something.'

'As long as it's not Twizzlers, I'm good.'

'I only eat those when I'm ghost hunting.'

Jeanie laughed. She swung her legs out of bed, his shirt riding up her thighs. She pushed strands of hair from her face. The delicate skin of her neck and chest was red from the roughness of his beard.

Jeanie brought a hand to where his gaze had stalled right above the enticing V the shirt made. He was staring. He was staring and not getting her food like he was supposed to be doing.

He shook his head and strode over to the kitchenette. He did most of his eating in the big house, but he kept some stuff here for occasional late-night snacking, or for when he was hiding from his nana. Which this past week had been kind of a lot.

Jeanie joined him and was rooting through his cabinets like she lived here.

God, did he love that idea.

Not yet, but someday. He could picture it so clearly.

Jeanie caught him staring at her again. A delicious blush crept up her cheeks. 'What?'

He cleared his throat. 'Nothing.' *Just picturing you being here forever.*

'Ooh, Cup a Noodle! I haven't had these in a million years.' She pulled down two of the styrofoam cups filled with dried noodles and seasonings. 'I want these.'

'Okay.' *You can have whatever you want.*

She grinned at him.

He boiled the water while she made herself comfortable at his little table. Outside the weather was gray and cold. Logan wouldn't be surprised if there was a layer of wet snow on the ground tomorrow morning. But today it was warm and cozy inside his little apartment and suddenly it seemed like plenty. Like more than enough, like the only thing his life had been missing before was this woman at his table, wearing his shirt.

The kettle whistled and he poured the water into the plastic cups, watching as the noodles magically plumped up and the broth turned golden. He carried them to the table.

'Yay!' Jeanie clapped. 'I love these things. We used to

eat them during late nights at the office. So bad for you, but so good.' She sighed as she breathed in the salty scent of the noodles. And for the first time since he met her, the mention of her old life didn't send Logan into a panic about her leaving.

He believed Jeanie. He trusted her. And he knew this thing between them was more real than anything he'd felt before.

She happily slurped her noodles, her legs tucked up under her. The rain ran in streams down the window behind her.

'How do you think Noah did at the café?' she asked after a few minutes of slurping and chewing. It was after four, so the café was now closed for the day.

'Fine, I'm sure. He tends the bar for Mac. He knows what he's doing.'

Jeanie nodded. 'It was nice of him to help out.'

'He's a good guy.'

'I think he has a thing for Hazel,' Jeanie added, with a secret smile.

Logan choked a little on his noodles. 'Oh, he definitely does.'

She giggled. 'They'd be good together.'

Logan shrugged. He still didn't feel the need to weigh in on town gossip, even if it was out of good intentions for his friends. If Noah and Hazel wanted to be together, that was their business. He loved this town, but he still wasn't about to join the book club anytime soon.

'I think you should tell Dot about Norman,' he said instead.

Jeanie wrinkled her nose like the idea did not appeal to her in the least. 'I don't know. I don't want to cause more drama.'

'Jeanie, that was really shitty what he did to you. He was tormenting you.'

She shifted in her seat. 'Tormenting seems a bit strong.'

Logan frowned. 'He also caused actual damage.'

'I took the money to replace the window and fix the dishwasher out of his last paycheck. Nothing else was really ruined.'

'Jeanie.'

She sighed. 'He just seemed so sad about the whole thing. The café. Aunt Dot. Everything. I don't know, I feel bad.'

'You have nothing to feel bad about. He should feel bad.' The words came out angrier than he meant them to, but he was pissed at Norman. He'd made Jeanie doubt being here and that was enough to make Logan consider fighting a man nearly as old as his grandfather.

Jeanie cracked a smile. 'I know. He does feel bad. I think.'

'Dot would want to know.'

Her lips twisted to the side as she thought about it. 'Let me get things back in good working order, then I'll tell her.'

She still wanted to prove she could do it. His heart ached a little for her, but he understood that. He'd felt the same way when he took over management of the farm.

'Okay, deal.'

'That way Dot will be back from her island-hopping trip, and I won't ruin her vacation.'

'Makes sense.'

She slurped the last of her noodles and licked her lips. 'Delicious.'

'Mmm-hmm.'

Jeanie's eyes darkened. *Okay, she was fed, back to more important activities.* Logan pulled her chair closer and dropped to his knees in front of her.

'What are you—'

Her question hung in the air as Logan tugged her to the edge of her seat and dipped his head to her thighs, kissing along the warm flesh. He pushed her shirt up to her waist and her legs fell open for him.

He tasted her and she groaned, her head tipping back on the chair.

She tangled her hands in his hair, putting him right where she wanted him. Logan's moan rumbled through them both. She held him there; licking her, his fingers digging into the flesh of her thighs until she came apart for him, gasping his name, her hands tugging his hair. The weight of her legs on his shoulders, the taste of her on his tongue, her little moans and sighs surrounding him; another perfect moment.

'Holy shit,' she whispered as he sat back on his heels. Her legs slipped from his shoulders. She leaned forward and pressed her forehead to his. 'Best. Day. Off. Ever.'

He grinned and she kissed him, and as the rain poured outside, for the first time in a long time Logan felt safe enough to be happy.

'I love you, Jeanie,' he whispered. He would whisper it every day, he'd shout it in a crowded café. He'd hold a damn town meeting about it if she wanted. He'd tell her every which way.

She smiled. 'I love you, too. And I'm not going anywhere.' She planted a kiss on the end of his nose.

And he believed her.

A knock on the door that connected to the big house dragged Logan's attention from Jeanie's beautifully flushed face.

'Yeah?'

'Do you kids want to come have some dinner?' Nana's voice came through the door loud and clear. 'I cooked.'

Logan glanced at the empty soup cups on the table and Jeanie's current state of undress. 'Uh... I already ate.'

'I know Jeanie's in there with you.'

Jeanie giggled.

'*We* already ate,' he amended.

'It was probably junk food. Come have a nice home-cooked meal.'

'That sounds nice,' Jeanie whispered.

'That's because you've never had her cooking,' he whispered back. Jeanie shoved him playfully.

'I'm sure it's not that bad.'

He gave her a grim look. She did not know what she was getting into, but if she wanted to eat dinner with his grandparents that badly, he couldn't save her.

'Okay, Nana. We'll be over in a bit.'

'Wonderful! I'm sure you two worked up an appetite.'

Heat rose to Logan's face while Jeanie bent over in a fit of laughter. 'I love her,' she gasped.

Logan stood from his spot between Jeanie's legs. 'Yeah, she's a real hoot,' he said, as his grandmother's footsteps receded.

'I guess I better get cleaned up and dressed.' Jeanie stood and headed for his shower.

'I should probably come with you.'

She glanced at him over her shoulder, a smile playing around her lips. 'Oh, really?'

'The knobs can be kinda tricky.'

'The knobs?'

'Yeah, they can stick. I better come in and adjust the temperature for you.'

Jeanie's eyes crinkled with laughter. 'Okay, I guess you'd better. You're just so thoughtful.'

Logan wrapped his arms around her from behind and planted a kiss on her neck. 'Very thoughtful. I have a lot of thoughts actually of what we can do in the shower together.'

'I thought you were just going to help with the temperature.'

He bit the soft flesh of her neck, and she squirmed in his arms. 'And maybe some other things...'

'Your grandparents are waiting for us.'

'Trust me, Nana's food isn't going to be any better if we get out there early. And my grandfather will be puttering around for at least another hour.'

'Well, in that case...' Jeanie broke free of his grasp and hurried into the bathroom, shucking off his flannel shirt on the way. She glanced over her shoulder again, laughter dancing in her eyes, and he followed her in.

If Jeanie was going to suffer through Nana's cooking, she really ought to be rewarded. At least a few more times before dinner.

Jeanie was down on her knees in the shower looking up at a surprised Logan. Warm water ran down her back, but the shower was big enough that she was fairly confident she could do this without drowning.

She wrapped her hand around the base of his erection and put her mouth around him.

A garbled sound that might have been her name rumbled through Logan.

She smiled around him.

'Jeanie,' he gasped as she took him deeper. 'You don't have to...'

She stopped and pulled away, looking up at him through wet lashes. 'I want to.'

He blinked. 'Oh.' And by the expression on his face, Jeanie thought maybe no one had ever said that to him before, but she did want to. She wanted to make him feel good. Even here, in the shower where she might drown, but probably wouldn't.

'Do you want me to?'

'God, yes,' he groaned, his head tipping back to rest against the tiled wall behind him. She took him in her mouth again, letting the long, hard length of him slide against her tongue. She rested her hands against his thighs, felt them tense and flex beneath her palms.

He coiled his fingers in her damp hair, holding her close but not pushing her. Polite, even now, while he groaned and tensed above her. Jeanie thanked him by taking him even deeper.

'Shit, Jeanie,' he swore, his hands digging deeper, his hips making small thrusts into her mouth. 'So good,' he gasped and then pulled away, tugging her up abruptly.

'That was ... you are—' At a loss for words, he devoured her mouth instead, communicating perfectly how he was feeling at the moment. Jeanie melted against him, breathless. He wrecked her with his kiss and then spun her toward the wall.

'I need you,' he rasped in her ear, reaching around and finding where she was already wet and aching for him.

'Me, too. I need you, too.' *Again. Always. Forever.* She was still amazed by how much she needed him. Wanted him. Loved him. And how many times they'd managed to do this today. Good for us, she thought as Logan spread her legs and thrust into her from behind.

She groaned, pressing her forehead against the cool tiles. *Very good for us.*

He pushed in deeper, his hand still stroking between her legs, until he hit the spot inside her that made her breath catch.

'Logan,' she moaned, only a little worried that the

acoustics in the bathroom were too good and that they might be giving Logan's grandparents a show.

'Yes, Jeanie,' he whispered against her ear.

She gasped, 'Harder.'

Logan groaned, dropping his forehead to her shoulder, and thrust harder. He held tight to her hips and drove into her again and again until she forgot everything. Who she was, who she wanted to be, her actual name.

But she remembered his.

'Logan,' she cried as the orgasm broke around her, crashing into her until her legs were trembling and the only thing keeping her upright were Logan's hands still on her hips as he thrust one more time and came with a curse.

'Damn, Jeanie.'

He turned her around gently, which was good since she was pretty sure her limbs had turned to goo. He pressed a kiss to her forehead, pulling her tight against him. She smiled against his bare chest, listening to his still-racing heart.

Her stomach grumbled.

'What do you think your nana is making for dinner?' she asked, and Logan's laugh tumbled through her.

'Let's get cleaned up and find out.'

Chapter Thirty-Two

'He just carried you out of here?' Annie asked, her eyes so wide Jeanie nearly laughed.

'Yep.'

'Over his shoulder, or like a bride?'

Jeanie tapped her pen to her lips. 'It was more that I was climbing him like a tree and the tree grew legs and started walking.'

Annie nodded like that made perfect sense. 'Okay, like a baby koala situation.'

'Exactly.'

Hazel rolled her eyes and took another sip of tea.

'I just can't believe I missed it!'

It was after-hours at the café, and Annie and Hazel had come for their afternoon pumpkin-spice drinks and chat. It had become somewhat of a routine over the last week. They all sat at a round high-top table, mugs and plates of leftover goodies from the bakery laid out between them. It was another day of rain and the café was dim but cozy, the windows fogged up with the warmth from inside. Someone had drawn a heart in the condensation earlier in the day and it was still there, a happy little doodle standing out in the gloom.

'It was pretty romantic,' Jeanie said with a smile she knew must be dreamy and ridiculous, but she couldn't seem to help it. 'And then we went back to his place and spent the whole day—'

'Nope!' Hazel held up her hands as though she could physically stop Jeanie's words from reaching her. 'No way. That's where I draw the line. I cannot hear about Logan doing whatever it was you two were doing yesterday. Nope. Sorry.'

'Okay, okay. I won't get into the details.'

'Thank you.'

'I'll just say he was very good at it.'

'Agh!' Hazel covered her ears and squeezed her eyes shut.

Annie cackled beside her. 'Good for you, Jeanie. Glad to hear our dear Logan is up to the task.' She took a bite of her scone. 'But, seriously, no details.'

Jeanie nodded and peeled Hazel's hands away from her ears. 'No details. I promise.'

Hazel blew out a long dramatic sigh of relief. Jeanie smiled thinking of the first time the two women had come in to warn her about Logan, and, she now realized, tried to protect their friend's heart. It made her more than happy to know that not only did Logan trust her, but his best friends did as well.

A sharp rap on the front door startled them all.

'Who on earth?' Annie muttered.

A tall figure in a black raincoat stood outside the door. Rain ran in streams down his hood and the wind crashed into him from the side. Jeanie was proud of herself for thinking it might be a murderer for only a second before realizing it most likely wasn't.

The figure raised a hand in greeting.

'Noah,' Hazel breathed, recognizing him first.

'Oh!' Jeanie hopped down from her seat and hurried to let him in. 'Noah, what are you doing out there?'

Noah came in with a rush of wind and rain, his entrance making an instant mess of the café floor. He pushed down his hood and grinned at her. 'Just a little rain.' His gaze flicked to where Hazel and Annie still sat, and his smile grew.

'I was looking for you,' he said, his gaze now fixed on Hazel, and Jeanie didn't miss the blush that was slowly creeping up her friend's cheeks.

'You were?' Hazel's eyes were wide behind her glasses. 'Why?'

Noah's grin slipped, some of his usual confidence faltering in the face of Hazel's shocked question.

'I ... uh ... was hoping that book I ordered had come in.'

'And you needed it right now?' Hazel asked, gesturing toward the storm out the window.

'Well, I was pretty excited to read it.'

Annie huffed a laugh, but Jeanie shot her a warning look. This thing between Noah and Hazel was too cute and awkward to interrupt.

Hazel sighed and grabbed her coat from the back of her chair. 'I did get some orders today. I guess we could go check.'

'Great.' Noah rubbed his hands together in excitement and Jeanie had to bite down on her own giggle.

'Come on.' Hazel flipped up her hood and headed for the door. 'See you guys later,' she said over her shoulder and Noah followed her out into the rain.

Annie collapsed onto the table. 'Oh, my God! Those two are ridiculous!'

'I think they're cute.'

Annie rolled her eyes. 'He has been ordering books for weeks now. Random books, Jeanie! Like I don't even think he looks at the title before he buys them. All just so he has an excuse to go in and see her.'

'That's so romantic!'

Annie scowled. 'It's painful. He should just ask her out and put us all out of our misery.'

Jeanie laughed, climbing back onto her stool. 'And what about you?'

'What about me?'

'You and Mac.'

Annie's jaw dropped and then snapped shut. 'Me and Mac are mortal enemies so I couldn't possibly imagine what you are talking about.'

'Right. Sorry. I don't know what I was thinking.'

'Stop smirking, Jeanie.'

'I'm not smirking.' The laughter was clear in her voice.

Annie narrowed her eyes. 'Just ride off into the sunset with Logan and leave the rest of us alone.'

'Of course. I plan to.' She took a bite of a snickerdoodle and grinned at Annie. Her new friend glowered back at her.

It was lovely.

'Where is he?' Aunt Dot stormed into the café on a quiet afternoon in November, her wool wrap flying out behind her like a cape.

'Aunt Dot! You're back!' Jeanie ran around the counter to greet her. Dot pulled her into a patchouli-scented hug, one of her enormous earrings smacking Jeanie in the face. Jeanie breathed in memories of her childhood visits here. The Pumpkin Spice Café and weekends with Dot used to mean freedom and fun and endless cups of cinnamon-spiced hot chocolate. It meant different things to her now. It was belonging, and satisfying work, and friends just a few steps away. It meant stumbling down the stairs in the early morning hours to share a cup of coffee with Logan before he drove back to the farm. Those quiet, pre-dawn moments were her favorite.

Her aunt's strong grip remained on Jeanie's arms as she pulled away from their hug, holding her niece still as she inspected her.

'You're happy?' she asked, her face softening as she took in Jeanie's smile.

'Very.'

Dot nodded, the starfish dangling from her ears swinging to and fro. Her salt-and-pepper hair was swept up into a topknot and she sported a golden tan. She even smelled like coconut. But Dot's face was anything but relaxed. In fact, her expression had slipped back into the determined one she wore when she first burst through the door.

'It looks beautiful in here.' Her aunt turned her attention from Jeanie to look around the small space. She tucked her arm through Jeanie's. 'You're keeping the place up nicely.'

Jeanie flushed with pride, temporarily forgetting to ask what was bothering her aunt. 'Thanks.' For the past few weeks without Norman, Jeanie had been perpetually worried she was one false move from running the café into the ground. But as it turned out, her years of working for Marvin had taught her to be organized and efficient. She was good with people, even the prickly ones. And she worked well in chaos and high-pressure situations. Maybe she hadn't given herself enough credit to begin with. Maybe she, Jeanie, was the right choice to run the café after all.

Maybe Dot had known that all along.

Adelyn, one of the café's newest baristas, smiled from behind the counter. 'What can I get you?'

'Peppermint tea, please,' Aunt Dot said, her gaze still flitting around the room. She was practically vibrating with nervous energy, and peppermint tea was another sign her aunt was keyed up about something. Dot always claimed peppermint calmed her nerves. And she was looking anything but calm at the moment. Jeanie had never seen her like this before.

'How was your trip?' Jeanie asked as they settled in at a table in the corner.

'It was good. Very nice.' She finally turned her intense gaze to Jeanie. 'I'm just so sorry I left you in such a bad situation.'

Jeanie winced. She'd told her aunt about Norman a few days ago, and she certainly hadn't been expecting a surprise visit.

'It's fine. Really. Everything is straightened out now.'

Her aunt huffed, as though in disagreement.

'Here's your tea.' Adelyn left the mug in front of Dot and scurried back to her post, obviously sensing the mood at the table. Jeanie was suddenly wishing she could hide behind the counter, too.

'It's absolutely not fine, which is why I demanded he meet me here today.'

'You what?' Jeanie had managed not to run into Norman since he quit, which had proven trickier than she expected. Just the other day in the grocery store, she had spent a full twenty minutes hiding in the frozen-food aisle while Norman finished up his shopping so they wouldn't accidentally meet at the register. Her fingers were so numb she could barely get her card out of her wallet when she finally went to check out.

'We need to settle things.' Dot folded her hands on the table, her stacks of gold rings clinking together.

Who needed to settle things? Dot and Norman? Norman and Jeanie? For Jeanie's part, she felt perfectly fine with never seeing the man again.

The bell above the door jingled and her attention snapped to the entrance.

Logan found her immediately, his lips tipping into a smile that transformed his face from stoic to soft in an instant. He noticed Dot next, and he lifted an eyebrow in a silent question. Jeanie shrugged as he strode toward their table.

'Hey, Dot. What brings you into town?'

'Logan! Please join us. I hear you and my niece have become quite an item.'

Jeanie watched in delight as Logan's cheeks turned red above his beard.

'Uh ... yes ... we ... I mean, I—'

'Just sit down, Logan,' Jeanie said with a laugh, and he gratefully sank into the seat next to her. Adelyn came over with his usual black coffee and he thanked her with a smile.

Dot's laser focus returned to the door. Her leg bounced nervously under the table, bumping into Jeanie's over and over. Was her aunt really this worried to confront Norman? Sure, he was grumpy, but the man wasn't exactly threatening.

'What's going on?' Logan whispered into her ear, breaking the uncomfortable silence.

'Aunt Dot invited Norman. So we can settle things,' Jeanie said, leaning into his comforting warmth.

'Good. I have some things I'd like to settle with that guy, too,' he muttered quietly.

Jeanie was about to remind Logan that under no circumstances was he allowed to fight Norman, when the door opened again and in came the man in question.

Norman's eyes scanned the room until they landed on Dot. Her aunt sucked in a little gasp of breath, her entire body going still. His gaze lingered on her like he was drinking her in, absorbing every bit of Dot that he could. Jeanie could feel the longing. The angst. The *love.*

Holy shit. Hazel was right. There was something big going on here.

Norman pushed up his glasses and ran a hand down his vest. Jeanie caught Dot tucking the wisps of silver hair that had escaped her bun behind her ear as Norman strode toward them. An uncharacteristic blush crept up her aunt's cheeks.

'Dorothy,' he said with a small nod.

'Norman.'

Jeanie glanced at Logan. He raised his eyebrows and

shrugged, at as much of a loss with the whole situation as she was.

'I'd like to apologize,' Norman began.

'You damn well better,' Dot snapped, the imaginary cartoon hearts circling her head crashing to the floor. Logan stifled a laugh and Jeanie kicked him under the table.

'I'm sorry for the damage I caused to the café, and to Jeanie's state of mind, as well. Things went much farther than I ever intended them to.' He caught Jeanie's eye, and she gave him a small nod of forgiveness. Beside her, Logan, feeling much less forgiving, glowered at him. Norman snapped his gaze back to Dot. Not that she was being any more sympathetic. Poor guy. Jeanie really did feel bad for the man. This level of awkward conversation seemed like more punishment than was really necessary.

'You terrorized the poor girl. Scaring her half to death in the middle of the night!'

'To be fair, that wasn't him,' Jeanie cut in, but ignoring her, Dot didn't take her eyes off of Norman. Beads of sweat formed on the poor man's forehead.

'I never intended for that to happen. I just thought I could cause a little trouble. It went too far. I paid for the damages.'

'Well,' Dot huffed and crossed her arms over her chest. 'That was the least you could do.'

Norman gave a stiff nod. 'I know. My actions are unforgivable.'

'Already forgiven, Norman,' Jeanie said, and Dot cut her a look, but her aunt's face was already softening. Jeanie's attention flicked back and forth between Dot and Norman, but she might as well not exist with the way they were locked in each other's gaze. She gave her aunt's shoulder an encouraging nudge.

'I suppose, if Jeanie forgives you, I could, too. Maybe.'

Norman let out a sigh, his posture relaxing but the angst still etched into his features. 'I was hurt,' he said. 'When you left, I thought, well, after all these years working together, I thought it just made sense for me to buy the café. That I should take it over for you.'

'Or you could have come with me.'

'What?' Jeanie clapped a hand over her mouth, not meaning to cut in again, but really, what?!

Norman blinked, his mouth opening and closing before words finally escaped. 'Dorothy ... I don't understand?'

Her aunt let out a long sigh. 'Of course, you don't. I suppose that's half my fault. But the reason I didn't leave you the café was because I hoped you might retire, also, and that we could ... we could finally...' Dot's words trailed off as Norman sank down into the nearest chair.

'I d-didn't know,' he stammered.

Dot gave a feeble shrug, all the anger draining out of her. 'I never told you.'

Jeanie had never seen her aunt be anything other than confident and strong, moving through the world in exactly the way she wanted to. But now, looking across the table at the man she had apparently been in love with for years, Dot looked shy, nervous even, and Jeanie could feel the butterflies reflected in her own stomach.

'Maybe we should go—' Logan whispered, but Jeanie waved him away.

'Shush.' She wasn't about to leave now. Things were just getting good. This town was really rubbing off on her.

Norman reached across the table and grabbed Dot's hands. 'Dorothy, I've been in love with you for years.'

Dot sniffled and Jeanie slid her a napkin. She'd never in her life seen her aunt cry. Dot dabbed her eyes and then placed her hands back in Norman's.

'I should have told you sooner,' she said. 'But I was afraid, I guess.'

'Afraid of what?'

She shrugged. 'That you wouldn't love me back.'

Norman shook his head. 'Impossible.'

Jeanie smiled, even as Logan took her hand under the table and tried again to tug her away, to give her aunt some privacy.

This time, Jeanie agreed, and the two of them got up and stood together behind the counter, watching Dot and Norman scoot closer and closer together until her aunt's head rested on his shoulder.

Jeanie sighed. 'Imagine loving someone for so long and never saying it,' she murmured.

'I *can* imagine it,' Logan said, the gruffness of his voice hiding the emotion Jeanie knew was behind it.

'You can? You told me you loved me after like a month,' she said, leaning her shoulder against his, loving his sturdiness.

He let out a small laugh. 'I know, but you made it easy.'

She smiled. 'I did?'

'Yeah. You were kind of obvious.'

'Hey!' She swatted him playfully on the arm. 'You were pretty obvious, too.'

'Oh, really?'

'Well. Nothing says I love you like installing new locks.'

'Is that so?'

'Anything that involves a toolbox really. Fixing something, making something. Big giant 'I love you' gestures.'

'Wow, I had no idea.'

Jeanie leaned into him again. 'Yep.'

'I'm glad we were both obvious about it,' he said, before their attention drifted back to Dot and Norman's reunion. Jeanie couldn't imagine working next to Logan every day and not being able to tell him how she felt, or hold his hand, or kiss him. It would be torture.

But she could imagine how someone might worry that they were unlovable. It might have crossed her mind a time or two. The fact that her brave, strong aunt felt the same way made Jeanie think that maybe no one had things really figured out.

And maybe that was okay.

Maybe she could be cheerful and dark, messy and competent, sunshine and rain, New Jeanie and Old Jeanie mixed together.

Logan pressed a kiss to the top of her head, and she felt the warmth of it down to her toes.

It certainly seemed to be working out so far.

Maybe the picture-perfect small-town life she had imagined didn't exist, but the one she had found was pretty damn perfect for her.

Epilogue

Jeanie's apartment was filled to the brim with people – people and empty, moving boxes. Logan stood by the front door, collapsing the boxes one by one as they were emptied. He already had quite the satisfying stack beside him. And every box he added to the pile just reminded him further that this was real, and Jeanie was staying.

But even if she didn't, he was still worthy as a person. Or so his new therapist liked to tell him. He was working on untangling his issues once a week with Dr. Stephens and Jeanie was adapting to her new life, but most importantly they were doing it side by side.

The unpacking party was Isabel's idea. She'd recruited the book club, Annie, and Hazel to come and help Jeanie finally get settled in her new apartment.

Noah had begged Logan to invite him, too, so the tiny apartment was now crammed with all of Jeanie's new friends.

She beamed from the center of the room, instructing Noah on just where she wanted everything hung.

'I think a little higher on the left,' she said.

'No, no. Now it's crooked,' Hazel protested, pointing to the higher side. 'Lower that side again.'

Noah held the giant framed painting of a purple cow above his head and struggled to adjust it again. 'How's this?'

'I don't know. Now the right seems too high.' Hazel stifled a giggle.

Jeanie put a hand on her hip and cocked her head to the side. 'Maybe I don't even want it on this wall at all.'

Noah lowered the painting with a groan. 'You two make up your minds. I need a drink.'

Jeanie and Hazel collapsed into fits of giggles on the couch. 'Sorry, Noah! You're the best,' Jeanie told him as he walked by to grab a beer from the kitchen. Logan followed him in, passing a very flustered Jacob, who was on his way to ask Jeanie why she owned so many chunky scarves.

Noah grabbed two beers from the fridge and passed one to Logan. A stack of pizza boxes sat on the counter. Payment for everyone's help. It was the day before

Thanksgiving and Jeanie said this was the feast before the feast. Tomorrow they would close the café and head out to New York to spend Thanksgiving weekend with Jeanie's family. He was only a little nervous about meeting her parents and her brother, Ben, who'd decided at the last minute to fly in from California to celebrate. Jeanie said it was because he was dying to meet her sexy farmer. A comment that while always welcome from Jeanie's lips, did nothing to settle his nerves.

'I think she hates me,' Noah said, not needing to specify who he meant.

'Probably not.' Logan took a swig of his beer, pushing aside thoughts of meeting Jeanie's family for the moment.

'I'm pretty sure she does,' Noah said with a grim smile. 'But I'm good at wearing people down.'

Logan laughed. 'That is one of your special talents.'

Noah nodded and took another sip of beer to fortify himself against Hazel and Jeanie's teasing. 'Okay. I'm going back out there.'

'Good luck, man.'

'Thanks.' Despite his concerns, Noah was clearly eating up the attention from Hazel. His face lit up as soon as he was back in the room with her. He was so screwed.

Logan shook his head, watching Noah take up his

post at the wall again, while Hazel blatantly admired his ass. Yeah, she definitely didn't hate him.

Logan leaned in the doorway of the kitchen watching everyone pitch in, and slowly but surely Jeanie's apartment began to look like a home. He still secretly wanted her to come live with him in the big farmhouse someday, but he wasn't going to rush her. For now, things were just right between them.

She looked over the back of the couch and found him smiling at her.

'It's looking good, right?' she asked.

'It is.'

'Looks like I really live here.'

'You are a real Dream Harbonian? Dream Harboran?'

'A real Dreamer,' Hazel corrected, and Logan rolled his eyes, but secretly he loved it. He loved this damn town and these damn nosy people, and he especially loved the woman peering over the back of the couch at him.

Jeanie hopped up and came around to stand beside him, tucking herself into him the way he loved.

'Whatever it's called, it's a long way from having no one to help me out when I'm sick.'

'True. Look at all these people that would totally come over and clean up your vomit.'

Jeanie laughed and buried her face in his side. 'Don't

tell them that, though,' she said in a stage whisper. 'Or they won't want to be my friend anymore.'

'Don't tell us what?' Kaori asked, stepping into the living room from the bedroom. 'That you're a horrible slob. We already know and we still love you.'

'Gee, thanks.'

Kaori grinned. 'You're welcome.'

Jeanie pulled away from his side and climbed back over the sofa, perching on top. She cleared her throat.

'I just wanted to thank you guys for helping. For everything. Getting the café running smoothly again and for today. It means a lot to me.'

'Of course, dear,' Nancy patted her leg as she settled down on the couch next to Jeanie's feet. 'You're one of us now, for better or worse.'

Jeanie smiled. 'Definitely for better.'

Logan came up behind her and wrapped his arms around her waist. She leaned into him, and he couldn't agree more.

Everything was better in Dream Harbor with Jeanie by his side.

Bonus Epilogue

ONE YEAR LATER

Thanksgiving

'Are you mad at me?'

'Huh?' Logan's gaze snapped to Jeanie's before returning to the road ahead of them. The single syllable was the most he'd uttered in the past twenty-seven minutes. Jeanie knew because she'd been keeping track. They were two hours into their nine hour drive to her parents house in Buffalo for Thanksgiving and she definitely wasn't going to make it if Logan stayed this quiet the whole time. He'd been acting squirrely all week and she couldn't figure out what his problem was.

'Is something wrong?' she asked, trying again. Logan was never much of a talker, but this weird, loaded silence between them was new. And it was creating a low level of dread in Jeanie's gut.

She watched Logan's grip tighten on the steering wheel. 'No, everything's fine.' His furrowed brow and tense shoulders seemed to disagree with that assertion.

'Okay. You sure? You seem upset. Is it the whole Bennett thing?'

His gaze flicked to hers again, confusion in his blue eyes. 'No, of course not. Why would I be upset with Bennett?'

Jeanie shrugged. 'Well, I just thought maybe you didn't feel like driving him and his three dogs back with us and maybe you weren't super excited about me moving in with you for the month while he stays in my apartment.'

Logan grabbed her leg and gave a squeeze. 'I'm very excited about you moving in for the month.' His hand skated higher. 'Very excited.'

'Oh.' Heat flooded Jeanie's face at the feel of Logan's strong fingers on her thigh, but she still wasn't convinced. Something was going on with him.

When she'd brought up the idea of her brother coming to stay for the month of December, Logan had been the one to suggest she move into the farm house. He seemed excited. But the past week, he'd been a little too quiet. And then there was all the whispering she'd caught him doing lately. First with Noah at Friendsgiving and then with Hazel before they left this morning.

Maybe he'd changed his mind. Maybe he didn't want her in his space. Maybe it was too much too soon. Even though they'd been together for a full year and it didn't seem too soon at all to her, but what else could it be?

'Is Nana okay?' she asked, changing tactics. Maybe it had nothing to do with her at all.

'Nana's fine.'

'Grandpa?'

'He's fine too.'

'Annie? Hazel? Noah?'

Logan blew out a long breath. 'Jeanie, everyone is fine. I swear. Everything is fine.'

Fine, fine, fine. Hmph. Jeanie slid down in her seat, propping her feet on the dash. Logan glanced at them but didn't comment. He hated when she put them up there. Dangerous, he said. If they got in an accident her legs would go right through her body. He'd been unnecessarily graphic about the whole thing, but now he wasn't saying anything and the dread was settling deeper in Jeanie's gut.

'Jeanie…' His voice was a low grumble. 'Just…just trust me okay?'

She looked over at him. *Trust him.* She did trust him. Of course she did. He was Logan. Her Logan. Sturdy and reliable and still so freaking sexy it startled her sometimes. His beard was trimmed today and he was wearing his good flannel, the one he saved for special occasions instead of mucking out the goats' pen. He was broad and safe and she still wanted nothing more than to burrow her face against his chest and feel his arms around her.

But even when they'd fought over the past year, she'd never once felt like he was keeping something from her. She'd never felt like he had a secret. Logan was sparse with his words but he was always open with her, or at least she thought he was.

But now he was lying to her.

She was sure of it. And she had nothing to do for the next seven hours except obsess about it.

'I do trust you. But you're keeping something from me.'

Logan sighed. 'Maybe it's about your Christmas present.'

'No, I don't think that's it. You seem too…weird for it to just be a surprise present.'

'Jeanie…' he warned. 'Drop it.'

The more he refused to talk about it, the more keyed up she got.

'I can't drop it. You're being weird and lying to me and I don't know what to think! Are you planning to break up with me? Because don't bother waiting until after the holidays, just do it now…'

Logan jerked the wheel, cutting across three lanes of traffic, tires screeching, and rumbled to a stop on the shoulder of the highway. He slammed the truck into park and turned to stare at her. Jeanie's heart pounded against her rib cage. Logan's eyes were wide, cheeks red. He looked…furious.

Oh God, was he really breaking up with her on the side of the highway on Thanksgiving? She'd only said that as a last ditch effort to get him to talk to her but she hadn't really considered it could be true!

'Damn it, Jeanie. Of course I'm not breaking up with you. Jesus.' He ran a hand over his face, letting out a low groan and Jeanie thought maybe she'd broken him. He shook his head. 'This is not how I wanted to do this.'

Logan reached into the back seat where their overnight bags were. He rummaged around in his bag before turning back to Jeanie.

'I'm not breaking up with you,' he said. 'Ever.'

'Oh.' The word left her in a sigh of relief, but Logan still looked…intense. Serious in a way that made Jeanie stay on high alert.

He shook his head again. 'I was going to do this right. I was going to talk to you dad and everything, but maybe this is better. Just us is better, I think.'

'Logan, what—'

There was a box in his hands. A small black box. *Oh God…*

'Marry me.' He held her hand in his now, their fingers twined together and his face was blurry because, oh God, because she was crying. 'Move in permanently, Jeanie. Marry me and stay forever.'

Stay forever.

Logan was proposing to her, not breaking up with her, because of course he was! How could she have ever doubted him? This man who had been by her side for a year now, loving her, and she thought he was considering ending it? Sometimes she really needed to tell that voice in her head that jumped to the worst possible outcome to shut the hell up.

She should have just let him have his secret. His one little, lovely, amazing secret.

'I ruined your surprise,' she sniffled.

'Yeah, you did.' His smile was small, rueful, but at least he didn't look apocalyptic anymore.

'I'm sorry,' she whispered, guilt and regret clogging her throat.

'Jeanie…'

'Yeah?'

'You didn't answer the question.' His blue gaze was still on her, steady and unwavering. Like him. 'Will you marry me?'

She hiccuped a little sob. 'Yes.' She nodded just in case he missed it, her answer, the only answer she would ever give him. She nodded until he took her face in his hands and pressed his forehead to hers.

'Good.'

He brushed away her tears with a sweep of his thumb and then let her go so he could open the ring box. Nestled inside was a gold ring with an oval stone in the middle, delicate gold vines with small diamonds for leaves wrapped around it.

'It's a mint sapphire,' he told her as she studied it. She'd never seen anything like it before.

'It's perfect.'

He smiled, relief settling over his features. 'It was my mother's.'

'Oh, Logan…' her voice cracked with emotion. 'That's…it's…I love it.'

'Nana gave it to me when I met you. After that first day you came to visit the farm, actually.'

'Really?' That long ago? The day she felt crazy and insecure and like she shouldn't be there at all?

'Yeah,' Logan gave a small laugh. 'She gave it to me and said 'just in case' I needed it.'

'Nana's the best.'

'Funny she never mentioned the ring even existed

when I was with Lucy.'

Jeanie couldn't help her laugh. She loved Logan's grandmother as much as her own and it was nice to have such a strong vote of confidence from the woman. Even on a day when she'd been used as a chicken perch.

Logan shrugged. 'It was never meant to be her anyway.'

'Well, that's true,' Jeanie said with a smile. 'But I really am sorry I ruined your plan.'

He shrugged, taking the ring from the box. 'The plan was to ask you to be my wife, so…' he smiled, 'I'd say it went pretty well.'

He slipped the ring on her finger. It fit perfectly.

'How'd you know my size?' she asked, holding her hand up to the window to get a better look. The light greenish blue stone glinted in the sun.

'Annie borrowed one of your rings so we could get the size.'

'She never asked to borrow a ring.'

'Okay, she stole it, I guess. I'll get it back.'

Jeanie laughed. 'Does everyone know?'

Logan smiled ruefully. 'Of course they do. Honestly, I'm shocked I made it this far without someone telling you. I've been walking around with this ring in my pocket for months.'

'You have? Why? You didn't actually think I'd say no did you?'

'I don't have a great track record with proposals.'

Jeanie winced. Right.

He shrugged. 'I don't know. I guess I was nervous.'

Jeanie leaned across the center console, wishing she could get closer. She put her arms around Logan's neck. 'I would have said yes no matter how you asked.'

His lips tipped up in the corner. 'Oh yeah?'

She nodded. 'Yep.'

'Well, on the side of the highway in Thanksgiving traffic wasn't at the top of my list of ways to ask.'

Jeanie leaned forward and kissed the small smile on his lips.

'What was on top?'

'I was going to talk to your dad and then propose to you tonight after dinner.'

She shrugged. 'Good thing I'm not traditional like that.'

'Good thing.' He smirked.

'What other ideas did you have?'

Logan smiled, a memory lighting up his eyes. 'I almost did it on that day over the summer when you insisted we go out and look for fireflies and the field was lit up with them and you looked so beautiful in that little sundress it actually hurt to look at you.'

Jeanie swallowed hard. 'That would have been nice.'

'Yeah. And then I almost did it that day when Nana was teaching you how to make her absolutely horrible beef stew and you were being so patient and kind and listening to every word and you were so at home with my family that I knew I never wanted you to leave.'

The tears were back, sliding down her face. She let them fall.

'And then I thought I should do it at the fall festival because that's when I fell in love with you and because you smell like cinnamon spice and fall leaves and it's the season that reminds me of you.'

'But you didn't ask that day either.' Her voice was a whisper now, nearly drowned out by the traffic still speeding by their window.

He huffed. 'Jeanie, you are the best thing that ever happened to me. I couldn't screw this up. I wanted it to be…perfect.' He blew out another disbelieving sigh. 'And look how it ended up.'

'Perfectly,' she said. She brushed her lips against his. 'You are perfect. This was perfect. Logan, I would have said yes to you every single one of those times and I said yes to you today on the side of this road in the middle of nowhere Massachusetts and I will say yes to you every day for the rest of our lives.'

'Promise?' he said, his smile returning.

'Yes, I promise.'

He kissed her then, long and slow, with the sounds of traffic and their blinking hazard lights in the background. He kissed her and it was perfect even on the side of the road on Thanksgiving day. Kissing him always was.

And now she got to do it forever.

Acknowledgments

I've always felt I had a contemporary small-town book somewhere inside me and I'm so happy to have had the chance to write it. So, first of all I'd like to thank Jennie Rothwell for trusting me with this series (and for the permission to run with it!). And a big thank you to everyone else at One More Chapter, especially my editor Ajebowale Roberts for all her thoughts and encouragement and excitement for this series.

Another thank you to my parents. To my dad for always being willing to talk shop with me and to my mom for her endless enthusiasm for pretty much anything I do.

To my husband, for never thinking this writing thing was a crazy idea and to my kids for being the first ones to fill in 'writer' under the 'what does your mom do?' question on every Mother's Day worksheet at school. If you guys believe it, then I guess I do too.

And lastly, a big giant thank you to the readers because without you, these books are just me talking to myself. Thank you for taking a chance on me and I hope you come back for more!

ONE MORE CHAPTER

The author and One More Chapter would like to thank everyone who contributed to the publication of this story…

Analytics
Abigail Fryer
Maria Osa

Audio
Fionnuala Barrett
Ciara Briggs

Contracts
Sasha Duszynska Lewis

Design
Lucy Bennett
Fiona Greenway
Holly Macdonald
Kelley McMorris
Liane Payne
Dean Russell

Digital Sales
Hannah Lismore
Emily Scorer

Editorial
Kate Elton
Arsalan Isa
Charlotte Ledger
Bonnie Macleod
Ajebowale Roberts
Jennie Rothwell
Caroline Scott-Bowden
Emily Thomas

Harper360
Emily Gerbner
Jean Marie Kelly
emma sullivan
Sophia Walker

International Sales
Peter Borcsok
Bethan Moore

Marketing & Publicity
Chloe Cummings
Emma Petfield
Christina Storey
Jo Surman

Operations
Melissa Okusanya
Hannah Stamp

Production
Emily Chan
Denis Manson
Simon Moore
Francesca Tuzzeo

Rights
Rachel McCarron
Hany Sheikh
Mohamed
Zoe Shine

The HarperCollins Distribution Team

The HarperCollins Finance & Royalties Team

The HarperCollins Legal Team

The HarperCollins Technology Team

Trade Marketing
Ben Hurd

UK Sales
Laura Carpenter
Isabel Coburn
Jay Cochrane
Sabina Lewis
Holly Martin
Erin White
Harriet Williams
Leah Woods

And every other essential link in the chain from delivery drivers to booksellers to librarians and beyond!

When a secret message turns up hidden in a book in the Cinnamon Bun Bookstore, **Hazel** can't understand it. As more secret codes appear between the pages, she decides to follow the trail of clues… she just need someone to help her out.

Gorgeous and outgoing fisherman, **Noah**, is always up for an adventure. And a scavenger hunt sounds like a lot of fun. Even better that the cute bookseller he's been crushing on for months is the one who wants his help!

Hazel didn't go looking for romance, but as the treasure hunt leads her and Noah around Dream Harbor, their undeniable chemistry might be just as hot as the fresh-out-of-the-oven cinnamon buns the bookstore sells…

Kira North hates Christmas. Which is unfortunate since she just bought a Christmas tree farm in a town that's too cute for its own good.

Bennett Ellis is on vacation in Dream Harbor taking a break from his life in California. And most importantly, taking a break from his latest run of disastrous dates.

After a run in with Kira in her fields, Ben has no intention of offering to help the grumpy owner set up her tree farm, despite the fact she's clearly got no idea what she's doing.

Kira knows she should stop being so stubborn, but her farm is not all cute and cozy like people always show on social media, it's borderline dangerous with no heating, and she'd rather no one saw it.

But somehow fate finds Ben at Kira's farm once more, and as Kira watches him swing an ax at the first tree, she finds herself appreciating his strength and questioning why she refused help in the first place..

Cafe